"Move over, Walt Longmire. There's a new sheriff in town. Virgil Dalton is the kind of character that comes along maybe once a decade—a classic Western hero and so much more. When you're done with Frank Hayes's stellar debut, *Death at the Black Bull*, you'll smell the sagebrush in the air and have to clean the dust off your boots. An absolute must-read for fans of Craig Johnson and Tony Hillerman."
—Reed Farrel Coleman, Shamus Award–winning author of
*The Hollow Girl*

"This is one of the most impressive debut crime novels I've ever read. There's such depth and humanity in the characters, such tension in the story itself, and the sense of place is as good as it gets. I know I'll be reading every book in this series!"
—Steve Hamilton, Edgar Award–winning author of
*Let It Burn*

"Virgil Dalton takes no prisoners in Hayes's satisfying debut novel, and fans of Craig Johnson's Walt Longmire will cheer the sheriff's desire to protect his town. With its strong sense of place, this series launch will also keep fans of Western mysteries enthralled."
—*Library Journal*

"Hayes's strong debut introduces a complex and likable lawman . . . readers will want to see a lot more of Virgil and friends."
—*Publishers Weekly*

"Hayes is a skillful storyteller and a deft hand at witty dialogue."
—*Booklist*

# Books by Frank Hayes

The Sheriff Virgil Dalton Mysteries

*Death at the Back Bull*
*Death on the High Lonesome*
*Shattered Dreams*

# Shattered Dreams

## A Sheriff Virgil Dalton Mystery

Frank Hayes

BEYOND THE PAGE
PUBLISHING

Shattered Dreams
Frank Hayes
Copyright © 2019 by Frank Hayes
Cover design and illustration by Dar Albert, Wicked Smart Designs

Beyond the Page Books
are published by
Beyond the Page Publishing
www.beyondthepagepub.com

ISBN: 978-1-950461-01-1

*To Joan, who introduced me to the world of fiction,
setting free my imagination,
and to Fran, whose adventurous spirit always inspired*

# Acknowledgments

To Bill Keller and Steve Hamilton, my constant support group, along with my family, who never fail me.

# 1

The early morning sun was just high enough to make him squint. A light wind caused him to shiver. Despite the chill of the mid-December day, a bead of sweat was evident above his upper lip. He could see the silhouette of the figure clearly, even though it was forty yards away. He had hit much tougher targets in Afghanistan and Iraq easily. But this was different. As he found the trigger he drew in a deep breath. It was all wrong. The weapon felt strange. He knew his position was right, the sight line perfect, but he couldn't feel the trigger. He had always been fairly ambidextrous, able to use his right or left hand, but he had always shot from the right side. He never thought why, just assumed he was right-side dominant to some degree, but it was his right hand that now was alien to him. Nevertheless he squeezed. A burst erupted, surprising him, the recoil a shock. He squeezed two more times with the same result. The distant figure bounced with the first shot then danced in the air at the impact of the next two. Then, when only the echo of the volley hung in the morning air, he lowered his weapon. He wiped the moisture from his upper lip and shook his head.

"What's the matter?" The words from the figure in back of him, reminding him that he was not alone. "A perfect kill." The figure answering his own question.

"It felt weird . . . like it wasn't me pulling the trigger." He shook his head again.

"Maybe that's not a bad thing, Simon, to feel a little more removed."

"I don't think you can rationalize the end result, Sheriff." Virgil didn't respond.

• • •

"Well . . . ?"

"Well what?" Virgil had just walked through the door of his office. Rosie was hanging up the phone.

"How did it go with Simon? Can he hit the broad side of a barn?"

"Oh, he can hit it all right. I think it's more a question of whether or not he is going to want to. It's been quite a while since he had to do it. I think he's had a lot of sleepless nights, remembering. Maybe, when he was in the midst of it all, the killing, the carnage, he was able to turn it off. Now it's been a while. He's allowed some perspective to creep back in. Today, when he said it didn't feel like he was pulling the trigger, I don't think he was talking about the prosthesis, the lack of physical feeling. I think he was remembering back to when . . ." Virgil hesitated.

"Back to when he turned off his humanity," Rosie said.

"Yeah . . . maybe," Virgil replied. "Guess, when your job is killing people, maybe you've got to turn off that part of you to survive."

"Or just stay sane," Rosie added. "Guess that man wasn't joking when he said war is hell."

Before he went to his desk, Virgil walked over and poured himself a cup of coffee. It was cold.

"Damn."

"What's the matter?"

"This coffee is ice cold."

"I don't leave the pot on all day, Virgil."

"Why not? At least it would stay hot."

"Yeah, and after a couple hours it would be strong enough to take the chrome off your bumper. Don't get your shorts in a knot. All you have to do is put the cup in the microwave."

Virgil dutifully did as he was told, standing by the microwave while the coffee was getting zapped.

"Who was that on the phone?"

"Good question. I don't know. Could hardly hear the person. Something about a man or men then it ended, abruptly." The microwave buzzer rang. Virgil opened the door then reached in for his cup.

"Jesus H. Christ!" He yelled as he took his cup out, dropping it on the yard-sale table that held the microwave. He ran to the sink, stuck his hand under the faucet, turning on the cold water.

"What did you do, genius? By the way, what does the *H* stand for, hopeless?"

"Figured it was cold, so I put it in for eighty seconds."

Rosie shook her head, went over to the sink, got a sponge along with some paper towels then went to the table. While she was cleaning up the mess the phone rang again. She went back to her desk, throwing the sponge in the sink as she walked by. "Sheriff's office." Rosie waited a few seconds with the phone to her ear. Virgil could see the immediate change that came over her. She reached the phone out to him.

At first he heard nothing more than random noise, then a baby's cry followed by a clear voice.

"Lady, shut that kid up or I will. Come on, hurry it up with that money." There was a pause, then a loud sound that caused Virgil to pull the phone away from his ear.

"Virgil . . . what do you think?"

"Valley Federal," Virgil answered as he ran across the room and guided a rifle from the gun rack.

"Call Simon. Tell him I'll pick him up in front of Margie's. Tell him I'll be there in a couple of minutes. Then call Dif and Jimmy. See if you can get a response from them. Tell them I think there's a robbery going down at Valley Federal."

Virgil was already at the door when Rosie was punching in the number for Simon.

• • •

Simon had just walked into the apartment he had moved into three days before. It was a little more than five minutes from the sheriff's office, so Virgil had dropped him off on their way back from target practice. He was thinking about a shower to wash away the nervous sweat from the shooting experience. He could smell himself. It was the familiar odor that he hadn't smelled since Afghanistan.

When he returned from his final tour, the end of his military career, the world had become a different place. After a couple of months, he realized he didn't fit into his old life. It was about the same time that he came to the conclusion that the skill set from his time as a sniper wouldn't hold much weight on a traditional résumé. That epiphany, with the physical reminder provided by his right hand hook, brought him to the point of considering that his chances of landing a job in law enforcement were little to none. It had always been a career goal. The IED on a dusty road to nowhere in a land far away changed all that. In addition, the girl who had promised to wait forever decided forever was a lot longer than she thought. So, one sunlit day, when he was feeling as dark as he had ever felt, he threw his belongings into the backseat of his car, then headed west to Chet, the one person he knew would understand. Here, almost a year after his separation from the service, a dream he had almost given up on suddenly had new life. This morning, now for the first time, after pulling that trigger three times in quick succession, feeling the nervous sweat on his body, he was questioning whether this was really the life he wanted. He had stepped into the bathroom, about to turn on the shower, when he heard his cell phone dancing on the end table next to the sofa, which had come with the furnished apartment.

"Simon, it's Rosita. We have a situation."

# 2

Main Street was quiet. One car passed Virgil going in the other direction. He glanced at the clock on the dashboard. It was 10:35. When he looked up, he saw Simon running across the street to Margie's. He pulled to the curb. Simon quickly hopped in while the car was still rolling. Virgil gunned the vehicle but did not hit the siren or dome light.

"A bank robbery? Rosie said a bank robbery."

"Looks like," Virgil said. "Get the rifle from the backseat."

"A Mauser . . . where did you get a Mauser?" Virgil didn't answer the question.

"It's locked and loaded," he said.

"Where's your weapon?" Simon asked. Virgil patted his sidearm. He could feel the question coming from Simon.

"If there is going to be any long-range or pinpoint shooting, you're it," he said. "I saw what you did with that target. I'm not the worst shot in Hayward County. I might be able to put one round dead center, but on my best day I could never cluster three, like I saw you do this morning." Virgil had driven almost a mile when he slowed the car. Valley Federal was at this point in time the only bank in Hayward. It was also in one of the oldest buildings in Hayward. It sat on the corner of Main and Mesquite. An imposing white stone building, it had an entrance on Main Street, another around the corner on Mesquite. Virgil guided the car to the curb a half block away. There was no indication of anything out of the ordinary. Then he saw a puff of condensation rise on the cold morning air at the corner. He pointed it out to Simon.

"There's a car idling around the corner . . . waiting."

"I see it," Simon said.

"Let's see if we can get close enough to that window to get a look in." They both exited the vehicle, then, hugging the wall, made their way alongside to get to the large window that looked out on Main Street. Virgil had to climb up on the tiered stone façade to reach a point where he would be able to look inside. Because it was winter, fortunately the shades were raised to let in the light. Simon stood by while Virgil climbed to reach his vantage point. He edged closer along the cornice, his hands gripping the rough texture of stone. He knew well the layout of the inside. Anyone who lived in Hayward did. At last he was ready to raise his head. Virgil had left his hat in the car, so only his hairline would be slightly visible. He could see six or seven people sitting on the floor against the far wall, to the right of the entrance onto the side street. Through the glass of that door he could see the idling car, along with the figure sitting at the wheel. It was too far away to make out distinctive features of the driver other than long, shoulder-length hair. Inside the bank he could see two men, each holding an automatic weapon, one at the main front door, the other leaning against the long counter in back of which would normally be two or three tellers. Everything appeared to be quiet. One of the women in the group huddled on the floor, appeared to be holding a baby. The baby seemed to be asleep. Virgil looked on for almost a minute but saw little movement of any kind. Finally, he stepped down from the ledge.

"What's happening . . . what's going on?" Simon asked in a low voice. Virgil kind of shrugged before answering.

"Nothing, nothing's going on. That's what's strange. I don't get it. It's almost as if they're waiting, waiting for something or someone. Take a look." Simon climbed effortlessly up to the perch Virgil had left. The scene initially was unchanged from what Virgil had described, then a man came from behind the counter pushing an older man in a suit ahead of him toward the front door. At a certain point they stopped. The second man looked at his wrist then said something to the man in the suit. The man in the suit nodded. Simon jumped down from the cornice and told Virgil what he'd seen.

"So there's three of them inside along with the one guy driving the car. That's Myron Wilkes in the suit. He's the bank manager. I don't get it. If they've got their money, why aren't they getting out? The car's waiting and running." Simon had no answer. "Just doesn't compute. This could be bad, something I'm not seeing."

"Maybe they don't have all the money yet. Maybe the bank vault is hooked up to some kind of a time mechanism and they can't get in. Otherwise what would they be waiting for?" Simon offered.

Virgil looked out at the street. A couple of vehicles had driven by in each direction. None of the drivers acknowledged the sheriff and his new deputy standing on the sidewalk, but Virgil knew Hayward was waking up. It was Monday, after all, a new week was beginning. Sooner or later some people were going to show up on the sidewalks. Some of them were more than likely going to head for the bank. He knew there wasn't much of a window before the situation could become a lot more serious. What was he missing?

"That's it," Virgil said. "Monday."

"What?" Simon asked.

"It's Monday, the beginning of the week. They're waiting for the armored car to come. They don't want to rob only the bank, they want to get what's in the armored car too."

Virgil ran back to the cruiser. Simon could see him on the radio. He returned in less than a minute.

"Get up on the wall," he said to Simon. "Tell me, what's happening?" Simon reached his perch in an instant. He stood there for a couple of minutes. "Anything, anything at all?"

"Nothing . . . nothing's changed, they're just . . . wait, Mr. Wilkes and the guy that's with him are walking back to a desk. The phone . . . the phone must be ringing. Mr. Wilkes is answering it. He put it down and he's talking to the guy. Something must be wrong. He's angry, that guy is really angry. Now the others are coming over to him. They're all talking at the same time. Yelling . . . gesturing. Something's gone wrong."

"No. I'm hoping something's gone right," Virgil answered.

"Wait . . . they're all going through the cash drawers, scooping up whatever's left in them. I think they're going to leave."

"Come down from there. I want you to run down this alley. It goes around the building. You turn left at the end. It will bring you to the side street. Get a description, the make, model and license number of the car. I'll stay here so I can get into the bank as soon as they're gone. Maybe we can get through this thing without firing a shot. Wouldn't that be nice?"

"Absolutely." Simon smiled. Then he turned and ran down the alley.

# 3

"Well, your day started off with a bang."

"Actually it didn't and that was a good thing," Virgil replied. It was a little after twelve.

Mayor Bob "Ears" Jamison smiled as he sat back in the chair opposite Virgil and crossed his legs.

"Virgil, I wish everybody in town could know now what happened today. How you handled a situation that could've headed south in a heartbeat. Not a shot fired and state police waiting for that car soon as it hit the interchange. Major Travis said those four were shocked when they came at them from all sides. How'd you know they'd head for the interstate?"

"Well, it's what I would've done if I robbed a bank. Try to get out of the area as quickly as I could. Figured, they planned it out pretty good. The interstate would be the quickest way out."

"They knew about the armored car delivery and schedule," Bob said.

"Yeah, as soon as I figured that's what they were waiting for, I made that call to Rosie. Once she got through to the company they were able to get a hold of the driver of the armored car. He called the bank with that story that they had a breakdown and were waiting for a tow truck. I reckoned that was enough of a wrench in the works to send those boys running. I was happy to see them go." Virgil reached over to his desk, picked up a file folder, took a couple of sheets of paper out and placed them on top of the folder, which he had placed in front of Bob.

"Virgil, there's something eating on you? For a guy that averted what could have been a disaster you don't seem too happy." Virgil's eyebrows furrowed, the pencil-thin scars on each cheek deepened, the one from the bull throwing him into barbed wire when he was running fence as a teenager, the opposite from the near miss of a bullet from Wade Travis's gun six months earlier, which wore a little bit deeper groove. Virgil leaned over the desk, pushing the folder along with the papers on top closer to Bob. Bob's eyes widened a little.

"What's this, some late-night reading material?"

"Night or day it's still gonna tell the same story."

"And what would that be?"

"After things quieted down today, I did a little research. These pages show the trajectory of crime in Hayward on a chart over the last fifteen years along with a separate breakdown, a narrative, as to the type of crime, etcetera. Interesting reading."

"Where are we going with this Virgil?" Virgil could see Bob shifting a little uneasily in his chair.

"Let's back up a little, Bob. Do you know the last time Valley Federal was robbed, there was a guy standing outside holding the reins of three or four horses so the gang could make their getaway."

"That's pretty good, one bank robbery every hundred years or so."

"Yeah, I'd agree with that if all the other statistics reinforced that probability. But I'm afraid that's not the case. If you take the time you'll see."

"Virgil, I'll ask again, where are you going with this?"

"Bob, Hayward is changing. Dave Brand tells me that he and Alex can't handle their day to day anymore down at the Redbud Substation. Says sometimes it's a two- or even three-day response time for some routine calls. That's not acceptable."

"Well, you just got a new hire, Virgil."

"Yeah, and it looks like I'm going to have to send him down to Redbud. Then that leaves me, Jimmy, Dif—a part-timer—and Rosie for the rest of the county, including the town of Hayward. Rosie gave me three calls just since I got back to the office after our uneventful morning. Two of them are over twenty miles away down near Wilbur Flats. Then there's what's going on down in Cielo."

"Hell, there's nothing out there but cactus and coyotes."

"You been out that way lately, Bob? There's a gravel and sand mining company with almost a hundred employees. A gas station and a Quick Mart opened within the last year, and I've been told the first phase of a housing development was just finished. I've also heard there's talk of building an elementary school. You must know about that." Bob was shifting more uneasily in his chair. "I've got no one for coverage out there. It's a forty-minute drive and then some one way from here."

"Virgil, I hear what you are saying but what are you asking?"

"I think we need another substation, more personnel. It also wouldn't be a half-bad idea for the county to negotiate a contract with that helicopter service down in Sky High for some occasional aerial surveillance and emergency response. I know they already have a contract with Hayward Regional Hospital. According to Doc Sam it's been money well spent. He said that was a factor in the consideration of expanding the hospital into a regional facility."

"Virgil, that hospital can rely on private endowments along with state and government support. We're endowed by the taxpayers. The kinds of things you're asking for are sure enough going to raise taxes. Hell, do you know what I had to go through just to get you that new hire? The council fought me tooth and nail."

Virgil raised his hand. "I know, I know. Your right arm, Hilda, says she'll turn me into a soprano if she could lay her hands on a sharp, rusty nail because she got stuck with that nephew of Lester's in the deal to get Simon hired. But, Bob, you've got to understand and they've got to see where we're headed. We don't have a choice here. It won't be that long before someone else decides they are going to make an easy withdrawal from Valley Federal."

Bob Jamison stood up from his chair. "Okay, Virgil, I get it. Would you be willing to come to the next council meeting to lay it out for them like you did for me?" Virgil got up from his chair to walk Bob to the door.

"If I have to, Bob, if I have to." Bob tipped his hat to Rosie and walked out the door. Virgil stood for a moment looking after him then turned to face Rosie, who had been listening to the exchange.

"Well, go on, say it."

"I think you'd have a better shot at milking a porcupine than trying to get those boys to become part of the twenty-first century, especially if you are going to confront them without warning at a council meeting. Helicopter surveillance. Virgil, they fought against putting in a traffic light on Main Street for over ten years. Look at how you had Bob squirming, and he likes you."

"You know I'm right about this," Virgil responded.

"Virgil, I'm not the one you have to convince. Remember, I'm the one who took those calls from Cielo and Wilbur Flats this morning, but if you're going head to head with the council like you did with Ears, you better take a deep breath. For openers, know who you're talking to. Let's begin with Lester Smoot. Ever since Dif busted his nose that night in this office a couple of months back, he's not likely to jump on any bandwagon you're leading."

"What are you suggesting?"

"Well, how about buying him a beer sometime when you accidentally on purpose run into Lester at the Lazy Dog or the Wagon Wheel. Then try reaching out to the others. You know you could use a couple of informal meetings to lay some groundwork, then when you drop it in their laps at a formal town council meeting they'll be predisposed to listen."

"Guess maybe you're on to something, but sucking up to Lester Smoot? I don't know. That isn't exactly my idea of a fun night out."

"Virgil, keep your eye on the prize. You're not buying furniture together, just having a beer. And scale back your demands. Don't send Simon down to Redbud, keep him here. I know what Dave told you but

Dave's inclined to exaggerate. Hell, he's been doing it ever since I met him. That's over twenty-five years ago. I can teach Simon the nuts and bolts about running the office if I'm not here. To help with the situation down in Redbud, get somebody to take care of the office like I do here. You know Alex has a sister who I know has been helping out since Alex and his wife came home with the new baby. That's not going to last forever. Offer her the job. I've met her a few times. Nice girl. Got a brain in her head but she's kind of betwixt and between right now. This just might be something she would like until she figures out what she's going to do with the rest of her life. Then maybe, setting up another substation out toward Cielo might be an easier sell. Virgil, make sure when you explain your proposal you get across the notion that the implementation will be gradual. I think it will go over much better."

"You know, Rosie, sometimes I wonder how this office would work without you."

"Well, you're about to see." Rosie got up from her desk, then went over to the row of hooks on the wall to the left of the door. She slipped on her coat.

"Virgil, I need to leave a little early today."

"Some last-minute Christmas stuff?" She hesitated before answering.

"That's it, Christmas . . . tidings of great joy." She smiled at Virgil then went out the door. Virgil watched her leave, puzzling over her comment.

Rosita had only been gone minutes when Dif and Jimmy came into the office together.

"You guys are a little early, aren't you?"

"Well, we heard what an exciting day you had. We both were feeling a little guilty that we weren't there for your shout for help this morning. Edna dragged me out the door just after sunup to get a Christmas tree over at Edgar Best's farm. Jimmy here . . . well, there's no excuse for him." Dif nodded toward Jimmy, Virgil's deputy.

"I'm sorry, Virgil. Mom and Abby weren't home when Rosita called. Abby was in school already and Mom was gone too. Just didn't hear the phone."

"Not surprised," Virgil said. "Trying to wake you is like trying to breathe life into a corpse. Don't worry, it all worked out."

"We heard . . . great work, Virgil. So we figured you might like to get out of here a little early. Simon is coming in later to do nightly rounds with Jimmy, Virgil . . . remember?" Dif said. Jimmy didn't say anything.

"I forgot that was starting tonight. Okay, guys, you convinced me." Virgil got up from his chair. "I am kind of tired." Ten minutes later Virgil was on his way out of Hayward heading for home. It wasn't quite dark yet. The road heading east was empty once he got beyond the town limits. It had been a day that he knew could have gone a lot differently. Virgil was not a man to dwell on what might have been, but for some strange reason he felt unsettled. He glanced at the top line of a far-off mesa. A strip of daylight rimmed its highest point. In the next couple minutes, a black thunderhead suddenly settled down on the ridge, blotting it out. Virgil spent the last few miles of the ride to the ranch wondering why that image bothered him.

# 4

"So, Jimmy, I'm about to see Hayward in the dark. Is it going to be much different from Hayward in the light?"

Jimmy wasn't sure how to answer. He was more than a little intimidated by Simon. Besides, he was uncomfortable with his role as mentor. Most of the time when Simon said something directly to him, he just didn't respond or he'd half smile or shrug. That had been okay when they were in the office and there were two or three other people there, but this was different. There were just the two of them alone in the cruiser. Jimmy had been dreading this all day.

"Jimmy, is there a problem? I know you're kind of quiet but I think there's more to it than that. Pull off to the side here. Let's clear the air."

Jimmy responded like he always did when told directly to do something. He pulled the car to the side of the road. They had come off the bridge on to River Road. They were about a mile from where Calvin Thompson had hit his own brother's car a few months before, sending it down the embankment almost into the river. His brother, dead from a broken neck, would still be lying there in his car if Jimmy hadn't spotted the headlights of the car before the battery died out. The incident had caused Jimmy to revisit the notion of his own mortality because of a near miss he'd had only a few months before. The motor quieted. Then Simon reached over and turned off the ignition. Absolute silence inside the car and out. Jimmy never took his hands from the wheel. He was looking straight ahead. After a minute the lights shut off and the two sat in the growing darkness.

"You know all this is really new to me. I mean, I grew up in a much different place. So, I'd really appreciate your take on anything that could help me fit in with the people here, the area . . . anything, so I don't feel so strange. To tell you the truth, I was a little apprehensive about tonight. I mean, you're kind of an old hand as far as the job of law enforcement is concerned. I'm totally new at it. I don't know squat about the people, Hayward, or even about the procedural stuff. Hell, if I was by myself now, I'd probably get lost." Simon stopped talking. Once again quiet invaded the car. A moment passed then Jimmy cleared his throat.

"I'm not that much of an old hand. I'm only twenty-three."

"I don't think it's about age as much as it is about experience. You

12

grew up with these people. You've known them your whole life. This place, the geography, you could probably do this patrol blindfolded."

"But you . . . you've been all over. I mean, the war, the military . . . you're . . . you're a lot older. I mean you must be . . ." Jimmy didn't finish the thought. Jimmy couldn't see Simon smile but he could hear his laugh.

"Now I'm really feeling bad. Maybe we've got to play a little one on one so you know I'm not ready to collect social security just yet."

"Do you?" Jimmy asked.

"Do I what?" Simon answered.

"Play basketball? We have a little pickup game down at the high school on Thursday nights."

"I think I could get out of my walker for that. Got a couple of layups in me yet, I think. But I better warn you, my unorthodox hook shot is deadly." He held up his prosthesis. It was Jimmy's turn to smile. He turned the key in the ignition. Then he looked at Simon feeling a little more comfortable in his new role.

"Okay. Lesson one. This is River Road, which runs along the river. Pretty much east and west, like Main Street runs through Hayward on the other side of the river. This is a 2009 Bronco with a hundred and ninety-five thousand miles on it. It's what you get if you're at the bottom of the totem pole."

"Got it," Simon said. "Guess that means I'm probably in line for a scooter. What's lesson two?"

• • •

Virgil was finishing his supper when he saw the lights of a vehicle carve out a path coming down the driveway to the house. By the time the truck came to a stop he was outside standing on the porch. He was surprised to see the Hayward Ranch logo on the cab, more surprised when Virginia, his newly revealed daughter, hopped out of the driver's side.

"What happened to your car?"

"Nothing. I just needed the truck for this chore. C'mon down from your perch. Give me a hand."

Virgil did as he was told, dog trotting to the truck.

"What's up?" he asked.

"Drove by a few times this week. Place looked like it always does."

"Is that a bad thing?"

"It is when Christmas is next week," Virginia replied. She had walked to the back of the truck. By the time Virgil got there, she had already dropped the tailgate.

"Consider it one of your Christmas presents." In the dim light Virgil saw a Christmas tree laying in the bed of the pickup.

"What's this?"

"What's it look like?"

"I know what it is, but why? I mean, there's nobody here but me and Cesar, and he usually takes off for a few days around Christmas. There's no kids here or anybody but me."

"Sooner or later hopefully that's going to change. In any event, one kid is going to be here. Remember your promise that we'd spend some time together around Christmas before I go back to school."

"I didn't forget," Virgil answered.

"Well, I want to see some Christmas around here, especially if we're going to have a party."

"A party," Virgil echoed.

"Yep. Rosita and I worked it all out. She's taking care of the invitations. I'm handling the food. Margie is going to do the catering. We got a long list of people. Bet you didn't realize you had so many friends. Of course, most of them are only coming for the free food and drink. All you have got to do is decorate the house and sign the check."

"Guess this is a done deal. When is this party going to happen?"

"We were figuring a week from Friday since Christmas is Wednesday."

"I don't have any lights or ornaments for that tree," Virgil weakly offered.

"Guess you're going to be pretty busy tomorrow then scaring some up. I'll come by later in the week. We can trim the tree together. It will be fun. We'll start a tradition." Virgil couldn't resist. He grabbed her in his arms.

"I can hardly wait," he lied with a straight face.

Later as he stood on the porch watching the taillights of the truck grow smaller on the way to the county road, he caught the scent of the tree, which was leaning against the side of the house standing in a bucket of cold water. It was not unpleasant.

"Wish you were here, Rusty. I think you'd get a kick out of this." Then he took a last deep breath of the cold night air and went inside.

# 5

"How did it go with you and Jimmy last night?" Simon had just come into the office. Virgil sat back in his chair.

"It went well. Little awkward at first. We had a talk, got on the same page, then everything was fine. I like Jimmy."

"Good. Glad you got along. I was hoping things would work out between the two of you. Jimmy's a little gun shy around new people. I was pretty sure you would figure that out. In a few minutes I'm heading down to the southwestern part of the county to look into something. I thought it would be a good idea if you could join me. Kind of important that you get oriented to the area. I'm hoping by next week you can have a regular shift, go on patrol on your own."

"That's one of the things we talked about last night. I'd like that," Simon said.

"Me too. We need the manpower and the coverage," Virgil added.

They shared a couple of cups of coffee along with some small talk while they waited for Rosie. Half an hour later, they were leaving the outskirts of town. The cold winter sun offered little in the way of warmth but the air was fresh under a cloudless sky. They drove for about ten minutes before the silence was broken.

"So what's up? I mean, why are we heading down here?"

"Can't give you too much in the way of an answer. Rosie got two calls. One from somebody who said they thought they saw some smoke coming from one of the arroyos. The other was a report of a person who hadn't been seen in a while. Don't know if there is a connection but thought it was worth a look-see. Called the fire department, but since it's all volunteer I thought it best if I went down to give it an official sanction. Besides, I haven't been down here in an age. Don't want folks to get the idea that I forgot about them. It is the most sparsely populated part of the county, but it's growing."

"This sure is a lot different from where I grew up. Not a high-rise in sight." Simon was looking out the window at mile after mile of empty space while Virgil spoke.

"Yeah, I guess it'll take some getting used to before you start thinking of it as home." They had just crossed over some railroad tracks at a crossing.

"I kind of think of that crossing as the unofficial boundary of this end of Hayward," Virgil said.

15

"Even looks different," Simon said as he looked out at a wide expanse of scrubland. For the next ten or fifteen minutes there was little change in the landscape other than the gradual flattening of the land into a more desert-like scene. The foothills to the north of Hayward ascending toward the interstate became part of the horizon, while the wide expanse in front of them looked like it could go on forever.

"Does this ever end?" Simon asked. "It looks like the moon."

"Guess it does look like forever when you first see it. Hard to believe there's this much open space without a house in sight."

"Reminds me of the first time I saw Vegas," Simon said. "I was driving west out of a place called Page when the sun was sinking. I had been camping with some friends at the north rim of the Grand Canyon back when I was in college. I was heading to California. Flat desert on either side for forty miles. Then, when I lost the light, it was just a full moon, a billion stars and me on this road alone. It seemed like it would never end. All I could see was the dark and the cactus. Then it was there. Out of nowhere, a light. It grew and grew as I drove, then disappeared. All of a sudden as I topped a rise, there was a sudden explosion of more light, like a jewel of many colors, Vegas. I hadn't intended to stop, but staring at it as I drove, I was mesmerized by it for almost forty miles, I couldn't resist. It just drew me in."

"Well, I don't think there'll be a jewel waiting for us at the end of this ride but there is a grade we'll start up shortly. Who knows, maybe there'll be a surprise on the other side."

• • •

"Is this the surprise you were expecting?"

"Not hardly," Virgil answered. Virgil and Simon were standing with another man in a canyon that dead-ended half a mile in at the base of the buttes that encircled it on three sides. The three of them were looking at what had been a double-wide trailer but was now nothing more than a burnt-out shell. One of the local firefighters came up to them as they stood there.

"Well, it's out. It was pretty much done on its own by the time we got here. There was nothing left to sustain it. Pretty much a burnt-out shell. The fire came from the inside out, so we just hosed it down, not that there was much chance of it spreading. Not much out here in the way of fuel." The fireman gestured with his arm. "Don't know what we are going to find inside, Sheriff. We haven't been able to enter yet."

"What are you thinking, Sheriff?"

Virgil didn't answer immediately but stepped toward the door. The burnt smell, heavy and rancid, overpowered every sense.

"Right now I'm just wondering if we're looking at an accident or something else." He saw a rag lying on the ground, bent down, picked it up and smelled it. Then he took a couple of steps till he could reach up with it in his hand to the doorknob. He tapped it lightly with his fingertips. "It's still warm." He tried opening the door but it wouldn't budge. "Must have been pretty hot, the door got welded to the frame because of the intense heat. Simon, if you look around in the back of my cruiser, I believe you'll find a pry bar. If it's not there, ask one of the firemen. I'm sure they will have something to pry that door open." Simon took off running toward the vehicle while Virgil backed away from the trailer. He looked at the elderly man who had brought them to this place. Lank and lean, this part of the country was worn into every wrinkle in his face. He stood tall and erect.

"If you wouldn't mind, Mr. Jessup, could you tell me why you called the office?"

The old man looked around like he was trying to take it all in. Simon had come back with the pry bar, handing it to Virgil.

"Mr. Jessup," Virgil prodded. The old man's eyes roved the landscape before he answered, finally settling on the trailer. Then he turned. He looked squarely at Virgil. "Christmas," he said. "Christmas."

"I don't think I understand," Virgil said.

"Everett always come by to get me at Christmas. Didn't come . . . didn't call. Thought it strange. Always has."

"But Christmas isn't till next week, Mr. Jessup."

"I know that." The old man spat on the ground. "What do you think, I'm senile? Everybody knows Christmas comes on twenty-five. This is only seventeen. But Everett always brings me out before to see the decorations. Everett always loved Christmas. Each year he'd do up the trailer different. Bring me out . . . other folks too, show us what he did. Always had a big party. Didn't call . . . I got to wondering why. Look there." The old man pointed to the front window over the hitch. The blackened wire of what would have been framework for a huge wreath moved slightly back and forth across the window, egged on by a slight breeze. It made a scratching noise against the glass. "And there." He pointed to a pole that rose above the roof of the trailer a good fifteen feet. "Betcha, he was gonna put a star on top. Would've looked nice. Never did that before. Bet you could see it all the way to the road." The old man showed a mostly toothless smile then shook his head and looked away.

"Sheriff, you want me to open the door?" Virgil nodded his head. Simon went over, kicked away the burnt remnants of what used to be two steps and a small landing that led to the door. He shoved the crowbar into a space he found between the door edge and the trailer frame. After a couple of strong pulls, the door popped open. One of the hinges snapped. The door sagged crookedly to one side. Simon looked at Virgil. Virgil motioned for him to come back.

"Why don't you keep Mr. Jessup company while I take a look?" Mr. Jessup said nothing but continued looking at the sandstone ridges that lined the arroyo from the road for a half mile or so to the end of the canyon where the trailer sat. Virgil left the two men then moved toward the door. He hesitated for a moment before entering the blackened hole that he saw inside. Then he disappeared. He emerged after a few minutes brushing black soot off his clothes as he jumped down from the trailer. Simon noted the slowed walk as he approached them. When their eyes briefly met Simon knew. Virgil cleared his throat then spat a couple of times before he spoke.

"Well, Mr. Jessup, you were right to call. I want to thank you for that." The old man squared his shoulders. "I'm sorry to say there's a body inside, burnt pretty bad."

"Knew something wasn't right. Everett wouldn't not call me at Christmas for no good reason. Had to be something, I knew." Virgil nodded.

"Mr. Jessup, do you know if Everett had any family, someone I could notify?" The old man glanced at the trailer, then put his hand to his desert-wrinkled face as if to brush away a nonexistent fly.

"No need."

"Well, we really have to notify those closest to him, Mr. Jessup." The old man worked his mouth, then looked straight at Virgil.

"You already did, Sheriff. I'm Everett's pa."

Virgil and Simon waited with Mr. Jessup until the EMTs came down from Hayward to get the badly charred body. There was no reason for the firefighters to stay. They all needed to get back to work. Virgil used the time to instruct Simon on procedure. He had Simon photograph the scene inside and out.

"Are you going to have the site investigated for arson?" Simon asked.

"It's part of the protocol. A fire marshal will automatically be notified, but we're not going to wait for him. I'll be more interested to hear what Doc Kincaid says. He'll be a lot quicker to confirm what I think happened here."

"What do you think happened, Sheriff?"

"I think Everett or whoever that is sitting in that chair in there was dead before the fire started."

"How do you know?" Simon asked. Virgil reached in his pocket and took out the rag that he had found on the ground outside the trailer and put it in an evidence collection bag. He opened the bag, handed it to Simon.

"Take a whiff." Simon raised it to his nose.

"Gasoline."

"It was more than twenty feet from the trailer. Just a snip of cloth, probably used by somebody to wipe their hands. I kind of think that somebody probably struck a match, then tossed it inside the trailer before they wiped their hands on that rag. By not throwing the rag inside when the fire started, they made our job a little easier, because now we know they stood outside and watched as the place went up in flames."

An hour later, when the EMTs were getting ready to leave, Virgil walked over to where Mr. Jessup was sitting on a rock.

"Sorry about Everett, Mr. Jessup. Do you need anything . . . somebody you want me to call?" The old man looked at Virgil through watery eyes then rose stiffly from the rock.

"No . . . I'll be all right, Sheriff. I've dealt with death quite a few times in my eighty-seven years. Thought I'd be long gone before Everett."

"Did Everett have anyone besides you? A wife or maybe a girl-friend?"

"No. Everett wasn't inclined toward women." The old man rubbed the stubble on his chin. "Guess he won't be making any of those trips up to El Morro to the Desert Rose anymore." One of the EMTs yelled. Mr. Jessup reached out, patted Virgil on the shoulder then walked over to him.

"Why would anyone want to live here? A long dusty road that dead-ends in a canyon? I mean, no one would even know you were here." Simon made the comment as they were headed out to the hard surface road on their way back to Hayward. Virgil glanced at him before responding.

"If you think about it, I think you just answered your own question." Then he gunned the accelerator as the tires gripped the asphalt.

# 6

A. R. Kincaid ME were the letters and name centered on the glass on the top half of the door. Virgil knew that Arthur Robert Kincaid was the first and only medical examiner in Hayward. He considered that a bonus as far as his job was concerned because he'd grown to have a lot of confidence in ARK, or Ark, as everybody called him. He was also Virgil's friend. Virgil rapped lightly on the glass. Ark looked up from his desk, smiled when he saw Virgil then waved him in.

"You look tired," he said to Virgil.

"Been a long day," Virgil responded.

"I get the feeling that lately all your days have been getting longer and longer. Heard about the bank robbery. Guess maybe you were hoping that would be the high point for the week. Then you had to go looking for trouble."

"I don't really go looking for it."

"But it does seem to find you, doesn't it? Now you're here looking for more." Ark got up from his seat. "Okay, let's go have a look." Virgil followed him down the hall to the morgue.

"Got to be the quietest place in the hospital." Ark gave Virgil a wry look.

"Yeah, by the time they get here they've run out of oxygen and words," Ark said as he went through the door. He walked to an examining table in the middle of the room.

"I haven't seen him since he was brought here but Chet told me what he saw. He said a Mr. Jessup came with him but he explained we wouldn't have anything definitive for him for a couple of days, and that you would be in contact with him."

"Mr. Jessup is more than likely the victim's father. Is Chet almost finished with his internship?" Virgil asked.

"Just about. Looks like he's going to be on staff. He's decided to stay in Hayward."

"Good. You know Chet and my new guy Simon have shared an awful lot together, emphasis on the awful. I think the adjustment for Simon will be a lot easier if he has a close friend here." Ark nodded in response.

"So let's see if what Chet told me holds up." Ark pulled back the sheet covering the presumed-to-be Everett Jessup. Even though Virgil had seen the body in the charred hull of the trailer, he turned away. The contrast of the blackened corpse against the white sheet was startling. Ark walked around the table viewing the body from every angle, then he got up close, bending down to within inches of the cadaver. Virgil saw him draw in some deep breaths, then after a moment he stood up. Stepping back, he turned toward Virgil.

"I tentatively agree with Chet Harris," he said.

Virgil waited for more explanation.

"This is strictly preliminary, but in a case like this unless I find something graphic, we'll never have a hundred percent certainty. I did detect a slight chemical smell but the accelerant was obvious."

"What do you mean, Ark?"

"Well, look at him, Virgil. He's almost a skeleton. Most of the soft tissue has been burnt away. Unless I can find something like a crack in his skull from a blow, it's going to be very hard to determine cause of death. The heat from the fire must have been exceptional."

"Everything inside was a welded mass," Virgil said.

"That's because the trailer became a virtual oven. The contents of that trailer, once they ignited, from whatever combustibles were used, actually exploded. That's why the fire became so intense."

"What are you saying?" Virgil asked.

Ark pulled up the sheet to cover the victim.

"Virgil, my guess is that this man was incapacitated in some way. He might have suffered a blow that knocked him out. If that is the case, I'll be able to tell when I take a closer look at his skull. Otherwise, he could have been given something to render him unconscious. Either way would be a blessing so he wouldn't suffer."

"So wait a second. You're saying, as I already thought, that this was no accident."

"I'm talking possibilities here. Chet told me the body was taken out of a chair he was sitting in. Unless this was a suicide, anybody would attempt to escape the inferno that trailer had become. They wouldn't stay seated in a chair unless they couldn't get out of it. No. They'd have at least stood up, tried for the door. My guess is that he was unconscious, then an accelerant was used to start the fire, then something highly combustible exploded into flame."

"I found a rag that smelled of gasoline outside on the ground, like maybe it was used by someone to wipe their hands."

"Gasoline could have been used to ignite what was inside but this wasn't just a gasoline fire. Chet told me that he also detected a chemical odor."

"Is that what you were doing when I saw you bending over him . . . trying to detect that smell?"

"I think Chet was right. There was something. It wasn't just gasoline."

"What do you think it was?

"Well, I'm no expert but Chet thinks that trailer might have been one part residence and one part meth lab. So we might be looking at the murder of an entrepreneur here."

"That's an interesting spin. If that's the case, then I guess we're looking at a whole range of possibilities."

"Yep, everyone from a dissatisfied customer to a partner who maybe isn't a good sharer."

• • •

Virgil was mulling over what Ark had told him on his way to the office. He was passing Talbot's hardware store when he glanced at the clock. He did a quick U-turn in the middle of Main Street and pulled up in front of the store. The bell over the door rang as he stepped through. There was that particular smell of age with the blend of the store's inventory. Everything from tools, paint, kitchen items like toasters and can openers filled the shelves. It was the ancestor of the box stores that were coming to larger population centers throughout the southwest. Selling virtually anything a homeowner could want or need. The store wore its age in every aspect from the uneven wooden floors to the sag in many of its shelves. Every time Virgil came in, he felt like he had stepped back in time. He had no doubt that the store looked pretty much exactly as it did when his father walked through the same entry that he had over fifty years before. In a true sense it became part of the town's identity in a way he doubted those huge depots of commercialism ever could.

"Hey, Sheriff? Can I help you with anything?"

Virgil looked into the familiar smiling face of a young man. He was fumbling for the name.

"Haven't seen you since you broke my last boss's thumb, when you leaped over his desk and smashed him into the wall. That was some day."

Virgil kind of shrugged as the not-so-pleasant image jumped into his mind. Remembering the incident helped him to recognize the young man.

"Wade almost shot your ear off. Never going to forget that day," the young man said.

"Sorry you lost your job," Virgil said, trying to let go of the recollection.

"We all did that day. Most of us didn't like Wade but we all liked cars."

"So you're back working in the family business. It is Joe, right?"

"Yeah, Joe Talbot, newly retired from the automobile business, now a hardware clerk in my father's store. Sounds real snappy, doesn't it?"

"I don't know," Virgil replied. "Sounds better than unemployed."

"I guess," the young man answered. "Anyway, Sheriff, what can I get you?"

"Lights for a Christmas tree," Virgil said.

"Gee, Sheriff, we're just about out of everything for Christmas. Think all we got left are some sets of white lights and some decorated wreaths."

"Will you be getting more in?"

"Not this late. Christmas is only a few days away."

"This is not good," Virgil said. "My daughter wants to see Christmas in a big way."

"You mean Virginia?"

Virgil smiled at the revelation that the word was out. If Joe Talbot knew about Virginia, it was a safe bet most of Hayward now knew Virgil had a daughter.

"Well, thanks anyway," Virgil said as he turned toward the door.

"Hey, Sheriff. Hold up a minute."

Virgil turned to watch as Joe ran to the back of the store. He was surprised when he was back a couple of minutes later carrying a cardboard box.

"Hope you don't mind slightly used," he said, going to the window that looked out on Main Street. In a couple of minutes he stripped the lights off the tree that stood in the window. Then he wound them around his arm. After placing the last string in the box, he brought it to Virgil. "Merry Christmas, Sheriff." He handed the box to Virgil.

"But that's your window display. What will your father say?"

"It's okay. Like I said, Christmas is almost here. I'll take those white lights and string them on the tree before I close up. It'll look fine. This way you won't disappoint Virginia. Pop won't mind a bit. He is always telling me the goodwill of our customers is what keeps them coming back." Virgil smiled at the comment.

Virgil left the store feeling like he scored a coup. Joe was standing in the doorway. Virgil waved as he pulled away. It was nice to see that one of the town bullies who had ganged up on Jimmy years before had become a different person.

A little over an hour later, he was admiring his handiwork on the front porch when Cesar came out of the barn. Virgil walked down the steps to meet him. Together they stood in the darkness, not even minding the cold chill of the night while the multi-colored lights from the tree worked a kind of magic on each of them.

# 7

"You want another cold one?"

Simon looked at the empty glass sitting in front of him.

"Sure . . . why not?" He pushed his glass across the bar.

"Couldn't wait for me?" Chet Harris was standing at Simon's shoulder. He signaled to the bartender for another beer. "Well, how's your introduction to law enforcement going?" Simon shrugged but didn't respond. "What's the matter, Simon?" Chet prodded. "The job or something else?" The bartender set two glasses in front of them. Simon took a swallow from his then Chet did the same.

"You know," Simon said, looking into the glass.

"Yeah. Guess it's never going to go completely away. We just have to figure out a way to live with it." Simon for the first time looked full on at Chet.

"You seem to be doing pretty good. To tell you the truth, I was amazed when I came out here to see how well you were doing."

"I got lucky, met some good people. Doc Kincaid for one. He's been great. You know, even in the hospital environment, a lot of administrators didn't jump at the prospect of a one-eyed intern. Even Virgil when we first met didn't flinch a second when he saw the eye patch, made a crack that maybe I should get a parrot. Guess he and Ark are cut from the same cloth. Then of course there's Karen."

"No . . . I got no problem with the sheriff or anyone, Rosie . . . Jimmy. It's just I feel haunted. I mean, you were a medic. You were always trying to help people . . . save lives. Now you're doing the same thing." He paused, then took another long drink from his glass.

"And you," Chet said. "You think you're going to be doing the same thing . . . fighting the enemy, killing people, taking more lives. Maybe you should talk to Virgil about the way you feel."

"Maybe. It's just that it struck me today." For the next few minutes, he told Chet about the trip he made with Virgil. "It hit me when I was standing outside that trailer. I didn't want to go in there. If Virgil had asked me I couldn't have. I didn't need to see another blackened corpse. There were more than enough of them in Afghanistan. I see them every night when I close my eyes. They wake me up in a sweat. They haunt me."

Chet looked at Simon. He was staring straight ahead but Chet knew he saw nothing except a deep, dark abyss.

"I know . . . I know." It was all he could say. He knew. He had worn that same haunted look for a long time. He also had spent many sleepless nights staring into that abyss.

# 8

"Well, I hate to be one of those people that says I told you so, but I detected a crack in the back of Everett Jessup's skull. Pretty sure he wasn't born with it."

"That just reinforces the verbal report I got from the fire investigation. Gasoline was used to start the fire but the chemicals inside the trailer finished the job. Thanks for the call, Ark. Guess I got another mystery to solve. Looks like I'm going to be making another trip down-county. Talk to you later." Virgil hung up the phone just as Rosita came through the door.

"Either I'm late or you're early," she said.

"I wanted to clean up some paperwork that I've been putting off. Now it looks like I'm going to have to make another trip down to Cielo. See Mr. Jessup about his son. Maybe try to get a leg up on this thing before Christmas. Everything here seems to be in good shape, but I'm going to have to leave some of this for you."

"We run a tight ship, Virgil." Rosita was standing at the sink by the refrigerator washing out the coffeepot. She was humming a tune that Virgil couldn't make out.

"I don't know if it's my imagination or what, but it seems to me you've been in an unusually good mood lately."

"Must be your imagination, Virgil. I'm the same cheerful person I've always been . . . happy-go-lucky and carefree."

"You can add delusional to that list." Before the rejoinder came, the door opened and Dif walked into the office.

"Morning, folks, or is it afternoon yet?"

"You're about an hour early for that," Rosie said.

"What's going on? Edna throw you out of the house again? I didn't expect you for another four or five hours."

"She and her sister are going to Vegas for three days, with Edgar. Guess he got a bunch of comps from some hotel."

"Why didn't you go with them?" Virgil asked. "We could have worked something out, Dif."

"No. That's okay, Virgil. I told them I couldn't get off because so much was going on around here. Told them about the bank robbery then the other thing down around Cielo. Tell you the truth, I can't stand Edgar. He's got about as much personality as road kill. I haven't heard an intelligent word out of him in the last two years. Those first three husbands of Lola's weren't so bad, but this one."

"Didn't one of those guys empty out the bank account on Lola?" Rosie asked. Dif hesitated before answering.

"Yeah. But he just needed some getting-away money. Hell, I woulda done the same thing to get away from Lola. I liked him best of all her husbands. I asked him one time why he married her. He told me that second husband of hers that got hit by the freight car was his best friend, so he thought he should comfort her. The comforting led from one thing to another. Next thing he knew he was staring at a preacher."

"Whatever became of him?" Rosie asked.

"Last I heard, he was managing a tiki bar on the beach in Mexico near Cozumel. He's probably happy as a clam. Bet every day he realizes how close he came to committing a felony, if he'd stayed with Lola."

Virgil was smiling as Dif's narrative came to an end. The door opened again and Jimmy and Simon came into the office.

"What's going on?" Virgil said. "Hasn't anybody got a life around here?"

"Simon wanted to take a ride before our shift starts. He wants to see as much of Hayward in the daylight as he can before he sets out on his own."

"It doesn't look any better in daylight," Dif piped up.

"Maybe," Simon answered. "But at least if I get lost, I'll know where I am." Dif was about to respond then stopped, stymied by Simon's response. Everyone started laughing.

"Yep, Simon. I think you're going to fit right in with this crowd," Rosie added. They were still laughing. Virgil had gotten out of his chair, heading to the coffeepot for the third time when the door opened again and Kyle Harrison, ATF agent, stepped through. The room got momentarily quiet.

Virgil didn't miss a beat. He threw his cup into the sink, shattering it into tiny pieces. Then he threw an ill-timed punch at Kyle, who sidestepped just far enough so that it brushed the side of his face. The momentum of Kyle's movement caused him to trip over his own feet. He crashed into the wall on his way to the floor. Virgil stood over him, his eyes dark with anger. Kyle held up a hand.

"I'm not going to even think about trying to get up until you put that gun back in your holster, Virgil. I know you got a bone to pick with me, that's why I'm here. But first I wanted to tell you that I'll be happy to come to your Christmas party."

"Well, I'm glad that's settled," Rosie said. "Virgil, you're not going to treat all your guests this way, are you?" Virgil looked at Kyle then at

Rosie. The fire had gone out of his eyes. "Virgil, go sit down. I'll get you and Kyle a cup of coffee."

Virgil extended his hand. Kyle grasped it, then Virgil pulled him to his feet.

Jimmy, Simon and Dif stood silently watching. Virgil walked to his desk and sat down. Kyle grabbed a chair, pulling it alongside. Virgil looked hard at him. There was a full minute of silence before he spoke. Rosie set a hot cup of coffee in front of each of them. When Virgil finally spoke everyone heard what he said.

"You lied to me. There never was a plane crash." The words hung in the air.

"I had to, Virgil. The story had to be convincing to everyone, especially you. Ruby is alive and safe. She has given us a lot of information that a lot of people would have killed her in a heartbeat to prevent. You've got to understand it was the only way. I did it as your friend."

• • •

"Can you tell me exactly what happened back there?" Simon asked the question shortly after he and Jimmy pulled out of the parking lot by the office. For the next couple of minutes, Jimmy brought Simon up to speed about Buddy Hinton, the Black Bull, but particularly about Virgil and a woman named Ruby.

"Bottom line is, I guess Virgil found out that the story about the plane crash in the Superstition Mountains was just that, a story. It evidently was made up to cover getting Ruby into the witness protection program. Virgil didn't take it kindly that they didn't let him in on it."

"Can't say I blame him," Simon said.

"Yeah, well, I guess at least one federal agent agrees with you. Too bad Virgil couldn't know that before he ended up sitting on the floor."

# 9

It was a little after three when Virgil left the office for Cielo. Whatever punch the sun had had was long gone. There was a cold wind blowing that caused him to turn up his collar. Once he got on the other side of the railroad tracks where the land was wide open and flat, he could see sand eddies, miniature twirling tornados on the prairie, along with tumbleweeds driven by that same wind. Every so often when he was alone on a landscape like this, he felt a certain sadness. It was hard to explain why. It wasn't a new experience and he knew exactly when it had started. He didn't know why it popped into his head just now. Maybe it was the resurrection of what might have been with Ruby, after the encounter back in the office with Kyle Harrison. Or maybe it went way back to that first time his world got turned upside down. It hurt to think on it but he couldn't stop himself.

He had just come home after a great day with Rusty. There was a stiff wind blowing that day too. But the difference was it was warm, filled with the promise of spring. His world was just about perfect that day, too perfect. He was anxious to work with Jack, who was a young weanling. His father had bred his favorite quarter horse mare to a Texas stallion with a pedigree that went back to Pegasus. Jack was the result. His father had made a present of him on Virgil's twenty-first birthday, even though the mare wouldn't drop him for another six months. Virgil knew what that meant. It would be the first horse he would start and finish all by himself. He didn't want to disappoint.

After he was foaled, Vigil worked with him almost every day, which at that stage was just a lot of hands-on touching. He had already gotten the colt to the point where he could almost put the halter on himself. He learned quickly. Virgil could pick up any hoof, curry any part of his body. That day he was going to put him on a lunge line, just to see if he could circle him so he could begin to learn his leads. He knew he was young for this, but he'd been so quick on the pickup to this point, he was curious to see how he would react.

Virgil wasn't too surprised when he pulled into the driveway that day and saw his Aunt Clara and Uncle Clyde standing by the corral fence talking to Cesar. Only when he saw no sign of his mother or father was he slightly puzzled. He knew if Clara and Clyde were coming that his parents would be there to greet them, since they were coming all the way

29

from just on the outskirts of El Paso. When he stepped from his vehicle and his Aunt Clara turned toward him, he knew that there was a serious reason why his parents weren't there. He was numb for the next three days. His world had changed overnight but it didn't impact him until he came home from the cemetery. Everything looked the same, yet somehow it was all changed. He had walked out of the house away from the noise and the people who filled the house after the funeral.

He was standing by the corral when his father's horse came over to nibble at his sleeve. He didn't even remember how it happened, but he soon found himself astride and headed for the high country. The horse needed little urging. He hadn't been under a saddle in almost a week. Virgil wasn't aware of the passage of time or the miles he rode. In a strange way, time stood still. It was only after the horse snorted a couple of times and Virgil instinctively reached forward to pat his neck, drawing his hand back covered in lather, that he came back into the moment. He slowed the horse's gait, coming finally to a full stop.

His immediate reaction as he dismounted was how angry his father would be to see his favorite mount with sides heaving, covered in moisture, nostrils flaring as he struggled to fill his lungs. He pulled off the saddle, then started rubbing the horse down with the saddle blanket. Steam rose from the animal's back. After the rubdown, Virgil began walking the horse, becoming truly conscious of his surroundings for the first time.

He had reached the flat land beyond the ridge way up on the mesa, an area of BLM land that his father leased and was the northern border of their grazing rights. It was the poorest part of the range. A high plateau, like the land in the eastern part of the county on the way down to Cielo. It seemed endless, stretching all the way to the end of the world. Virgil stopped, looking at the emptiness of the barren landscape. Barrel cactus, sagebrush, some bunch grass and not much more. Even the cattle deserted this land after spring rains. At least ten acres was needed to support one cow unit in the best of times here. He sat on an outcropping of rock while the horse dropped his head in a vain attempt to find something worth chewing. Virgil's eyes roved the wasteland looking for any sign of life. Nothing, not a bird or a sidewinder. He was literally alone. An insignificance. A profound sadness settled on him that he had never experienced before and he wept. Wept for his loss, but in reality mostly for himself. This new world was not of his choosing. He realized for the first time how little control he had and how vulnerable he was. It scared him because he knew that from now on whatever came at him, he would be facing it alone.

The dark mood Virgil had slipped into because of the recollection lifted a little when he saw the same rise ahead that he had pointed to when Simon had been in the car with him. At least, he thought this time hopefully, his journey would not end standing alongside the burnt-out hull of a trailer. He passed the turnoff for Everett Jessup's place, crossed another rail crossing, then passed by what he thought was the entrance to the sand and gravel company. He was surprised when he heard how much more it had expanded since he had last seen it. But then he realized he couldn't even remember when he had last been down this way. This was an area of the county that had been the least developed until the last couple of years. He was driving so fast he almost missed the turnoff for Roscoe Flats. He braked, did a quick U-turn, then headed away from the routed county road. About two miles down, pretty much in the middle of nowhere, there was a general store with a gas pump outside. Seven or eight houses were clustered together. There was even what passed for an eatery with what looked like a smaller scale version of the Lazy Dog next door. He could see a couple of pickups and a dump truck outside, probably belonging to somebody from the sand and gravel. To the right of the building a little further on was a driveway. The carved wooden sign at the head of it read Sundown Ranch. Beneath in smaller letters he saw E. Jessup Prop. He turned down it, followed it for a half mile or so until he saw a neat, one-story, small ranch-style house. He pulled up by a fenced pasture, stopped the car and got out. A horse on the other side of the fence raised his head, greeted him, then dropped his head to some graze. Virgil walked around the car heading for the house. He could see Mr. Jessup sitting on the front porch getting out of a chair to greet him.

"Hey, Mr. Jessup. Hope I'm not interrupting your routine today."

"Ain't had much of a routine for the last ten years, Sheriff. Pretty much take it as it comes these days. You know, when I look back now, it seems like I was always in a hurry. Now I wonder what I was hurrying to."

"My grandfather said something like that not too long ago." Virgil's eyes took in the little house as he got closer, noting how the shutters on either side of the windows that looked out from the front of the house onto the driveway and the front yard looked freshly painted. The windows themselves looked brand-new.

"Nice little spot you got here, Mr. Jessup."

"Yep. Everett's doing. The whole place from top to bottom. The old place stood for over a hundred years but Everett said it wasn't worth putting new money into it, so he just had it leveled and had this new place built. It's a modular. They did the whole thing start to finish in less than one week. C'mon inside, Sheriff. Got a fresh pot on the stove."

Virgil followed the old man inside. He was even more surprised when

31

he sat down at the kitchen table and got a chance to look around. Everything, appliances, cabinets, even the floors he had walked on to get to the kitchen and those in the kitchen itself looked brand-new. "Got some doughnuts if you'd like." Mr. Jessup placed a plate of doughnuts in the center of the table. "They're still warm. Gracie over at the Pit Stop brought them over about an hour ago. When I got your call, I told her you were coming and she brought them over."

"Thank you, Mr. Jessup. Didn't mean to have you go to all this trouble." Mr. Jessup held up his hand.

"Nice to have the company. Now that Everett's gone, I'll have plenty of time to be alone. Might as well get used to the idea. He was a good boy, kept me from getting lonely." He waved his hand again in a sweeping gesture. "Did all this for me. Said Pop, you earned this. Wouldn't take no for an answer. Funny, it was almost like he knew something was going to happen. Didn't want me living in the old shack. Funny." He bent his head slightly. Then Virgil saw him brush his hand across his brow as if he was swatting a fly. Virgil took a sip from his cup then reached across, taking one of the doughnuts from the plate. He took a bite, sat back in his chair, then took another sip from his cup. Mr. Jessup sat up a little straighter in his chair and took a drink of his coffee.

"So, Sheriff, how can I help you?"

"Well, I was hoping you could tell me about Everett, his friends, his job, anything that might help me understand why he ended up like he did."

"Don't quite understand, Sheriff. Accidents happen. Guess maybe Everett got a little careless."

Virgil took a breath.

"Well, Mr. Jessup. You see, that's one of the reasons I'm here. There is a pretty strong likelihood that this wasn't an accident." He waited for the words to sink in a few seconds before continuing. "So, if that's the case, anything you could tell me would be really helpful as the investigation goes forward."

The old man looked about the room, almost like he was looking for something. "Investigation . . . investigation." After he made the comment he paused. "So you think maybe somebody hurt Everett on purpose." He said it as a statement of fact rather than as a question. Then he looked at Virgil. "Why would anybody do that, Sheriff?"

"Well, that's what we're hoping to find out, Mr. Jessup."

For the next twenty minutes Virgil heard the life story of Everett Jessup, how he had worked at the sand and gravel company with his partner, Michael Stark, for the last five years, how everybody liked him and he didn't have an enemy in the world. Virgil chose to not point out that wasn't a hundred percent true. Everett, he knew, had at least one enemy. Finally, Mr. Jessup was showing signs that he wasn't just talked out but physically tired.

Virgil got up from the table, took his and Mr. Jessup's empty coffee cups and set them in the sink.

"Thank you, Sheriff. You know, I remember your father. Didn't know him real well but I remember he had a reputation for playing it straight down the line. 'Course, back in that day that was a line many people regretted crossing. Not everybody was happy about that. But he was known as an honest man. Didn't have his hand out waiting for a payoff or dipping into the till. Every time I read the newspaper these days or see the news on the TV, somebody in Congress or some local politician is being looked at for double dealing. No matter how much they have, it's never enough." He got to his feet with some difficulty.

Virgil reached out to steady him. Together they started for the door.

"Have you been here long, Mr. Jessup?" They had reached the small entry hall by the front door.

"All my life and then some." He pointed to the wall in the hallway leading to the door. It was covered with family history. Virgil saw cowhands in full regalia looking back at him from days long past. "That's me in the buckboard, alongside of my mother. We were bringing supplies out to where my father was running fence with a couple of hands and my older brothers. Ran over two thousand head on this range back then. This here was my grandmother. She was mostly Ute. My other grandmother was half-Apache. They hated each other. You got a little Indian in you, right?"

"More than a little," Virgil answered.

"Well, I always say the soup with the most ingredients has the best flavor. Never did understand how people got to hating one another because of race. Way I figure, we all come from the same pot of stew. Oh, that there is Everett." Mr. Jessup pointed to a photograph obviously taken much more recently than all the others. Virgil leaned in to get a closer look. "That was taken just before my wife passed, about four years ago." The man in the photo, all in white, towered over the woman standing next to him.

"Everett must have got his height from your side of the family," Virgil said.

"Well, my wife had a couple of pretty tall brothers. But Everett, yeah, he just sprung up like a weed. He was still growing when he was in the Army. He was the tallest of the three boys. 'Course, the youngest never got to full growth. He got hit by the haybine when he was eleven. Clint, well, he landed bad off a nasty bronc, so Everett's all I got now." He averted his eyes for an instant. Then he turned to look at Virgil. "By the way, Sheriff, do you know when I can get him?"

"I'll check when I get back to Hayward." They had stepped outside. "Guess you have to make some arrangements."

"No . . . that's all done. His spot is waiting for him."

Mr. Jessup stepped off the path that led to the front door then motioned to Virgil to follow him. They walked around the side of the house to the back. There were a couple of barns and a corral not too far distant. One of the barns looked in fairly good shape but the other looked like it wouldn't make it through the next windstorm. But then Virgil had seen old, forgotten outbuildings like these hang in there long after the people who owned them. Mr. Jessup walked to the sturdier of the two barns and opened the door. The sunlight flooded in while an old barn cat missing one ear ran out. Dust motes swirled in the air, while a cow somewhere in the depths of the structure bawled. Mr. Jessup walked a few feet into the alleyway that ran down the middle, then stopped. Virgil could see something covered by a canvas tarp sitting on a couple of sawhorses. Mr. Jessup picked up the edge that was hanging over, throwing it back on itself, exposing what was underneath to view.

"I made it for myself, like I did for my wife, but now it will be for Everett." Virgil looked down on the frame of the box that would hold Everett's body. "Hope it's long enough." Mr. Jessup said.

"You did a nice job." Virgil didn't know what else to say. Mr. Jessup pulled the covering back over then led Virgil back outside. He didn't say anything but the horse that had been grazing in the pasture had come over to the fence gate that led into the corral, which stood to the right of the barn. He called to Mr. Jessup like he had to Virgil.

"Not time yet, Ranger," Mr. Jessup said. "He's getting anxious for his supper." Again he motioned to Virgil to follow him as he led him down the opposite side of the barn, past the other barn that was struggling to stay vertical. When they got clear of both, tucked away on a little knoll that rose up in back was a small fenced-in area maybe a quarter acre in size. He led Virgil through a small gate that squeaked for lack of oil in the dry climate. Virgil realized immediately that they were in a family cemetery.

"Been putting family in here for about a hundred and seventy-five years. Looks like I'll be the last one, now that Everett's gone. Didn't think it would all end with me."

They walked a little further into the cemetery. Virgil noted the fresh paint on the metal fence that enclosed it. Every marker stood upright, every memorial on each was vivid and readable. The old man stopped in front of one headstone. It read: Mamie Jessup. Underneath were the dates of her life, and beneath that there was one word, BELOVED. Alongside, Virgil saw a freshly dug hole.

"That's for Everett," Mr. Jessup said. "I'll be on the other side of Mamie. You know I always had a dream that Everett would come back to the land. Oh, I know he decided to go to college, become an accountant. Always was smart as a whip, but I figured that maybe someday . . ." A minute passed in silence. A crow landed on the fence surrounding the little graveyard, gave a raucous caw, then flew away. Mr. Jessup looked at it. "Guess it's time to let that dream go, bury it here with Everett." He looked once more down at the empty hole in the ground. Then they turned and headed back down to the house.

Virgil looked in his rearview mirror as he pulled away from the house. Mr. Jessup was standing by the pasture fence. Ranger had walked over to him. He was nuzzling at his sleeve. Virgil had the feeling that he had come to find out about Everett Jessup Junior but was taking away a lot more than that. He mused over the last words of Mr. Jessup when Virgil asked him if there was anything he could do for him.

"Nope." He looked back in the direction of the graveyard. "After I've taken care of Everett, I've got to build another box. Make some arrangements for myself. Guess I ain't done living yet."

# 10

When Jimmy came into the office he was surprised to see Rosie still there locked in conversation with Dif.

"Hey, guys. What's going on?"

"Actually, we were talking about that Christmas party Virgil's having."

"Yeah, Virginia's getting into that big time," Jimmy said.

"Should be fun but we got a little problem. Rosie and me were just now talking about it."

"What's that, Dif?"

"Well, if everyone's at the party, who the hell is going to mind the store?"

"I don't get your drift. How do you mean?"

"Well, the town and county of Hayward ain't about to shut down just 'cause we are all having a good time over at Virgil's place." The door to the office had opened again. The gust of wind that came with it caught their attention. Simon had walked in on the tail end of Dif's comment.

"Don't mean to butt in but I might have a thought about that, if I understand correctly what you were talking about." Three heads turned toward Simon, who was still standing in the doorway.

"Well, spit it out, son," Dif said.

"Major Travis . . . the state police. I think after the way the attempted bank robbery went down, for a little payback I bet he'd be more than willing to cover the town and the area for a few hours."

"You know, Simon, I'm beginning to think I misjudged you. I wasn't sure whether or not you had enough sense to pour sand out of a shoe but that's a great idea."

"You know, Dif, I'm beginning to feel different about you too. When I first heard some of your stories, I figured you were just another old windbag living in the past. But now I realize you're not that old." A hush fell over the room. Then a spontaneous roar filled the room. By the time Virgil came in almost half an hour later, a transformation had occurred. Simon had definitely become a member of the club.

Simon and Jimmy left on patrol shortly after Virgil came in, spurred on by Virgil's revelation that he had spotted a lot of lawbreakers roaming the streets of Hayward with little evidence of any members of law enforcement on the scene.

"Everything all right, Virgil?" Rosie made the inquiry as Virgil slumped down into his chair. Virgil took off his hat and tossed it onto his desk before answering. She thought he looked tired. "What is it, Virgil?"

"Oh, I don't know. Guess I'm just thinking about how life sometimes tosses us a curve. We go along thinking it's a straight line. Like Mr. Jessup down there in Roscoe Flats. All alone now at the near end. Wife gone, now his son. Tough way to end up . . . all alone.

"Virgil, you are going to the dark side. That's not you. Look, you've got a daughter now. People who care. We all go through rough patches, but life is always a surprise waiting around the corner. There may be one for Mr. Jessup. Just when you think there is no more and you are ready to settle into that rut, something jumps up, smacks you in the face, to let you know you are not in control." Virgil looked across the desk at Rosie, who was smiling from ear to ear.

"You know, Rosie. I should pay you for the therapy. But what gets me is, here you are spouting this life philosophy and hell, your life has been going in a straight line forever."

"That's right, Virgil. Like I just said, that's when it hits. Just about the time you've settled into that rut. Dave and I, we finish one another's sentences. We're all set. Empty nesters, bills mostly paid off. Nice house, mortgage almost done, kids gone. Looking from the outside, the straight line . . . the rut. No more surprises, you think, then wham."

Virgil sat up in his chair.

"What are you saying, Rosie?"

"I'm saying, Virgil, just what I told you. Life is waiting to happen, just around the corner. It can be good or bad. You never know but it's there."

"You had any of those surprises lately? I don't think so," Virgil said, mockingly leaning back in his angled chair.

"Just one, Virgil," Rosie shot back quickly. "I'm pregnant, Virgil. Dave and I are going to have a baby. I'm a grandmother and I'm going to have a baby. How's that for a curve?"

Virgil caught hold of the desk to keep from going over as he came upright. Rosie swore Virgil to absolute secrecy, telling him that he and Dave were the only ones who knew about her pregnancy. She hadn't even told her son and daughter.

When Dif came back from the holding cells, Rosie was washing out the coffeepot while humming the same song she had been humming in the morning, before Virgil left to go down to Cielo and Roscoe Flats. Virgil had wondered why she had been singing that morning. Now he knew that Rosie had put a positive spin on this life surprise, but then knowing her as long as he had, he would have expected no less. He was still thinking about her news along with what she had said while on his way out of town. It was almost full on dark. He glanced at the clock on the dashboard. It wasn't even five thirty. He decided to take a chance on an unscheduled stop, turned off Main Street and backtracked to the hospital.

Virgil caught up with Ark in the hall leading from his office to the morgue.

"I thought maybe by chance I would get you."

"Trying to get caught up on a lot of overdue work so I can have a little more time at home next week with the kids."

"Guess Christmas can get a little crazy when you have little kids." Virgil was thinking of Rosie when he made the comment.

"You have no idea, Virgil. You will have to try it sometime. But we are looking forward to your party and a night away from the house. Toys will be all over the place. It's like walking through a minefield. It will be a nice change, stepping over some partygoers who didn't know when to stop. Hell, we might even join them. We can sleep in the barn if it gets that good."

"You will be more than welcome. Jack will be happy for the company. On another note, Mr. Jessup was wondering when he would be able to get Everett?"

"I guess that all depends on when Everett wants to show up."

"Not quite sure I get what you're saying, Ark."

"Well, I called you earlier but you were out of town."

"Never got the message," Virgil said.

"Well, Virgil, to answer your question, that poor soul lying on the table in the room at the end of the hall isn't Everett Jessup. I'd say it's somebody in their late teens to early twenties. And I'm not a hundred percent sure, but I remember Billy Three Hats contacting me a while back about a couple of youngsters he was looking for who had gone AWOL from their homes. Do believe drugs . . . meth was involved. Well, I think that boy in there . . ." Ark gestured toward the room at the end of the hallway.

"I think that boy's last home might have been on the reservation."

*A surprise, waiting around the corner,* Virgil thought, recalling Rosie's words.

# 11

By the time Virgil left Art Kincaid at the hospital the dark had settled in for real. Virgil's head was spinning a little with the new information he had learned. He was beginning to get that feeling that he'd been down this road before. For some reason, that phrase Kyle Harrison used that night he set up Virgil to see Ruby for the last time was stuck in his brain: "Things are not always what they seem." He actually said it out loud, as if by doing so there would be some kind of clarity. He drove another mile or two in anticipation but there was no epiphany. He had a deep-down feeling that as far as the mystery of Everett Jessup was concerned, there was a lot more that he didn't know than what he did. The burnt-out trailer along with its unknown occupant might be only a hint of what was ahead. Maybe that mantra that kept playing in his head like a phonograph needle stuck in the same groove was worth listening to.

The brightly lit Christmas tree that stood on his front porch could be seen on a moonless night like this a mile off. It pleased him to see it. It was a beacon to the one place on earth he held sacred. On this particular night, alone on a dark country road when he saw it, the day's events finally dropped away. Inevitably, it brought to mind his conversation with Rosie, then to thoughts of Virginia and how his life had changed in the blink of an eye. A year ago he didn't know he had a daughter. He was living day to day, which he now realized had been going on for much longer than he cared to think about. But now, like a fresh breeze, Virginia had come into his life. He would never go back to what was, he knew that. Rosie had only verified what he always knew, touched the tip of the iceberg. There's a surprise around every corner just waiting. For Rosie it was a new baby, for him it was Virginia. He couldn't think about Virginia without thinking about Rusty, her mother. Virgil didn't spend a lot of time on what-ifs, but in this case it was inevitable. For one thing, he knew as he turned into the driveway, if Rusty had been around this would not have been the first Christmas tree on the front porch.

He could see a light on in Cesar's apartment in the barn. The tree on the porch was the only light from the house. Instead of going right to the house, he went into the other new barn. Jack greeted him right away from his stall. He walked over to him. The newness of its construction was still there but now it was mixed with the animal smells, leather, and the tons of cut hay stored on the second floor. He was actually pleased to see some

39

hay chaff on the floor, which he kicked up as he made his way to Jack. There was even a little evidence of wear on the top rail of Jack's stall, where he hung his head in anticipation of a scoopful of grain or a late-night visit from Virgil. Virgil ran his hand along the smoothness of Jack's neck, pleased with the thickness of winter growth. All of the stock seemed to be in pretty good shape according to Cesar. Virgil was glad they hadn't had to thin the herd because of losing the last year's hay when the original barns burned down. Cesar said the hay they had gotten from High Lonesome ranch was good but not as good as what they had lost. Virgil smiled just a tad when he thought of the comment, because he knew in Cesar's eyes outside hay, wherever it came from, would never quite measure up. Jack's eyes were closing as Virgil stroked him. The only noise came from a snort or two from some of the other stalls that lined the runway. He looked down the row to where the only two overhead lights lost their way in the dark. He knew that in the last stall on the right his mother's mare, Star, was dozing, probably standing over the inert form of her six-month-old nameless foal, which had come as a great surprise in her old age. The link with his mother through her mare and Jack, who had been given to him by his father, offered a continuity that Virgil could now pass on to Virginia. He hoped she would like her Christmas present, which was now snoozing peacefully under the watchful eye of his mother, Star.

He stayed in the quiet longer than usual, even resting his chin on the top rail inches from Jack's head. It became a dreamlike state, listening to Jack's rhythmic breathing, feeling the warmth of his expelled breath, along with the nighttime noises that are only there in the dark. The barns were too new to groan but he could hear the wind pick up, tugging at any opening it could find. The suspension of time lasted until at last his eyes closed. His foot slipped off the bottom rail where he had anchored it, jarring him back to full consciousness. He wiped a bit of drool from the corner of his mouth as he straightened up.

"Guess I better get down the road or ask you to move over, Jack." He walked down to the door then turned, looked around once more, inhaled deeply the perfume that he loved and left.

# 12

Morning brought with it the new reality. There was no escaping it. When he got to the office he called Ark.

"You're sure of your findings?"

"Sure enough to tell you that's not Everett Jessup on the table in the back room. Not sure exactly at this stage who it is, but my guess, as I said yesterday, would be Native American, late teens, maybe twenty. Looks like the growth plates are done. Height, maybe five-eight, not much more. Sorry, Virgil, if this is going to make life a little more difficult for you, but that's what I see."

"Thanks, Ark. You know, yesterday I saw a picture of Everett Jessup hanging on his father's wall. He looked to be well over six feet so that kind of confirms what you just told me. As far as making my life easier, don't lose any sleep over that. I took this job of my own free will. I just want to make sure when I start going down the road I pick the right road."

"So, that is not Mr. Jessup's son." Rosie had obviously heard the exchange.

"Look's like," Virgil answered.

"Do you have any idea who it is?"

"I might but I'm going to have to speak with Billy Three Hats to see if my hunch is right."

"Sounds like a trip to see Grand Dad."

"I could call."

"Virgil, you haven't been up on the mesa in a while. Why don't you do both? Make the call, have Billy meet you there. Remind them both about the party on Thursday."

"Killing two birds with one stone. Sounds like a plan," he said.

• • •

*If you didn't know it was there, you wouldn't know it was there,* Virgil thought as he turned off the hard surface road into the desert west of Hayward, almost to the turnoff for Redbud. There were the slightest traces of wheel ruts in the hardpan, less visible on the frozen ground at this time of the year than when driving in during any other season. In spring and early summer they would be much deeper. In late summer and fall there would be a dust cloud in the wake of any vehicle turning off.

But on frozen ground in winter, nothing. Virgil didn't even slow down when he made the hard right turn or at any other time until he crested the butte to the flat land on which stood his grandfather's double-wide.

At almost any other time of the year his grandfather would be sitting outside at this time of the day, getting ready to enjoy another jaw-dropping southwestern sunset. But not in the winter, not up on the mesa. The dry northwest wind that hit Virgil in the face when he stepped out of his car made it feel twenty degrees colder than down in Hayward. He glanced around at the terrain as the door to the trailer opened. A couple of small tumbleweeds blew around the cleared spot where any vehicles would park. Blue sage, a bare cottonwood bent in an otherworldly shape by persistent winds over decades and a whistling noise through the rough corral fence that housed the small flock his grandfather still kept greeted him. All of it looked cold.

"Hello, Grandfather." Virgil pulled his Stetson tight as he jogged toward the open door. Once inside he grabbed his grandfather and gave him a quick hug. The old man pulled back.

"What is this?" he said.

"It has been too long. I am just happy to see you. I'm half-white. White people hug a lot. It is a nice custom."

"It was not unpleasant but it takes getting used to."

"I like it." The words came from Mary Hoya, who had just come into the kitchen. "You can hug me anytime, Virgil." Virgil walked around the table and hugged Mary, who vigorously hugged him back. Just then the door opened again. Billy Three Hats and one of his sons had come in.

"Hey, Virgil. You better be careful hugging Grandfather's woman. He might get jealous." Mary had proceeded to set the table for supper. Without being told, Billy's son went to help her.

"There's another white man's custom that has taken hold. Helping with the housework. Ah, for the days when a warrior sat and was waited on," Billy said.

"That was not from the white man, that change came from woman's liberation," Mary offered.

"Well, Billy, change is inevitable. You have to roll with it. On the other hand, you didn't have to go out in the cold on a day like this to hunt down the meat for tonight's supper," Virgil added.

"Just as well," Grandfather spoke up. "If that was how we were going to get tonight's food, I'm afraid our plates and our stomachs would be empty."

Billy feigned anger.

"I am a great hunter, just ask my son about my triumph today." He gestured toward the boy.

"Pop caught a mouse in a trap he set last night in the kitchen."

"Oh, great hunter," Virgil said. "We will drink a glass of wine in your honor. Your feat will be told around the fire for generations to come. There will be dancing and feasting."

"Thanks. I'll skip the wine and have a soda. I'm a friend of Bill W. now."

"Good for you, Billy. Good for you," Virgil said.

"I'll join you in the soda." Billy Three Hats raised his hand.

"No. You and Grandfather have your glass of wine. This is my problem, not yours. I have to learn to live with that. Besides, as head of tribal law enforcement, I should be able to show the restraint that I'm trying to instill in the other tribal officers."

"Come on, sit. Dinner is ready," Mrs. Hoya called, and everyone responded.

"Don't take this the wrong way, Billy," Virgil said after eating a mouthful of the steak from his plate, "but that meat tastes better than anything you could have caught out in the desert." Other heads nodded in agreement.

They finished the rest of the meal flavored with small talk. Most of it about life on the reservation. Virgil had never lived on the Rez but had spent much of his early youth there because of his mother. Now, sitting at his grandfather's table, after having been removed from daily life there for decades, it became so apparent that in many respects it was a mirror image of Hayward. Not so much a different world but a parallel one. Billy Three Hats, his counterpart in this scenario, was dealing with many of the same societal issues that Virgil faced. Admittedly, there was more or higher rates of some problems, but the fallout was just the same. Broken families, single mothers, addiction, it was all there. The only singularity that Virgil considered a positive was the common tribal culture, which bonded the people in a way he didn't see as much in evidence in the society in which he lived.

"A Christmas party, I have never been to a Christmas party. I like the decorations, the lights. I think it is a good tradition. I like to see you taking part in a custom like that. It gives meaning to your life, causes you to pause, look inside of yourself."

The words of his grandfather, Virgil felt, were another example of Virgil's tentative grip on the spirit world. Here, as he sat musing on the comparisons of the two different cultures, his grandfather was reading his mind. It was not a new phenomenon. It had happened many times before. So often in fact over the years that it was one of the primary reasons Virgil could never fully deny the life of the spirit. One time he had spoken to his mother about this.

"In this way," she said, "it is a gift, I think. Maybe given to very few people, marking them with a special kind of wisdom to see beyond this world. I have not been given it but I think your grandfather has. In your father's world I have heard it called second sight. Why certain people have it, I do not know. Maybe it is to keep us who may be a little more cynical less so."

Virgil had considered her words often, especially when he witnessed the darker side of life and struggled for understanding.

"So, Virgil, why did you come today?"

"Isn't it enough that I wanted to see you, Grandfather?"

"It is more than enough but the fact that Billy is here also suggests to me that there is another reason."

"Grandfather, I hope that someday I will be as wise as you."

"You will be. I will share the secret to being wise with you and Billy." The dishes had been put in the sink and were being loaded into the dishwasher by Billy's son and Mrs. Hoya. Billy had just placed three cups of coffee in the center of the table and sat down.

"What are you talking about?" Billy asked.

"I told Virgil that I was going to share the secret of wisdom with him and you."

Billy took a sip from his cup, sat back in his chair then rolled his eyes.

"This better not involve going and sitting on a rock for three days without food or water waiting for a vision. My lower back would never make it."

"No. It is much easier. All you have to do is grow old. That is the secret. When you are young you are in a hurry. When you are old you realize that to get to the same place you don't have to hurry. You will get there. It is the story of the old bull and the young bull standing on the hill looking down at the cows. The young bull says, let's run down there and have a good time. The old bull says, no. Let's walk down there and have a great time." Virgil and Billy looked at each other, then both broke out into laughter.

"Grandfather, that is the first time I ever heard you tell a joke," Billy said.

"There can be a lot of truth in a joke," Grandfather said as he stood up from the table. He picked up his coffee. "I am going to watch the news now, to see how all the people in the world are doing without wisdom. You and Billy speak about why you came tonight." After he stepped into the other room, Billy turned to Virgil.

"What's the problem?"

"You remember when you came to me a few months back looking for a couple of boys who had gone missing from the Rez? I believe you said they were dealing or using crystal."

"I remember," Billy said.

"Did you ever catch up with them?"

"Only one. He's in treatment now."

"What about the other one?"

Billy took another drink from his cup.

"No. I never did find him. He was a good kid too. Looked hard but he pretty much dropped off the map. Why do you ask?"

Virgil hesitated.

"If you have an idea of his whereabouts, his folks will be thrilled. He's Broken Nose's boy. You remember him. When you were kids, you and he used to hang out together when your mom used to bring you over. Broken Nose will be thrilled if you got a line on him. Where is he?"

Virgil hesitated even longer. Then he picked up his cup, looking into it as if he was going to find another answer to Billy's question. Billy repeated the question. "Where is he?"

"I think he is laying on a slab in Hayward Hospital."

# 13

By the time Virgil got back to Hayward, they had already taken in the sidewalks. There were a couple of cars outside of the Lazy Dog but that was pretty much it. Even Margie's place was almost empty as far as he could see. He had enjoyed the visit with his grandfather but was feeling a little guilty. He knew that first thing tomorrow, Billy Three Hats would be making a call to Broken Nose and his wife. Virgil had made those kinds of calls. They were the kind that stuck with you. A permanent scar on your memory.

His first call was only two weeks into his role as sheriff. He would always remember the haunted look on the faces of the Tylers when he had to tell them their daughter Cassie had been pulled lifeless from her boyfriend's car. The fallout wasn't temporary. The boyfriend who survived had become a raging alcoholic. Years later his bloated body was pulled from the same river where he and she had gone over the embankment. Guilt comes at a high cost.

Virgil was surprised when he pulled into the lot in back of the office to see Dif's car was not there.

"Hey, Jimmy . . . where's Dif?" He asked the question as he stepped through the door.

"I told him he could take the night, Sheriff. Simon was ready for a night on the town without me."

"An executive decision, I like that. Since you are in an administrative frame of mind, maybe you would like to share your perspective on Simon. After all, you are my right-hand man."

"Sheriff, you don't have to say those things anymore. I'm pretty secure now." Virgil looked at the boy he knew as Jimmy. For the first time he saw a trace of something that hadn't been there before.

"Besides, if you keep lifting that shovel, you are likely to get a hernia."

"Not only do I get a declaration of manhood, but I get a kick in the pants at the same time. Okay, Officer, in your professional opinion what is your assessment of our new hire's abilities?"

"I think he is going to be a good addition. He's smart, quick and he's got a mean hook shot." Virgil's eyes widened at the last comment. "It's kind of an inside joke of Simon's. We have been playing basketball on Wednesday or Thursday nights. I think he has the skill set to make a good

46

officer. The only thing is, I think he needs to have a little more time to get his feet on the ground."

"How do you mean?"

"Well, he has talked to me a little about some of his past experiences. Pretty bad. Between the loss of his hand and those memories, I think it's going to be a while before he can put all that in back of him." Virgil sat back in his chair reflecting on what Jimmy had just told him. "There a problem, Virgil?" It was rare that Jimmy called him by his first name.

"Not a problem as such but I've been mulling something over today. How do you think he would like working with Alex down in Redbud, at least temporarily?"

"But what about Dave, Rosie's husband? Why the change?"

"Well, something has come up. I'm thinking about bringing Dave up here, at least for a while."

"Well, I think Redbud would be a good fit for Simon. Alex is a real nice, easy going guy. It is a little less hectic down there. It would give him that time, like I said, to get his feet on the ground, along with more time to become familiar with the geography. I think he still feels a little like a fish out of water. We're quite a bit different from New York City."

"Yes, we are," Virgil said. "Not a parking meter in sight. Glad we had this talk, Jimmy." Virgil stood up. "Since everything looks good here, I'm heading home. But do me a favor. Don't mention anything we talked about to Simon when he stops back. Want to make sure I got it all worked out before I say anything to him or to Dave Brand, and to Rosie, for that matter."

"Can you tell me why you are thinking of making this change?" Jimmy asked. Virgil had picked up his hat and was standing by the door.

"Not just yet. If I told you, I'd have to kill you or else Rosie would kill me." Virgil stepped out, leaving Jimmy with a puzzled expression on his face.

• • •

There were times when he felt the weight of his job more than other times. This was one of those times. He was sorry he hadn't stopped by Margie's before he came home. He would have liked to have sat over a cup of coffee along with a slice of one of her homemade pies. There might even have been some social interchange. Margie kept him up to speed on local town gossip. On a personal level he hadn't had much social interaction out of the office since Ruby. He could hear Cesar, his stand-in Mexican father, telling him to work at not being alone.

The inventory of the refrigerator for a late-night snack a few minutes after he got home did nothing to stimulate his appetite. There was a covered dish with some mystery meat that looked like a laboratory experiment gone wrong. Cesar always said when in doubt dose it with hot sauce, but Virgil just didn't feel like taking a chance. He dumped it in the trash bin then settled on a couple of hot dogs, which he threw into a fry pan along with a can of beans. A few minutes later he was pushing them around on his plate, wondering why he had bothered. Even the cold beer he had opened tasted doubtful. Most of the meal ended up with the mystery meat, the last of the beer emptied into the sink. Twenty minutes later, after a warm shower, he was flat on his back in his dark bedroom staring at a spot on his ceiling that he couldn't see, wondering how he was going to tell Mr. Jessup that the charred body from the trailer was not his son. On the other hand, he had no idea where Everett was and whether he was alive or dead. People talk about closure but Virgil knew he had none to give. This was not going to be an easy call. In any event, he knew that with the daylight he was facing another trip down to Roscoe Flats. The thought of it was ruining his night's sleep.

# 14

The horses were blowing condensation from their nostrils when they stepped out of the barn. It was the coldest day since Virgil had been up in the high lonesome country on the Thompson ranch at Thanksgiving. Another reminder that they were getting deeper into a new season was the layer of frost that had settled over everything. It would only last until the rising sun had a chance to do its job. Cesar stepped out of the barn with a couple of Plymouth Rock hens following at his feet. They immediately ran ahead, pecking and scratching at the ground, whipping up ice flurries as they did. By the time Cesar reached the steps leading to the front porch Virgil was standing at the top, a steaming mug of coffee in his hand. He handed it to Cesar as he stepped onto the porch. Then he reached over to get his own cup, which was perched on top of the railing. Together they sipped the hot liquid while they silently watched the day begin.

"It'll all be gone by nine o'clock," Virgil said.

"Si, but it is pretty while it lasts. Maybe we get more this winter."

"Could be . . . been a little colder than usual. Horses' coats are pretty thick. How's the stock look?"

"All good. Time to wean that foal off the old mare. Probably going to be tough. She likes being a mom but it's got to be done. He's almost seven months."

Virgil drained the last of his cup.

"Why don't we wait until after the first of the year? We don't want the two of them carrying on when everyone is here for that party. Couple of days more or less won't make any difference."

Cesar took Virgil's cup along with his own, then went inside. Virgil stayed on the porch until he returned.

"Heading into Hayward?"

"Nope. Other direction. Down toward Cielo and Roscoe Flats. Got some news for an old-timer down there. I want to tell it in person."

"Long drive when you could just pick up the phone."

"Yeah." Virgil was watching the frost starting to drip down from the barn roofs. "Kind of feel like this is the kind of telling should be done face-to-face since it's good news. Besides, I like this old man."

"Those are good reasons," Cesar said.

Virgil gave a half wave then walked down the steps and got in his car.

49

Once on the road he called Rosie to tell her his plans for the morning. Not being her usual responsive self, he questioned her on it.

"I'm okay. It's just that it's been over twenty years since I had morning sickness."

"You and Dave break the news to the kids yet?"

"Last night."

"How did that go?"

"Well, one of the boys said, how did that happen? Dave said, if you don't know then you mustn't have paid much attention in that biology class you had in high school. The other boy said he thought he'd have a tough time relating, since he would be twenty when the baby was born. My daughter wanted to know if we knew anything about birth control. All in all, Dave and I would have to say the conversation wasn't the highlight of our day."

"Don't worry. They'll come around."

"I guess. It's just . . . Oh, I don't know. Guess I was thinking just when I was wrestling with the prospect of middle age, I kind of get a reprieve. Now, I don't know. I mean, this child is going to be an aunt or uncle to someone older than he or she will be. Like I said, I'm a grandma, Virgil."

"Listen, you and Dave will have plenty of time to contemplate getting old when you're old. In the meantime, you will be too busy with this little one to think about it. That's a good thing. Take it from someone who is trying to figure out how to be a father for the first time when he is on the north side of forty. By the way, I'm liking it."

After the conversation ended, Virgil spent part of his drive time mulling over his own words. For the first time he confronted the fact that it was true. He was happy to be Virginia's father. His only regret was that it took twenty years to find out.

It was a little after ten by the time he was knocking on Mr. Jessup's door. After a few minutes with no response he was beginning to wonder if maybe he shouldn't have just made that phone call, like Cesar had suggested. He stepped off the front porch. The field to the side of the house that ran the length of the half-mile driveway was vacant. No sign of the horse that had greeted his arrival when he came the previous times. He was contemplating his next move when he noticed a pickup by the barn in back. Virgil walked down along the side of the house to the barn. He slid the barn door open, then gave a call. He was about to give another when he heard a response from deep within. Following the sound, he began walking the length of the barn. The almost finished casket was still up on a couple of wooden horses covered with a tarp so he stepped around it. He hadn't realized how big the barn was until he started walking its length.

"Mr. Jessup, it's Sheriff Dalton." There was a momentary silence following his shout-out.

"Down in the last stall, Sheriff. Could use a little help." Virgil broke into a trot, running the length of the walkway until he reached the last stall. He saw Mr. Jessup then heard the cow. He remembered hearing a cow in the barn on his last visit.

"What's up?" Virgil asked the question as he scaled the top rail of the stall then dropped down to stand next to Mr. Jessup. The cow bawled again.

"She's having a hard time bringing this calf," Mr. Jessup said. "Straining so hard I'm afraid she's going to cash her whethers, if I don't get it out soon." It had been a long time since Virgil had heard the phrase. He knew it meant a prolapsed uterus, when a cow pushed so hard trying to deliver her calf that she literally pushed her uterus out right after the calf. The cow was obviously working hard trying to deliver her calf. If she succeeded then kept pushing she could expel part or all of her uterus. Getting the calf out quickly would help to avoid this. Coming alongside Mr. Jessup, Virgil saw the calf's feet sticking out.

"Here, let me have a go," Virgil said. He slipped off his belt then looped it around the calf's protruding feet. Once he had a snug fit he began to pull with a slow steady pressure. The cow bawled again, then Virgil could sense a contraction. He pulled steadier. The calf's legs almost came all the way out, then he saw its head. He reached forward, pushing the calf's head down into a diving position. There was a sudden gush of birth fluids, then the head came through as the calf in its diving position fell into the soft bedding that covered the floor of the stall. Virgil dropped to his knees, then pulled as much of the birth sac off the calf's head as he could to open up the mucous passage. Mr. Jessup handed him a towel. He rubbed the calf vigorously but there was little response. Virgil spied a full water bucket in the corner of the stall, so he jumped up, grabbed it, then poured the cold water on the calf in a torrent. There was an immediate response. The calf's eyes widened while it took in a couple of gulps of air. Its rib cage filled with oxygen and it gasped. Its breathing after a couple of minutes became regular, then it tried to lift its head.

Virgil stood up. Mr. Jessup put a hand on his shoulder.

"Thank you, young man. You saved the day."

By this time, the cow had turned around, giving her full attention to the calf. She began to vigorously lick the calf, which was showing more and more animation in response. The two men watched in silence for a while. After about ten minutes the calf struggled to its feet.

"As many times as I've seen it, I still find it a wondrous thing."

Virgil nodded in assent.

"Hey, that's a Jersey cow." Virgil made the comment as if he was seeing the cow and calf for the first time. The rust-red tint of the calf was matched by its mother.

"So it is," Mr. Jessup replied. "Don't see a lot of them in beef cattle country, do you?" Virgil waited for more to come. The old man reached over and pulled a wooden crate from alongside the wall of the stall, which he had obviously been using to sit on while he was waiting for the cow to calf. He sat down heavily, his breathing somewhat labored. Virgil saw for the first time that his shirt was soaked through with perspiration. "My people came here from New England over a hundred and fifty years ago. All they had by the time they got here were a few possibles and a Jersey cow. My grandmother told me that if it weren't for that cow they never would have made it through that first winter. Her mother's milk had dried up. The cow saved her life. Ever since, there has always been a Jersey cow in the family and on any land we owned. You might say it has become a kind of tradition. That calf can trace its history all the way back to that first Jersey cow that came into this country." He paused for a moment.

"Guess old Ginger there and her new baby are going to be the last of the Jessup cows." He paused again. "Always thought Everett would keep it going." There was a noticeable sag to the old man's shoulders. He stood up off the box.

"Come on, Sheriff. Let's get on over to the house, get something to drink." A few minutes later they were sitting at the kitchen table. "I think we earned this today." He set two cold cans of beer on the table then popped the tab on each. "Need a glass?"

"No. This will do just fine." Virgil took a long drink from his can, then set it down on the table. "Mr. Jessup, I wanted to talk to you about Everett, that's why I came today."

"Didn't figure it was to deliver a calf. Is it about getting Everett, so I can put him up on the hill?"

"Not exactly," Virgil answered. "You see, that body that came out of the trailer wasn't Everett."

"Not sure I understand." Mr. Jessup leaned forward in his chair.

"Well, Dr. Kincaid examined the body. Says, it belongs to someone younger then Everett and not as tall. We think there's a possibility it might be a young man from the reservation." Virgil could see the old man trying to put the pieces together. He was working his mouth and fingering the beer can on the table.

"Are you saying Everett is alive? I know he told me he had someone over there helping with the decorations." The note of hope in his voice could not be missed.

"We just don't know, Mr. Jessup, but there's a possibility. But I need to ask you a favor."

"A favor?"

"Yes. Because I'm not sure what's going on exactly. I think it would be best if we could keep this information between us for a while."

"But why?" Mr. Jessup asked. Virgil took another swallow from his can before answering.

"Because, maybe if Everett was the target and whoever was after him think they got him, there's a chance they will stop looking. I think Everett has a better chance staying alive right now if he stays dead."

# 15

Virgil had intended to drive straight back to Hayward but the last couple of days had made him aware of how out of touch he really was with this part of the country. When Rosie had referenced the sand and gravel company, along with the other changes to the area, it just reinforced the notion that not only was the county too large for the size of his staff to patrol, but its profile was rapidly changing. When he reached the intersection after leaving Roscoe Flats, he made the right turn toward Cielo. If Roscoe Flats was not much more than a wide spot in the road, Cielo had definitely taken a step up. The first sign was the gas station and the Kwik Mart. Virgil pulled in off the road, parked and went inside. It even smelled new. The smiling dark face behind the counter greeted him. By his accent, Virgil judged him to be Indian or Pakistani. Virgil went to the back of the store, where he figured the cold drinks would be located. He took two bottles of Snapple from the shelf, then returned to the front of the store. Another younger man had joined the first man in back of the counter. Virgil asked for a turkey and Swiss hero with lettuce and tomato. The older man went to make his sandwich. Virgil nodded to the younger man.

"Nice store . . . looks new," he said.

"One month, we're open one month," he answered in precise, slightly accented English.

"How's business been?"

"Very good," he replied. The door opened, a couple of men came in and went to the back of the store. A minute later they were standing alongside Virgil. Virgil could see their trucks outside. Each of them ordered a sandwich. The man standing next to Virgil, sporting a mustache and beard and wearing a brightly colored headband, broke the ice.

"Howdy, Sheriff. Little way from Hayward, aren't you? We don't see much law down here."

"That must mean everyone down here is law-abiding or the state police are doing a great job."

"Well, we try to stay out of trouble, don't we, Lou?" The other man just rolled his eyes. Virgil's sandwich was placed on the counter. Virgil reached in his pocket. The man behind the counter made a waving motion.

"No . . . no. It is my pleasure. We are happy to see you." He looked at the younger man, who Virgil now took to be the older man's son. He said nothing.

"Thank you for the gesture," Virgil said. "But it is on me. As a matter of fact, I'd like to treat these two gentlemen here." Virgil put thirty dollars on the counter.

"Well, if that don't beat all, Lou. The law is buying us lunch. That's a first. Sheriff, I ain't always had positive interactions with the law. Thank you very much."

"Enjoy your lunch," Virgil said as he picked up his change and turned toward the door. He was standing next to his vehicle when the two men came out of the store. "Would you happen to know where the sand and gravel company is?" he asked them. He remembered seeing the sign on his last trip but didn't know whether that indicated the actual turnoff.

"Can do better than tell you, Sheriff. Follow us."

Virgil followed them for three or four miles. As he did he noticed a small plaza that had sprung up around the local post office. He glanced at five or six stores that were open for business—a deli, a florist, a hardware store, and at the far end of the row of buildings, what would pass for a restaurant and a bar. There were a couple of vacant storefronts but the plaza itself looked well maintained. A little further on, he passed two churches, one on either side of the road, and then a feed store. They came to the railroad crossing, which Virgil vaguely remembered, then a half mile after the crossing the two trucks turned left just past the sign he had seen, on to a recently blacktopped drive. Virgil saw another bigger sign a quarter mile down for Diamond Sand and Gravel. He followed the two trucks through the gate then pulled up next to them in the paved parking lot. He shut off his engine and got out of his vehicle.

"You guys didn't have to go out of your way," Virgil said. The bearded man had rolled down his window.

"Not a problem, Sheriff. We work here. If you follow that path it will take you right to the main office." He pointed to the path that edged the parking lot. "We're continuing on to the plant. We park there. Anything else you need?"

"No. Thanks for leading me here. I might have missed the turn after the railroad tracks. I thought it was Mesquite Sand and Gravel."

"It is. Diamond's the old name. It's just been changed to Mesquite recently. They just haven't gotten around to putting up the new sign."

"By the way, would either of you happen to know an Everett Jessup? I understand from his father that he works here."

After a slight hesitation, the bearded man's silent partner stuck his head out of the window of his truck.

"I know Everett, Sheriff."

Virgil left his spot then walked to stand between the two pickup cabs.

"Everett and me play on the same softball team. Company has sponsored a team last couple of years. We play in a league. Everett's a pitcher." The image from the photo on Mr. Jessup's wall immediately popped into Virgil's head. Everett had been dressed in white. Virgil realized it had more than likely been a uniform. Tall and lanky, Everett looked the role of a pitcher. "Ain't seen him lately, though. 'Course, there's no softball now. He maybe is on vacation. Lots of people in the office take time in the winter when things slow down a little. Guys like me and Jesse spend a lot of time now crushing rock, building up stockpiles for the spring when it gets busy. Jesse, you know Everett. We was drinking with him at the end-of-season barbecue."

"I know who you mean now but didn't remember his name. Nice guy but doesn't drink nothing but beer."

"That's right. Never touches the hard stuff. Doesn't smoke neither. No vices but a real good guy."

"You sure that's Everett you are talking about? I kind of got the idea that Everett liked to party, maybe smoke a little weed," Virgil said. Lou raised his eyebrows at Virgil's comment.

"Sheriff, I don't know where you are getting your information, but that's about as far away from the Everett I know as you can get. Hell, he don't even cuss. Doesn't even like to throw inside. Afraid he's gonna hit somebody and hurt them. Drove the coach crazy but he's got a mean fastball. He's our best pitcher. He don't actually work for the company. He's an accountant. I think he and his partner have been contracted by the company for the last couple of years. Keep forgetting he's not just a regular employee. Come to think of it, he said last year that it might be his last year on the team unless him and his partner got a new contract for their work."

"Lou, we got to go. Got to be back to work in twenty minutes."

"Okay, Jesse. Sorry, Sheriff. We got to eat these sandwiches you bought us." Each started slowly backing up. Virgil gave a wave then watched as they drove out of the lot. He continued watching them as they drove toward the plant, then disappeared around the side of the building. Virgil could hear dull, thunderous noises coming from where they were headed. He didn't know much about rock crushing but it sounded to him like a noisy job. Lunch break for some workers was apparently over.

He stood for a couple of seconds looking at the building at the end of the path bordering the parking lot. The main office, as Jesse called it. It had been his intention to go in, ask to speak to a Human Resources person about Everett, but now he was having second thoughts. Knowing what he had just found out about Everett had him in a quandary. Lou's words had painted a different picture than what he had started to put together in his head. The contradictions were nagging at him.

There was one Everett who decorated his home for Christmas, which turned out supposedly to be a meth lab, containing the body of a young Indian charred beyond recognition; and there was the Everett who didn't want to throw an inside pitch for fear of hurting a batter and didn't drink much or smoke. Virgil looked once more at the building at the edge of the path, then, remembering his own words to Mr. Jessup, decided he better try to keep Everett dead for a while so he could work out some of the contradictions he was wrestling with now.

He turned and got in his cruiser, retracing his steps until he got to the main road, then made a right turn and went over the railroad tracks and headed back toward Cielo. He stopped when he reached the gas station, pulled in to fill up his tank. It was early afternoon. Despite the chill he was standing in full sun. It felt good. The air was clear, a blue sky filled his view overhead. A hint of a breeze tugged at his collar while he pumped the gas. The smell of the fuel lingered in the air while he ran the county credit card through for his gas. The smell of the gasoline usually never bothered him—sometimes he kind of actually liked it, but not today. It somehow spoiled the crisp, clear air and the sunlight. When he pulled out of the station for the second time that day he had intended to drive straight back to Hayward. The thought of stopping at Everett Jessup's trailer hadn't struck him until he saw the actual turnoff. The long road in looked the same. There hadn't been any recent rain. Even though he was going slowly, he could see roiling dust clouds left in his wake. High sun was bouncing off the sandstone walls of the arroyo. Mica glistened like little diamonds as it caught the direct rays.

At last the double-wide came into view. He could still see the yellow crime scene tape, some of it torn, fluttering in the light breeze. When he stepped out of the car the distinctive smell of burnt-out wreckage was still heavy in the air. He stepped under the tape to approach the trailer. When he reached the front door, which was still hanging crookedly to one side, he stopped. He wasn't sure why he had decided to come. Nothing looked any different from his recollection of the last time he was here. On either side of the trailer at the back stood a couple of large green specimen bushes standing in stark contrast with the trailer and the red stone buttes that framed the back of the landscape. Virgil moved toward the right side of the trailer, realizing they completely obscured the back from view. He was moving along the side almost to the rear when he saw what he took to be the headlight of a vehicle. He moved forward to take a closer look. As he stepped around the rear corner, suddenly the daylight disappeared from view. The blue sky, greenery, red sandstone, and glistening sun reflecting mica, all of it was gone. Instead, sharp pain followed by an instant blackness swallowed Virgil whole. He felt disconnected from the world as he fell into the bottomless darkness that absorbed him.

# 16

"Hey, Rosie, what's going on?" Dif had just stepped into the office.

"Actually, it's been pretty quiet. Guess the population realizes that Christmas is around the corner. Instead of law breaking, they are out Christmas shopping."

"Yep. That's why I'm here early. Lot quieter here than at home. Edna gets a little crazy at Christmas."

"If she wasn't a little crazy she would probably have never married you." Dif didn't react to the barb. "I'm only teasing, Dif."

"I know, but seriously, she becomes almost obsessed, whether it's buying presents, decorating or baking. She keeps a list on the night table. Wakes up in the middle of the night to add to it. I don't see you get crazy like that."

"Well, we all have something that sets us off. In Edna's case, maybe something from long ago. Didn't you tell me once that her mother died when Edna was young?"

"Yep, she was only five or six. Her sister and brother were younger."

"That must have been tough. What happened?"

"Guess they were tenant farming. Her dad was also working a couple of extra jobs. They were hard at it. You know that old saw when you're young . . . working can to can. Can't see in the morning till you can't see at night. Evidently, her mother got on the tractor pulling the manure spreader one morning because Edna's father had worked real late the night before. Rained hard all night till morning. Guess the tractor went over on her mom, on her way out to the field to spread some manure. Edna's father got up when the kids were running around the house. When he found out that she had let him sleep, he figured she had gone out to do one of his chores. He gave the kids breakfast then went looking for her. She was dead when he found her underneath the tractor. Edna said nothing was ever the same after that."

"I can believe that," Rosie said. "Christmas maybe got forgotten for a long time. Kids are resilient but hard times leave their mark."

Dif sat down heavily in a chair.

"Yeah, I guess," he said. Just then the phone rang. Dif continued to sit slouched in the chair while Rosie spoke on the phone. When she hung up, she sat quietly for a moment or two. Dif noted the change of expression. "What is it, Rosie?"

"That was the oddest call. Whoever it was said someone should go down to Everett Jessup's trailer. Before I could ask why, they hung up."

"Isn't that the trailer that got burnt up down there in Cielo? Where they found that body?"

"Yes, but why should someone go down there now? Virgil's in that area, I'll give him a call. He can check it out." For the next few minutes Rosie tried connecting with Virgil. "No response," she said after her fourth attempt.

"Try his cell," Dif said. "He obviously isn't in his vehicle."

Rosie tried Virgil's cell. After a couple of tries, she called Cesar at the ranch. Following a brief conversation she hung up the phone.

"I don't like this, not one little bit. Virgil's not answering, Cesar says he hasn't spoken to him since he left this morning. Said maybe we should call Mr. Jessup. I'm going to call Jimmy instead."

"What are you thinking?" Dif asked.

"I'm thinking somebody better get down to that burnt-out trailer. But I don't want to drop it in the lap of an old man."

Within twenty minutes Jimmy and Dif were in Jimmy's patrol car tearing up the road on their way down to Cielo.

"Ain't been down in this part of the county in years. Just used to be mesquite and desert. Sam, Virgil's dad, used to say it was like the dark side of the moon. No one would live here except the coyotes and the sidewinders. I think he would be more than a little surprised if he could see it now." Dif made the comment as the distant red buttes came into view.

"Don't know what it was like back then. Virgil says they got kind of a mini-boom going on down here now. This country sure looks a lot different from most of the rest of the county. Seems like it takes forever to get down here."

"Guess that's why Virgil keeps telling the town council we need more manpower, more coverage. Hell, Hayward County is as big as some countries." Dif raised his hand, pointing to a mailbox on the side of the road. "I think that's the turnoff." Jimmy barely slowed. Road dust rose up while rocks were scattered to the sides of the dirt cutoff. Dif grabbed the sidebar. "Holy shit, Jimmy, slow down or we're going to become part of the landscape."

"We got to find Virgil."

"I get it. Just don't want to be picking cactus thorns out of my ass while we are looking for him." When they reached the end of the canyon they saw the burnt-out hulk of the trailer. Alongside was Virgil's car. Jimmy skidded to a stop. Dif had his door opened before the engine quieted. Each had reached for his gun.

"Wow, they weren't making it up. What a mess. This thing's not much more than a shell now."

"No sign of anyone here," Jimmy said.

"Well, he must be within earshot. His vehicle is here, so he's on foot. Maybe he went up one of those draws for some reason and that's why he is not answering his cell." Dif pointed toward the wall of rimrock, where there were crevasses and breaks in the red rock. As they stepped out of the cruiser, each started calling Virgil's name. Only the echo of their own voices came back to them. Then Jimmy took his sidearm, raising it above his head.

"Cover your ears, Dif." Jimmy shot off two rounds, which echoed and rolled around the canyon like thunder.

"Well, if I wasn't already half deaf, I'm a goner now for sure."

"Don't worry, you'll still hear Edna whispering sweetly in your ear."

"Yeah, that's a good enough reason to fire off another couple of rounds." Jimmy fired again.

"Nothing," Jimmy said after they stood for a minute in silence. "Nothing."

"You don't think he could be in the trailer?"

"Why would he go in there? Nothing but charred wreckage. Besides, he certainly would have heard us. Let's just check it out." The two of them walked the fifty or so feet to the trailer.

"I can still smell the fire. What a mess," Dif repeated as they approached. "Must have been like an oven in there."

"Yeah, Sheriff said the body was close to being cremated." They both walked to the door and looked in.

"What are we going to do now?"

"It doesn't make sense. We were told to come here. His car is here. He's sure not in the trailer, and if he's up one of them draws, he ain't answering." Dif stood back as he made the comment. "Look." He pointed to the ground. "There's a boot mark."

"There's another," Jimmy said. "Another." He followed the scuff marks to the end of the trailer.

"Around back," Dif said. Jimmy started running. Before Dif got to the rear of the trailer, he heard Jimmy.

"He's here. He's here."

• • •

Two hours later, Virgil was in a hospital bed in Hayward Memorial, looking up at a circle of faces. They parted when the doctor came to the side of his bed. "Virgil, look at me. Okay, now follow my finger." He moved his finger from side to side, then up and down. "How do you feel?"

"Headache," Virgil answered.

"Not surprised. You took some hit. We put six stitches in your scalp, but more than that you have a concussion. The fact that you were unconscious for so long confirms it, even without a scan."

"When can I leave? I've got things to do."

"You are not going anywhere. Look, in the past year you have been operated on for a brain aneurysm, then there was that incident out at the Thompson ranch that you wouldn't let me check you out for, which probably also was a concussion. Now this. Virgil, you ought to try avoiding taking these hits to your head. Unless you want to fill that vacancy for village idiot.

"I'm serious. We've found out a lot about brain injuries in the last few years. I don't have to remind you that when we were in school you took some pretty good hits on the football field."

"You did too, Sam. You were blocking for me."

"I know. You don't have to remind me. The thing is, I don't want either of us to spend our declining years sitting on the front porch trying to remember our first name."

"Point taken," Virgil replied. "I'll settle in here until you tell me I'm fit to be in polite society."

Sam smiled at Virgil's remark.

"Trouble is, Virgil. You gotta avoid the not-so-polite society."

"Kind of tough to do in this job, Sam."

Sam didn't respond but Dif spoke up.

"Virgil, do you have any idea which one of those not so nice polite people nailed you?"

"Can't say for sure Dif, but I have an idea it just might be a guy who doesn't like to throw inside fast balls for fear of hurting the batter."

# 17

Virgil had just finished the last of his supper. It wasn't the worst food he had ever eaten, but he would much rather have been sitting over at Margie's contemplating the homemade pie that would come with his coffee. He was feeling better and would have liked to have gotten out of bed to walk around but he had promised to stay in bed until an aide was available. As much as he hated to admit it, he knew Sam was right. The pounding headache had subsided but the woozy feeling was still there. He felt it when he sat up in the bed to eat his meal. Now he suddenly felt tired so he laid back and closed his eyes. The next time he opened them the twilight had softened all the sharp edges and Micah Hayward was sitting by his bed.

"Hey, Virgil." Virgil started to sit up. Micah put his hand out. "No, relax."

"Mike, it's been a while. How are you doing?"

"I think a lot better than you. From what I'm hearing, you have to learn to duck more often."

"If they would give me some warning I would. I remember you hitting the ground pretty hard not too many years back."

"Yeah, but I always tried to land on my feet and I never went near the bulls. Didn't have that much of a death wish. I'm mighty happy to see those young guys wearing those metal baskets on their heads these days in those events. What are you smiling about, Virgil?"

"I was just thinking maybe I ought to start wearing one of those."

"If you had, Virginia wouldn't have been calling me to get in here and check on you."

"I was wondering how this visit came about."

"Welcome to fatherhood, Virgil. The first twenty years you were off the hook, now it's your turn to step up to the plate. Having a daughter worried about you and planning a Christmas blowout is just the beginning."

"Well, if that's the case, why did she send you as a substitute?"

"She's down in Redbud. It's probably her last day there before she goes back to school. We are closed next week because of Christmas, and after the first of the year we do inventory. So there is not that much for her to do then, and I'm pretty sure she'd rather spend the time getting ready to go back to school. I'm sure she will be here tomorrow. I had to be in town today to go over something with our new accountants, so when I heard about you, I told her to stay down there and that I would get in here to make sure you're in one piece."

"Well as you can see"—Virgil held up his arms—"still got all the working parts."

"Glad to hear it. By the way, I'm looking forward to that party next week, should be interesting. Too bad Mom's not here to see it."

"Well, if Audrey was there, it would be a lot more than interesting. Probably be more like the Fourth of July than Christmas." Micah Hayward stood to leave. "Did you get together with your accountants?"

"Yes. They weren't my first choice but we don't always get what we want."

"Who would that have been, Micah?"

"Well, last year when we were getting ready to make a change, I met with a nice guy who had been highly recommended, Michael Stark. He and his partner were looking for a new client. Evidently, there had been a significant reason for him to leave the previous client. He was extremely ethical, wouldn't discuss it, which I admired, and it really swayed me to him and his partner. We were all set to sign a contract. The very next week they found him at the bottom of a canyon off High Ridge Road. He died after lingering in a coma for a couple of weeks. So then I had to go back to square one and here I am."

"Well, thanks for coming by even if it is only to relieve my daughter's anxiety."

"Virgil, you know it's not just that. Rusty knew it too. If I'm going to share fatherhood with anybody, there's no one I'd rather share it with than you. You're the best brother-in-law I never had."

"Thank you for that, Micah. I just wish Audrey and I could have gotten on the same plane before she died. But like you said before, we don't get everything we want in this life. We all have to live with that reality."

Micah gave a half wave and turned toward the doorway of Virgil's room.

"One last thing, Micah, before you leave. I was wondering about Michael Stark's partner. What was his name? What became of him?"

"You know, I really don't know, but I do remember his name. It was Jessup, Everett Jessup." Then he turned into the bright light of the hallway and left.

# 18

Virginia looked about the room, more than a little angst-ridden. She had never done anything like this before.

"Don't worry, the place looks beautiful." She had been so locked up inside of herself she hadn't heard the car pull up outside or the door to the kitchen open. "I knocked a couple of times, but when I looked through the window . . . well, I just sorta figured maybe you were feeling a bit overwhelmed. That's actually why I came a bit early. Thought you wouldn't mind a little moral support."

"It's just that I never planned a party before, much less actually put one together. My grandmother, Audrey, she always took care of anything like this."

Rosita smiled.

"And knowing Audrey, I bet she did it without a hair out of place."

"Omigod, I hadn't thought about that. I haven't even begun to get ready. I must look a mess."

"Honey, on your worst day there would be females in this town who would give their eye teeth to look like you do right now. You go upstairs. See if you can improve on perfection. I'll handle things down here."

"Thanks, Rosie. I'll be back soon as I can." Rosie could hear her running up the stairs as the kitchen door opened. Virgil came in, staggering under an armload of firewood.

"I'll get the door, Virgil." As she walked by she grabbed a couple of split pieces of firewood off the mound he was carrying. A few minutes later she brought them into him where he was kneeling in front of the fireplace building a fire. A small glow in the kindling had started to emerge for his efforts. He stood up. The two of them stood there waiting to see if the fire would catch. After a couple of feeble mis-starts, there was a sudden hiss followed by a burst of flame that started licking up the side of a good-sized log.

"Looks like we got liftoff." Virgil said. "I'll go get another load." He turned to go. Rosita put her hand on his arm.

"Virgil, let somebody else get the rest of the wood. You just got out of the hospital."

"I'm fine, Rosie. Feel like I ought to do something. After all, it's the first ever Christmas party in this house."

"Tell you what. You go sit at the kitchen table. Slice up some cheese, make some appetizer trays. It's got to be done and you probably won't get light-headed doing it. Dave is outside looking for something to do. He'll get the wood." Virgil

After a little nudge, Virgil headed for the kitchen.

He had just finished his fourth tray when Virginia came downstairs. His back was to her. She came over to him and wrapped her arms around him, kissing him on the cheek.

"If I knew that was the payoff for slicing up this cheese, I'd have done it a lot sooner."

She sat down next to him.

"Guess people will be coming soon."

"Sure as hell better, otherwise we are going to have to eat all of these apps that I just made."

She reached over and grabbed a cracker with cheese and an olive on it, popping it into her mouth. Then she stood up, gave Virgil another quick hug.

"I'll put some of these in by the fireplace."

Virgil heard footsteps on the porch. Looking outside, he saw Dave Brand with a load of wood. He got up and opened the kitchen door.

"Rosie said you needed more wood." He walked by Virgil. A minute later he was back. "That should hold for a while."

"Dave, have a seat. I'm almost finished here." Virgil motioned to the kitchen chair.

"I'll get us a beer."

"Make mine a bottled water or diet soda if you have it, Virgil." Virgil sat down after placing two bottled waters on the table. "What are you looking at, Virgil?"

"You," Virgil replied. "Never saw you opt for water over beer before."

"Yeah, well. Making some changes."

"You look good, Dave."

"Lost twenty pounds, stopped smoking over a month ago."

A slight smile crossed Virgil's face.

"Would this have anything to do with Rosie's news?"

"More than a little," Dave said. "Rosie told me if we're going to have a baby at this stage of our lives, she doesn't want to be raising it by herself. To put it in her own words, 'I didn't get into this situation without help, so you better not drop dead from drinking too much beer or smoking your head off, because I'll be too busy to bury you I'll just take you out to the desert. Let the buzzards and the coyotes have you.'"

Virgil smiled.

"Sure sounds like Rosie. Don't bet she wouldn't do it either." He paused for a moment. "Anyway, I've been thinking. Four or five months from now, when the apple's getting ready to fall from the tree, I was thinking you would come back to Hayward. I figured I'd send Simon or Jimmy down to Redbud. That way you would be close by."

Dave shook his head.

"I was going to ask you about that, Virgil. Maybe even sooner, if it's okay with you. I think Rosie is having some anxious moments. We're not kids, you know."

"What about you, Dave, any anxious moments?"

"Well, I can't say I wasn't floored by the news, but after the smoke cleared, I got to thinking you know it's going to be a lot different this go-round. When the other three came on the scene we were busier than squirrels getting ready for winter. I was always working a couple of jobs, Rosie too. Then one day when I finally caught my breath I looked around. They had all grown up. Felt somehow like I had missed out. Me and Rosie talked about that a couple of nights ago. We're not running so hard now, so we can catch our breath. I'm actually kind of feeling like I got a second chance. Kind of like a dream come true. I think Rosie is feeling like that too."

"Yeah. I kind of get that second chance thing," Virgil said. A shaft of sunlight broke through the cloud cover, splashing the kitchen with its light. "Looks like Mother Nature is cooperating for this party."

"Looks like," Dave responded. "Also looks like some of your guests are here."

Virgil looked out the window to see a couple of cars coasting to a stop past the corral.

"Could be wrong." Dave said. "but I think that's Aunt Clara leading the charge."

"I'll be damned. So it is," Virgil answered as he jumped up. Together they walked out onto the porch. Clara was already out of the car.

"Well, it's nice to be greeted by two of the best-looking men in the county." A broad smile crossed her face as she came toward them. She greeted each with a big kiss and a bigger hug. "That alone was worth the drive."

"Clara, I didn't know you were coming," Virgil said.

"Couldn't miss a good time like this. Chance to see some hometown folks I haven't seen in a long time. Is that old Indian coming down off that mesa?"

"If Billy can drag him," Virgil answered.

"I hope so. I love that old man."

"Sorry, Clara, he's taken. Got himself a significant other," Virgil said.

"Good for him. No good being alone."

"But you are alone."

67

"It's easier for a woman. Women get out more, connect. Men don't. Guess it's the way we are hard-wired. Anyway, Dave, where's that pistol of a wife you have?"

"She's around, Clara. She'll be mighty happy to see you. She's got some news. Has to do with putting off that empty nest thing for quite a few more years."

"My, oh my. Virgil always said you were the best shot in the county. Guess you are still holding on to that title. Let me get inside and lend a hand. Give Rosie a hug. Virgil, could you put my stuff in my room?" They watched as she gamely climbed the stairs.

"Her room?" Dave said.

"Yep. Always was, always will be. The fact that she has been gone over fifty years doesn't change a thing. She was born in that room. I'm going to try to get her back here now that Clyde's gone, so she can die in it. That's a long drive from outside El Paso and I can't get down to her as often as I'd like."

"Yeah. It's a worry when folks get older. Clara has got to be in her eighties now. My folks are getting up there too, but at least they are close. What about her boys?"

"One's up near Seattle married with two or three kids, the other's single, works down on the rigs in the Gulf. Gets up once or twice a year." While they had been talking, other cars had been pulling in and lining up along the driveway.

"Looks like you need a traffic cop, Virgil."

"Think I'm looking at one, Dave. Do you mind?"

"Not at all. I'll stay out away from the food and the beer as long as I can. Go do your thing."

• • •

It was a little after eight when Virgil finally got out of the house for a breath of air. It was clear and cold. Stars crowding the night sky seemed brighter without the glow of the moon. He walked to the corral, then turned along the driveway toward the road. His lungs filled with cold night air, his breath escaping in small wisps of vapor. By the time he reached the road, he no longer felt the nighttime chill. He opened the two top snaps of the blue denim jacket he had grabbed off the hook on the wall just inside the kitchen door. He occasionally referred to it as his barn jacket, to be used whenever he was going to engage in some strenuous and maybe dirty work in the barn. The truth of it was, he hadn't worn the jacket in quite a while. The state of his present life had not allowed much time for the luxury of barn chores. He couldn't even detect the sweet manure smell that had infused the jacket in the past when he had more time to participate in the day to day on the ranch. Again, it was a marker of how much his life had changed.

He stood at the end of the driveway looking across into the darkness that hid the fields on the other side of the road from his view. There was absolute quiet. No night creature stirred, no car divided the road with the glow from headlights in either direction. He held his breath for a moment, straining to see if he could hear any of the merriment from his home at the end of the long driveway. Nothing, not a sound. No music, no tinkle of a glass or spontaneous laughter to inform the night. He was for an instant the only man alive, the only one on the planet. He let out a long-overdue breath, watching the small cloud rise then dissipate in the night air.

Finally, he turned to walk back. He had a momentary image stirred by his boots scraping the loose stone underfoot of the boy he once was, getting off the school bus running and scattering some of these same stones. He looked at the house, every window lighted. The music of the coming together of so many friends spilling out. The warmth he now felt came from deep within as he retraced his steps. He wished his mom and dad could have been in the waiting group, but that again was a reminder that change is the only constant. He knew to embrace it, to hold on to the moments like this. He quickened his pace as a smile of anticipation grew.

# 19

Clara looked out the window in the bedroom she had been born in over eighty years before. Looking through the same blue eyes but now framed by a face that wore the cares of a long life in every wrinkle. The scene she saw conspired to make time stand still. She could see clear to the ridge where she would ride Nugget every day after she came home from school. Sometimes she would take Sam, her little brother, with her, but most of the time she was alone. She saw herself racing out of the barn on the dry bed of the tractor road, which snaked its way to the first of the low-lying hills. Her father, if he saw her, would yell at her to slow down. "Ease up," he would say. "Give Nugget a little time to work into it. That's not a starting gate you came out of. It's a barn." She could hear his voice even now, though he'd been gone over sixty years. She barely had any remembrance of her mother. She had died shortly after giving birth to Sam. She thought maybe that was why she grew up more boy than girl.

She could do and did everything there was to do on the ranch. And she loved it. Sam used to tease her. Boys in school did the same when they saw her rope and ride. She wasn't much like the other girls. She never really worked at being a girl. Her father and her brother even talked to her about it a couple of times, but she was happy doing the things she did and being the way she was. When she got older she came to understand that she didn't exactly fit the mold. Boys didn't come around often. Not that she was unattractive. She mentioned it one time to her father when she didn't get asked to the end-of-year school dance.

"Clara," he said, "boys don't like it much when a girl can ride better, rope better and shoot straighter than they can. Unless you plan on not doing those things, the situation ain't likely to change. Sorry I wasn't a better mother to you."

Pop was right. Clara never did stop doing those things and the situation did not change, until Clyde came along. Of course, by then she was closing in on forty. But then like she, Clyde was cut from different fabric. He wasn't threatened by a woman like Clara. He thought she was a hoot and spent most of his married life bragging about her every chance he got.

She sat at the window a long time until the winter sun finally cleared the highest butte, flooding the room with cold light. She was sitting at the table in the kitchen enjoying a second cup of coffee when Virgil entered the room.

"You're up early." He made the comment after glancing at the wall clock, noting it wasn't quite seven.

"Old people don't sleep as soundly or as long as young people. Maybe it's because they know they are running out of time. Don't want to be caught napping when the reaper comes knocking."

"That's a pretty grim thought on a nice morning after a great party," Virgil responded.

Clara reached out, covering Virgil's hand with one of her own.

"You are absolutely right, Virgil. And it was a great party. Don't let an old hag like me drag you down. Guess it's just that a lot of memories get stirred up when I come here. Can't escape them. Then last night, seeing folks that I haven't seen in a long time. Sleeping in my old bed, looking out the window and seeing the world just like it was when I was a girl. Then just when I'm getting ready to buy into the illusion, I get up. My bones are speaking to me, saying, Clara, you are not that young girl anymore. Get over it."

"Guess we'd all like to stop the clock sometime. I know there's been more than a couple of times when I would."

"Maybe the lesson is, we should all try to live in the now more often. Clara replied. "More parties like last night."

"Definitely. I'm going to make sure of that. If it wasn't for Virginia, I would have spent another Christmas looking instead of being part of it."

"Virgil, I'm telling you that girl might just save you from yourself, being swallowed by the world and all its troubles. Your father had your mother to do that, now you have Virginia. Audrey did a good thing not taking that secret to the grave. Then again, she never was predictable. I sometimes wonder how it would have turned out between her and your father if things had been different."

"Well, for one thing you and I wouldn't be sitting here having this conversation."

Clara smiled.

"Guess we wouldn't have had that nice party we enjoyed either. Guess the only loser in that whole what-if scenario was Audrey, and she died the wealthiest woman in town carrying the town's name." Clara paused for a moment, glancing out the window at the bare branches of the cottonwood. "Guess there's a lesson to be learned in there somewhere." She made the last comment as she got to her feet. "Time to start the day."

"Me too," Virgil replied.

"Can I ask you what you're about?" Virgil had made it a rule to never discuss details of whatever had his attention at the moment, following the advice of his father: *Remember, Virgil, small towns have big ears and even bigger mouths.* But this was Clara, who would have to be turned on a spit before she would give up a confidence. He sat back in his chair. Clara sat back down opposite. For the next couple of minutes he talked about his trips down to Cielo and Roscoe Flats and how they had ended with him in Hayward Memorial nursing a bad headache.

"Last night, Ark told me they had to release the boy from the trailer to his family. So now it will become public knowledge who he was and who he wasn't. I am more than a little concerned about the fallout when whoever is behind this finds out they missed their target. I like Mr. Jessup. Don't want to see anything happen to him."

"Did you say Jessup?" Clara asked.

"Yes. He's a nice man even if I do believe his son put me in the hospital."

Clara smiled.

"Always was, and I'm mighty glad to hear he still is."

"You know him?" Virgil asked.

"If his front name is Everett, I surely do. He gave me my first kiss. If Clyde hadn't come along he would've been my second choice if he had been available, but he was snapped up pretty quick. Back then the good ones didn't hang on the tree too long."

"But how did you ever get to know him? I mean, Roscoe Flats is almost forty miles away."

"Virgil, don't you know a thirsty man will go a long way for a drink. Sixty some odd years ago I doubt there were more than three thousand people in the whole county. Boys on ranches would think nothing of riding thirty miles just to get a look at a pretty girl. Guess it is hard to imagine in a world filled with cell phones and computers and instant messaging. Must seem like a different world to you." She glanced out the window. Virgil thought he saw her eyes moisten. "There I go again. Getting lost in the past." Virgil squeezed Clara's hand.

"Guess it's part of the cycle of life. We spend the early part looking for what's coming next. When we get there, it's flying by so fast we don't really take notice. Then one day we realize we are spending more and more time looking back. You know, last night when everything was going full-tilt, I took a walk out to the road. Did some remembering of my own. Thought of Mom and Dad. Wished they could have been there having a good time. Thought about getting off the school bus back when it was still a dirt road. That's when I thought about Virginia. Maybe the key to rolling with life is just that. Knowing that as things, people slip away, other things, other people come along to fill in the vacuum. That's what keeps us in the present."

"You know, Virgil, you are a lot older than you look. Hell, you might even be older than me." Clara stood up again. "Come on. Let's go for a quick ride before you start looking for lawbreakers." Before Virgil could respond she was walking out the kitchen door. He caught up with her on the front porch.

"You sure about this, Clara? I mean, the ground isn't getting any softer. I mean . . ."

"Thank you for the concern, Virgil. But if it's a choice of breaking my neck falling out of bed or off a horse, I'll take the horse. Besides, I saw old Sugar out in the pasture when I drove in yesterday. I'm more liable to fall off my rocking chair than off her. Let's go."

Twenty minutes later they pulled up to look at the new day from atop the ridgeline Clara had looked at from her bedroom window. "There's a view I never get tired of looking at." A slight breeze brushed her gray hair. They sat looking down on the ranch house, along with the collection of barns and outbuildings, as the morning sun drove the last of the shadows away. For an instant as she turned Sugar toward the back country, Virgil lost her gray hair in the brightness of the day. Then he saw only the figure of a young girl cantering ahead.

# <u>20</u>

It wasn't until early afternoon that Virgil got a chance to reach out to Mr. Jessup. He had gotten bogged down in the mundane work of the office. He couldn't pass it off to anyone else because he was alone. That was fallout from a successful party. When he got to the office a little after nine, there was no freshly brewed coffee aroma greeting him. Moreover, the first job of the day had to be getting over to Margie's to pick up the bagged breakfast that was waiting for the sole occupant in one of the holding cells.

"Here you go, Cecil." Virgil stood in the space of the opened cell door holding a breakfast tray, waiting for a response from the figure on the bunk. After the second summons there was an indication of life. Cecil Summers sat up and swung his legs around, hitting the floor with his stockinged feet. He was bleary-eyed and looked like he was just coming off a two-week bender. This was not the first breakfast he was about to eat at the county's expense.

"Thanks, Sheriff." He made the response as Virgil set the tray down next to him.

"You know, Cecil. This situation isn't going to have a good ending unless you move on. Getting a snoot full then going to your ex-wife's door banging on it at two o'clock in the morning isn't the answer. This has been going on much too long."

"Was my house for fifteen years."

"*Was* is the operant word here, Cecil. That isn't likely to change."

Rosie came into the office a little after nine. Virgil hadn't had any success reaching the older Everett Jessup.

"Virgil, I can't say when I've had a better time at a party. Everything was great. It was one of those nights that I wished would never end. You know, seeing all those people."

"You see them all the time," Virgil replied teasingly.

"I know, but it was seeing them there all together at the same time. You know what I mean. Your Aunt Clara locked in conversation with your grandfather and Dif. I mean, between the three of them they got about half the history of this county covered in their stories. Then who joins them but Eustace and his wife. I mean, an old Indian whose grandfather was with Cochise, the town's first librarian, a couple who brought aviation into the skies over Hayward, and for good measure Dif,

74

one of the town's first deputies and a storyteller who can make up more history than ever really happened. It was fantastic. Wish we could have got it on YouTube. It would have had a thousand hits in the first five minutes."

"Yeah, and they all would have come from assisted living facilities, caregivers trying to find something to calm restless patients," Virgil said.

"Well, I don't care what you say. It was a great party and you better send Virginia a huge thank-you."

"Thanks for the heads-up, Rosie. Have to be thinking about that. She did do a great job. Next year I'll tell her to get it all on video." Virgil got up slowly from his chair.

"You leaving?"

"Yeah. I've been trying to reach Mr. Jessup. No luck. Ark told me last night they had to release the body of that young boy to his folks."

"You know the parents?"

"Through Billy Three Hats. The father and Billy were real close. I didn't know the mother. Billy said they were great with their kids. But in some ways I guess life on the Rez can be a little claustrophobic, especially when you hit those teen years and realize there's a whole other world beyond the Rez."

"Yeah, but the lure is not just for the kids on the Rez, Virgil. Believe it or not, kids growing up in Hayward feel like they are on the Rez. Remember how you told me you couldn't wait to get out of here."

Virgil stood by his desk fingering the rim of his Stetson.

"Seems like at some point we all think that what's on the other side of the hill is going to be so much better than what we have. Then when we get there we find out it's not a whole lot different. The problem is a lot of people get lost along the way before they find that out."

"Like your friend's boy. Probably another casualty of the technology."

"How do you mean?" Virgil asked.

"I think a lot of people these days are living in the virtual world. But they forget it's not the real world. A lot of the anchors that kept them grounded are gone. All bets are off. People do things, say things to a computer or smartphone that they wouldn't have said or done in the past to a person."

"Don't think the internet or the virtual world is going to go away, Rosie."

"You're right, but everyone better remember living in a cloud isn't really living."

"With that profound thought, I'm heading down to Roscoe Flats." Virgil opened the door.

"Virgil, what about Cecil Summers?"

Virgil hesitated.

"Has Elvira sworn out a complaint?"

"I don't think so. She didn't any of those other times either . . . no order of protection."

"Damn." Virgil leaned against the doorjamb, his frustration obvious. Then he stood up straight, slapping his hat against his leg. "Guess we gotta let him go. No complaint, no way we can hold him."

"But, Virgil. He's done this a few times now. Simon said he was real belligerent this time. Mouthing off big time."

"Did he do anything we can charge him on, hit Simon or physically resist arrest?"

"Let me check." Rosie rifled through the papers on her desk until she came up with Simon's report on the incident. Virgil saw her shaking her head as she read it over. Finally, she looked up. "Can't find anything, just a lot of shooting off his mouth about Elvira not letting him see his kids while she's running around."

"Elvira running around? I think Cecil's got that a little backward if I remember correctly."

"Yeah, well, I think it's that O.J. thing. Tell a lie often enough you start believing it. Elvira should have thrown him back in the tank years ago. Cecil was no great catch to begin with. Guess some women will take any man rather than face life alone."

"Maybe Elvira didn't have a lot of prospects. Anyway, to the problem at hand, let him go," Virgil said.

"But, Virgil."

Virgil held up his hand.

"No buts. We can't keep him. No complaint filed. No charges. We have to let him go. I'm out of here. You can get me on the radio if you need me." Virgil gave a half wave with his hat and stepped out into the cold sunshine.

All the way down to Cielo and Roscoe Flats he was thinking about how the law sometimes gets in the way of common sense. He remembered Dif telling him how his father, Sam, would handle someone like Cecil. A little private talk in the parking lot. Then Sam would come through the door into the office, occasionally brushing some dirt off his clothes. On a couple of rare occasions pouring some peroxide over a bruised knuckle or two. Dif said he didn't say much on those occasions, but he couldn't remember a time when he had to have one of those parking lot conversations more than once with the same person. Virgil knew he wasn't Sam Dalton, but once in a while he wished he was. Then again, he knew that had been a different time in a different world.

Before heading over to Mr. Jessup, Virgil drove to the sand and gravel company. He knew from Mr. Jessup that his son worked there as an accountant. Beyond that, he now knew from Micah Hayward that Everett Jessup Junior had been in partnership with a man named Michael Stark. A man who not too many months before had ended up in the bottom of a canyon off High Ridge Road. These were the kinds of intersections that always caused the hair on the back of Virgil's neck to stand up. He parked in the lot, then started down the path toward the office building.

"Hey, Sheriff. Nothing tastes as good as a free sandwich." Virgil immediately recognized one of the truckers who he had bought lunch for coming toward him.

"You looking for another one of those free meals?" Virgil asked.

"No. My next one will be at home. I'm done for the day. Worked an early shift."

"You got far to go?"

"Only about ten minutes. Just got a place a couple of months back in Mesquite Meadow."

"Oh." Virgil obviously didn't get the reference.

"The new development. Company financed it. You work here you don't have to deal with credit checks, closings or any of that BS. Company takes care of it all. Yeah, we got ourselves a nice little casa. Wife loves it. Well, good seeing you, Sheriff. Thanks again for the lunch."

Virgil stood for a moment watching as the man walked away. A few minutes later he was sitting in a reception room waiting for a Human Resources person to show up.

He didn't know what he had expected, but he was quite sure this wasn't it. From the moment he walked through the front door, it was as if he was in any other modern-day corporate environment. If you didn't look out the window, you could have been in downtown Phoenix or Houston. An atrium stood in the middle of the entry hall on a polished stone floor. Lush plantings with waterfalls trickling through them offered shelter and drink to numerous brightly colored birds. To one side was a desk and a receptionist who offered Virgil a seat then put in a call to an inner office. As he sat and waited, it dawned on him just how out of touch he had been with this part of the county, along with all the changes that had been taking place. This was definitely no pickup truck, dump and deliver operation. He had seen the fleet of trucks lined up in the distance out back waiting to be loaded, and now this. He was thinking of another substation in this area like the one down in Redbud when his train of thought got interrupted.

"Good afternoon, Sheriff Dalton. How can I help you?"

The voice attached to the words was no truck driver. Virgil judged her to be in her early thirties, almost as tall as he, ash blond hair pulled into a French twist and two of the bluest eyes he'd seen in a long time. As she extended her hand he noted what looked like a dimple on her left cheek that could have been a small scar.

"I wanted to speak to you about one of your employees."

"In that case why don't we go to my office?" She opened the door she had come through and Virgil followed her down a long hallway till they reached her office. Again, it could have been an office in the middle of a corporate park or any urban environment. The only thing that gave it away was the window view. Obviously, this annex was far away from that part of the company that was the reason for its existence. The scene outside was of rolling prairie broken by mixed desert vegetation. Random varieties of cactus stood their ground while a steady wind drove some small tumbleweeds toward the far line of buttes that marked the blue-gray perimeter of the horizon. Virgil took the seat in front of Miss Allison, as she had introduced herself.

"I'm sure you know because of privacy laws I'm limited in what I can talk about regarding employees, but I'll help you as much as I can." Virgil nodded. "Could you give me the employee's name?"

"Jessup . . . Everett Jessup."

She quickly typed the name into the computer on her desk. A minute later she asked Virgil if he was sure about the name and the spelling. After he repeated the name along with the spelling, she entered it again into her computer. "What exactly does Mr. Jessup do?" she asked.

"As far as I know, he is an accountant," Virgil said.

"That explains it. He is a contract employee. We don't have our own in-house accounting department. That's why his name is not coming up. We contract it out. There's been some discussion of changing that, but as of yet . . ." She left the thought unfinished as she went back to the computer. "I have to open a different file. Ah, yes, here it is. I remember . . . it was too bad. He was a nice man." She sat back in her chair. "Stark and Jessup, we had contracted with them the last four or five years. I don't think I ever met Mr. Jessup more than two or three times, but Mr. Stark, Michael, was a very nice man."

"Was?" Virgil repeated.

"Yes. He died in a car accident right after last year's audit and filing. About seven or eight months ago."

"What about Mr. Jessup?"

She looked again at her computer screen.

"I don't know. There's nothing in here about him. Maybe he is just doing . . . handling small accounts. We were probably the largest client they had."

"Isn't it kind of strange using a small firm for an operation this big?" Virgil asked.

"You know, I never really thought about it. They were already on board when I came here four years ago right after Mr. Zambrano took over the business. Maybe there was a personal connection."

"Well, it sure looks like business is booming," Virgil said.

"Oh, yes. These last few years have been unbelievable."

"And yet the company continued with this small accounting firm," Virgil repeated.

"Yes. But like I said, maybe there was a personal connection. You would have to speak to Mr. Zambrano about that. This is not a publicly held company. He pretty much makes all the corporate decisions."

"Does he oversee the housing development also? I think it's called Mesquite Meadows?"

"As far as I know, but that's a separate entity. I mean, as far as the accounting aspect. I believe Mr. Stark handled everything for sand and gravel while Mr. Jessup took care of the housing development."

Virgil stood up.

"Thank you for your time, Miss Allison." He extended his hand.

"It's Jessica, I hope I've been helpful." Virgil nodded. "I'll walk out with you. Need to stretch a little." They walked together down the hall. She walked with him through the lobby out into the cold.

"Well, thanks again," Virgil said. "You better get inside. It's cold out here and you don't even have a jacket."

"I'm fine. It feels good to me."

"Well, Miss Allison . . ."

"My friends call me Jessie. Maybe I'll see you out in the Lazy Dog some night." Virgil hesitated before stepping onto the path to the parking lot. "I saw you there one night. You were with some friends. One of them sang that night. You seemed to be having a great time." Virgil smiled, remembering the night along with the good time. It seemed a long time ago.

"Yes. That was a good night. I'd like to have another night like that."

"Well, maybe we'll meet up, Sheriff."

"That would be nice. By the way, Sheriff's not my name. It's Virgil." He reached out and took her hand in his. A couple of minutes later as he was walking to his car, he was thinking a man could drown in those blue eyes.

# 21

Virgil was still looking into those blue eyes when he drove the long driveway to Everett Jessup's house. There was no sign of the horse in the pasture along the driveway, or the Jersey cow and her calf for that matter. Virgil thought it a little odd that on a nice day like this they would be shut up in the barn, especially since the best part of the day, considering the time of year, was just about gone. He had stopped at the same gas station and gotten a sandwich along with a drink, as he had on his last trip down to Cielo. He took the last drink from his cup as the engine quieted outside of Mr. Jessup's house. Now that the winter sun was slipping toward the horizon, the day was fast getting colder.

As soon as he stepped out of the vehicle, he buttoned up his jacket. He called out at the same time but there was no response from inside or out. He went to the front door and knocked. All was quiet. After a few more vigorous knocks and callouts he walked back to his vehicle. He stood for a moment or two looking around, trying to figure out his next move.

He'd had no luck calling from the office earlier when he was trying to reach Mr. Jessup. Now that he was here, for all intents it looked like he was still just spinning his wheels. Of course, he hadn't had contact in a while, so the old man could be anywhere. He thought about checking in the café across the road from the driveway, but he was reluctant to call attention to his presence. At the last moment, as on his last visit, he decided to check out the barn. Maybe Virgil thought, Mr. Jessup had corralled the horse and the cow because he was going to be away for most of the day.

As soon as he opened the barn door, he knew that was not the case. Everett Jessup was lying in a pool of his own blood in the dim light on the floor, right alongside the casket he had almost finished. Virgil rushed to the old man and turned him gently on his back. He had been beaten so badly Virgil almost didn't recognize him. Detecting no response or sign of life, Virgil got to his feet, the smell of blood heavy in the closed-up barn. He threw both barn doors wide open, letting in the daylight along with the cold while sucking some of that cold air into his lungs.

When he glanced back at the body, he was shocked to see one of Everett's fingers twitch. Realizing he had made an amateur's mistake, being thrown off because scalp wounds bleed so profusely, he ran to his car, put in a call for emergency responders, then grabbed his bottle of water from the console along with a first aid kit.

For the next fifteen minutes while he was waiting for the EMTs, he carefully washed the head wounds, two of which were going to need a lot more skill than he could provide to stop the blood flow. The old man felt real cold, so Virgil took off his own coat and covered him with it. He also managed to get some liquid past the old man's bruised and bleeding lips. The blood flow seemed to have slowed somewhat. He figured that was attributable to the cold. The only reward for his efforts was the moan that came when the EMTs arrived and slid Mr. Jessup's body onto a stretcher.

"That's as bad a beating as I've seen in a long time on this job." The comment came from one of the attendants as they rolled the gurney into the back of the ambulance. "Why would anyone do an old man like that?"

"Likely they wanted something from him that he wouldn't give up," Virgil responded.

By the time they pulled out of the driveway, the old cowboy was hooked up to an IV and his eyes had opened. For just an instant they locked on Virgil. Virgil thought he saw a glint of recognition, then the back doors swung shut. By the time he got to the end of the long driveway, he saw a couple of people standing on the porch of the café across the little square. Virgil crossed the road, pulling into the small parking area in front of the roadhouse. He felt their eyes on him as he sat in the cruiser. Before he got out, he called Rosie, updating her on the events of the day.

"Did you cut Cecil loose?"

"He's long gone, Virgil. When I had lunch at Margie's she said she saw him heading into the Lazy Dog." Virgil switched off the radio and got out of his vehicle.

"Howdy, Sheriff. Mr. Jessup having some trouble?" The words came from a man named Clint, who extended his hand and introduced himself as the owner of the café. "Come inside, sit a minute."

Virgil followed the man through the door. The rustic décor was full-on western. Saddles on wooden frames were lined up facing the bar. It was bright and clean, polished wide-board floors, checkered tablecloths on round tables in the middle, while compatible booths lined the walls. Bridles and hackamores hanging randomly on wall pegs were interspersed with rodeo posters along with some western art. Virgil was impressed. He even saw an authentic-looking McClellan cavalry saddle, set on one of the wooden frames. He had the feeling that this place could be really jumping on a Friday and Saturday night. For just a moment he thought about the Black Bull. This place might not have been on the same scale but it was more evidence of the growth in this part of the county.

"Did you happen to notice any activity over at the Jessup place?" Virgil asked.

"Sorry, Sheriff. Not a thing, but that driveway is close to a mile long. Besides, we don't open until noon." Virgil gave a brief accounting of what happened. The man was genuinely shocked.

"Can't believe it. That kind of thing just doesn't happen around here. I mean, he was a real gentleman. Come in once in a while, sometimes with his son. Tells me stories about the old times, the way it used to be around here. How his folks were the first settlers in this part of the country. Used to sit right over there." The man gestured toward a booth near a raised platform, where Virgil could picture a couple of musicians standing on a weekend night. "He enjoyed sitting over a meal with a couple of beers listening to the music. Even liked some of the more current stuff."

"What about his son?"

"He was just like his dad. Everybody liked him. But I don't think he was much interested in ranching. Think he was an accountant. Some of our regulars used to go to him at tax time. I do believe he gave me his card a while back. He was partnered with some other fella."

"I understand he did some work for the sand and gravel company."

"Don't know about that, but it don't surprise me none. Nine out of ten of my customers work for Mesquite Sand and Gravel. Hell, if it wasn't for Mesquite, I'd still be commuting to Hayward selling tires in that Firestone store. Yeah, last couple of years this area has changed a lot because of Mesquite."

"Wonder why it didn't happen earlier?" Virgil commented.

"Can't say. It all started when it got sold five or six years back. Before then, it was mostly a cash-and-carry kind of operation. The office was in an old trailer. Folks would drive in with their pickups, load up whatever they needed and pay on the way out. Sometimes there wasn't even somebody to help you load up. You had to do most of the shoveling yourself. No delivery. Now it's a totally different operation, streamlined, all kinds of options, delivery, the works. Best of all they hired a lot of people when they expanded, then built that development, keeping a pool of employees nearby. Most folks are just happy the new management showed up and took over. The place has been humming ever since. That's the main reason why I decided to try becoming an entrepreneur. Got tired of working for other people." Virgil stood to go.

"Well, thank you for your time. Listen, Clint, could I ask a favor?"

"Sure, Sheriff."

"I'm trying to get a hold of Mr. Jessup's son, but until I do he's got a horse and a cow and calf over there. I let them out in the fenced-in field before I came over here, but they're going to need some looking after. Can you take care of it?"

"Not a problem. I have a young boy who does odd jobs for me. I'll put him on it. He'll probably jump on that horse, do a little cowboying, if it's okay."

"Sure enough," Virgil said. "It's a nice-looking horse. His name is Ranger. Probably could use the exercise. I'll be happy to pay," Virgil said. Clint waved his hand and shook his head.

"I'll take care of it, Sheriff. Be happy to do that for the old man. I like him. Didn't deserve the hand he was dealt. Hope he is going to be back sitting in that booth listening to some music over a couple of cold ones."

Virgil shook hands with Clint then went out to the front porch, glad that he had made the stop. He took note of the sign as he left the parking lot, Clint's Dream.

· · ·

By the time Virgil got back to Hayward, nighttime shadows were drifting across the landscape. He noted a few stars already visible in the sky when he stepped out onto the crushed stone in the parking lot. Rosie had left. Dif was alone in the office. Virgil took off his hat as he stepped inside.

"That's showing some serious wear," Dif said as Virgil dropped his Stetson on the desk. Virgil looked down at the hat.

"Yeah. I guess."

"Looks good on you. Looked good on Sam too."

Virgil picked the hat back up, fingering the brim in a couple of places where the piping was seriously worn. The sweat stains at the base of the crown from years of wear had permanently discolored the felt. No amount of cleaning would remove them. He looked at it in the midst of a flashback. He was so much younger, standing outside the old corral and the old barns. It was raining slightly. The sky was leaden, that gunmetal gray color that offered the promise of a lot more rain. The man holding the hat, who was standing in front of him, looked like he'd rather be in any one of a thousand places other than there.

"Don't know what to say, Virgil. I'm sorry, but I thought you would want this. Can't resurrect a picture of your dad without it." Virgil reached out and took the hat from the extended hand of the state trooper. He had worn it ever since.

"Lot of history there." Dif made the comment as Virgil once again lay the hat back down on his desk.

"Anything going on, Dif?"

"No. Real quiet. Jimmy's been in and gone. Making his first rounds.

Rosie left early because Dave was home. Guess he's planning on heading down to Redbud now that the holidays are almost done."

"Just one more holiday . . . tomorrow night, New Year's Eve. Then it's back to normal, whatever that is. Dave might as well wait for the New Year with Rosie. He can head down to Redbud after that. If you are talking to Rosie later, tell her what I said. I'm going to call over to the hospital. Get an update on Mr. Jessup, then I'm heading home."

Ten minutes later Virgil was on the road heading out of town feeling a lot better. Mr. Jessup's condition was stable. As the doctor put it, he could still take a punch. Fortunately, most of the beating was confined to his upper body, which although it looked real bad, did not result in any major organ injury. He wouldn't look good for quite a while, but barring any complications he would walk out of the hospital. The last thing the doctor told Virgil was that the knuckles on the old cowboy's right hand were cut and swollen. He said he was pretty sure somebody was walking around with some loose teeth in their head. Virgil had smiled after hearing that remark as he hung up the phone. He shared the last comment with Dif as he had stood to leave the office.

"If you're going down, go down fighting," Dif had responded.

# 22

New Year's Eve and New Year's Day were surprisingly quiet in Hayward. It was almost as if everyone was partied out. Clara had decided to stay on at the ranch until after the holiday season was over. Virgil was surprised by her request on New Year's Day to be dropped off at the hospital. He had told her he was going into the office for a couple of hours.

"Think maybe I'll go sit with Everett for a while. Do a little catching up. Doesn't look like he's going to have many visitors."

"No. Don't think that's likely. Wherever his son has got to, he might not even know about what has happened. Probably just as well. Someone wants to find him real bad. Just hope I can get to him first."

While Virgil was in the office he took care of some paperwork, answered a couple of calls. He wrote a note to himself about getting something for Virginia. Rosita stopped by, reminding him again of his obligation.

"What did you get Virginia for Christmas?"

Virgil hesitated.

"Don't tell me you didn't get her a Christmas present?"

"Not exactly," Virgil answered.

"What the hell does that mean? You didn't get her something for all the work she put in on that party. Now you're telling me you didn't even give her a Christmas present. Virgil, I've been coaching you about this stuff for over ten years. Damn it all. You're making me feel like a failure."

Virgil raised his hand.

"Calm down, Mama. Didn't say I didn't get her a present. Just haven't found quite the right time to give it to her, and I've finally decided on what I'm going to give her for the great job she did putting together that party."

"Well, there's no time like the present." Rosie picked up the phone. Virgil reached across his desk, taking it from her and shaking his head.

"You are worse than my conscience." He put in a call to Virginia. After a few seconds Rosie heard him leaving a message.

"She wasn't there. I left a message."

"I heard. She's a young girl, Virgil. She's got a life. She's not sitting by the phone waiting on a call from you. If you want to be part of her life, you have to work at it. Don't forget, in another couple of weeks she's going back to school. Relationships take work."

Virgil looked at Rosita almost like he was seeing her for the first time.

"Is Dave allowed to have an original thought?"

"He did once. That was when he asked me to marry him."

While Virgil was laughing, the door opened and Dif walked in.

"Hey, Virgil, Rosita. What's going on?"

"Let me guess," Rosie said. "Edna suggested you get out of the house for a while. Probably said Dif, why don't you go down to the office for an hour or two."

"Why, that's exactly what happened. How did you know?"

Rosie looked at Virgil.

"See, Virgil. There are people who have original thoughts. Then there are people who just have to follow the script as they've been told."

Virgil jumped to his feet.

"Omigod. You're killing me." He grabbed his hat off the desk while he headed for the door.

"Where you going, Virgil?" Dif asked.

"Ask Rosie. She can tell you. If you're interested, she can probably tell you where you are going after you leave here. Also where you are going tomorrow and the day after that.

• • •

Clara was waiting for him when he pulled into the hospital parking lot. On the way out of town she filled him in about her visit with Everett Jessup.

"He recognized me right off. It was like we had seen each other yesterday. Real nice. We had a nice time. Promised him I'd come again." They had reached the driveway to the ranch. "You know, Virgil, I was thinking you ought to do something or get something for Virginia for all she did to make that Christmas party such a success."

Virgil looked at Clara as the car slowed to a stop in front of the corral.

"You know, that's a great idea, never would've thought of that." He smiled at her as he opened her door.

"Sure you would, Virgil." She patted his hand. "Eventually."

He stood there in the sunlight watching as she navigated the stairs up to the porch. She missed the second smile that crossed his face. Rosita and Clara were cut from the same cloth, he thought. Then he followed her into the house. They ate a late lunch together. Cesar came in as Clara was cleaning up.

"Virgil, you should be doing that." Virgil was sitting at the table over a cup of coffee Clara had just poured for him.

"It's okay, Cesar. I need to move a bit. When I sit too long my bones get cranky. Here, have a cup of tea with us."

Cesar pulled the chair away from the wall, placing it in front of the table where she had just placed a cup. He took off his hat, laying it across his knee. She filled his cup with tea from the brightly flowered teapot. Wisps of steam rose in the air as she poured. Virgil passed the sugar and milk across the table.

"You know, this teapot belonged to my mother. It's nothing special but somehow just knowing that makes the tea taste better."

"Si. I still have a sweater that mi madre made. I take it out sometimes on cold nights. I have other sweaters but that one keeps me warmer." Clara nodded. "I also have those old bones you spoke of, but yours did not keep you off Sugar."

"No, they didn't. I really enjoyed that ride. Like to do it again at least one more time before I go back home. Virgil, do you ever visit that cabin in the back country that Grandpa Dalton built when he first came to this country?"

Virgil had a distant look in his eyes.

"No, ma'am. Haven't been there since . . . since I found out about Rusty. Don't even know if it's still standing."

"Didn't mean to bring up a bad memory."

"I have no bad memories of Rusty," Virgil said. He took a sip from his cup. The only sound in the room after his comment was Cesar stirring the sugar in his cup. The quiet was finally broken by the sound of a car's tires scattering stone as it came to a stop outside the house. Cesar pulled the curtains on the kitchen window aside to look out.

"It is Miss Virginia."

"Right on cue," Virgil said. "Guess it's time to give an overdue Christmas present." He got up from the table. By the time Virginia got out of the car, Virgil was waiting for her at the bottom of the steps.

"Saw you called as I was driving decided to just stop by. So here I am. Hope it's okay."

"Anytime, always." Virgil smiled then drew her close, wrapping her in a bear hug. "Take a short walk with me." Virgil took her by the hand. He led her across the driveway, then they walked the length of the barn, opening the stall doors as they went. Cesar had already mucked out the stalls and provided the evening grain ration. A flake of hay was in each stall. At the end of the barn Virgil threw open the double-wide doors. The fading day flooded in as they stepped outside. Virgil gave a high-pitched whistle. Two more followed in quick succession. More than a quarter mile away, a young bay mare who was swollen with her first foal raised up her head at the first sound and pricked her ears. When she heard the second whistle, she started at a light trot for the barn. Immediately picking up on her response, the others at some distance from her called, then started for the barn. Within seconds, they had all come together, breaking into a full-on gallop with the young mare out in front. Virgil and Virginia stood side by side enjoying the scene as they charged toward the barn, a cloud of dust rising in their wake.

For an instant they morphed into one pulsating mass. As they drew closer, Virginia and Virgil could feel the earth beneath their feet tremble. Virgil stepped to one side, drawing Virginia with him. With only the slightest hesitation, the horses thundered past into the barn. Virginia let out a slight gasp as they ran by. Inside, as if it was choreographed, one by one they slipped into their respective stalls. It all happened before the dirt they had stirred up in their charge had settled. As the light once again filtered into the barn through swirling dirt clouds, its slanting beams showed that each horse had found their true home except one. Alone, standing outside the stall he shared with his mother, Star, stood the little six-month-old colt.

He snorted as he threw his head from side to side, resisting the temptation to go inside, join his mother at the grain bucket and give up his outside freedom. But the slurping crunching noises he heard from her and the others proved too much to resist. He bolted through the opening. Virgil then went quickly down the passageway, closing each of the stall doors. When he returned, Virginia was standing by the first stall, where Star and her colt were cleaning out the last of the grain from the buckets hanging on the wall.

"He's beautiful," she said, looking at the colt that was nibbling at his mother's neck. After a playful bite, the mare laid her ears back and stomped her foot. The colt backed away while she ate the last of the feed.

"Yes. He's looking good."

"Is he going to be black like his mother?"

"I don't think so. There's enough of his father in there that I think he is going to be a kind of mahogany color with some reddish highlights. Probably won't know for sure until he sheds out next spring. It's funny about color. Some foals born black turn gray by the end of their first year. Those Lippanzanner horses almost always turn completely white, no matter what color they are when they are first dropped." While he spoke the colt had walked over. Virginia reached her hand through the rails to stroke his nose. He tentatively extended his neck while she ran her fingers over his muzzle then alongside his jaw. He seemed to settle under her stroking.

"Looks like you've got the touch. He likes you. That'll make it easier."

"What do you mean? Make it easier?"

"It's always easier to school a horse that likes you. He will learn quickly from you."

"I don't understand."

"Merry Christmas," Virgil said. "He's all yours. I think he was meant to be. A present from me and your grandmother."

"But . . ."

Virgil raised his hand.

"No buts. Like I said, this old girl who was my mother's horse picked this time to finally drop a foal. Now I know why. Some things, I think, are meant to happen for a reason. Maybe some people call this karma. I like to think my mom is reaching across to her granddaughter."

Virginia's eyes filled.

"I don't know what to say."

"You don't have to say anything. I'll keep him here until he's weaned. Cesar and I will work with him while you are back at school. Then when you return, you can take over."

She turned toward Virgil.

"Thanks, Dad." He drew her close. Virgil was truly feeling like a dad for the first time.

# 23

Dave Brand was standing in the doorway of the bedroom down the hall from his and Rosie's room. A cup of steaming coffee in his hand, he was looking at the newly assembled crib and patting himself on the back. It was the first day of the workweek, January fifth. He would soon be on his way down to Redbud, but he took a little extra time to admire his handiwork. Sunlight was flooding into the room, falling on the crib like the centerpiece it was. There was no other furniture in the room. It was way too early. Rosie had finished her third month, the unsaid marker of a secure pregnancy. In her fourth month she was now comfortable with the idea of public knowledge of her condition but still thought it way too early for baby furniture. The crib had been Dave's idea. She told him he was crazy but didn't fight him on it. She recognized that he was in a way surprisingly renewed by her news. That was unexpected. She realized a lot of men his age would not have reacted like Dave. Rosie knew things could have been a lot different. He was still standing in the doorway when she came down the hall.

"You know that crib is going to collect a lot of dust before it gets an occupant."

"Yeah, I know, but since the kids grew up and moved out . . . I don't know. Guess in some ways it just felt like this house had lost its purpose. Two empty bedrooms, one with no furniture at all. Then me gone most of the week down in Redbud. You coming home from work to an empty house. I don't know. You never said anything but I can't believe you didn't wonder, why bother cleaning an empty house or fixing something that broke. I know I did, even though I was hardly here. I remember one day last spring, right after Carrie had her baby, thinking when I was looking at the swing set in the backyard that she might as well take it since we had no more use for it. Downsizing, I thought. That's what this is. Then I remember thinking, I'm only forty-four years old. It's over. I'm shifting into the next gear. Really brought me down, made me feel like life was passing me by. Then when you told me about the baby a few months later, I felt like I was getting a second chance." Rosie smiled. "Guess you think I'm going through a midlife crisis."

"Well, maybe you are, but you better understand that this baby is going to move out in twenty years or so like the other three did and I ain't planning on having one of those Guinness old-age pregnancies just to keep you from avoiding the fact we're getting old. So this is it. You did a great job with the crib, and I'll remind you about that second chance at two o'clock in the a.m. when I ask you to change that crying baby. Come on, lunch is on the table."

• • •

Rosie glanced at the time on the microwave as she was putting the lunch dishes in the sink. It was a little after two.

"I should have been out of here long ago."

"Thought Virgil said you didn't have to go in while I was here."

"Virgil's too easy on other people and too hard on himself. That office is busier than it has ever been. He just takes more and more on himself to keep up."

"Well, leave that cleanup to me. I'm in no rush. I told Alex I'd get down to Redbud by five so that gives me some time."

Rosie stopped what she was doing, then left the kitchen. A couple of minutes later she was back, coat on and ready to leave. Dave had loaded the last of the dishes into the dishwasher and was wiping off the counter. She gave him a quick kiss then stepped into the doorway.

"Just for the record, Dave, if I'm going to have a baby with anyone in middle age, I'd rather it be with you than anybody." She blew him a kiss. Dave reached up as if to catch it, then Rosie smiled and went out the front door.

• • •

"Rosie, what are you doing here? I thought Virgil said you wouldn't be in today." Dif was alone in the office.

"Well, Dave will be heading down to Redbud in a little while so I didn't want Virgil having to come in just to attack that pile of paperwork from last week. Did Jimmy check in yet?"

"He has been here and gone. Starting his rounds. So far everything has been pretty quiet. Hoping it stays that way. Don't need to start the New Year off with a bang."

"You and Edna made any New Year's resolutions?"

"Just that same one we make every year. Try to stay one step ahead of the gravedigger."

"Guess we all make that one, Dif."

"Yeah, but once you hit seventy you can feel him breathing down your neck. Hell, you don't have to worry for a long time about that. You and Dave are getting ready to start a second family. We were talking to folks last week at the party. Edna said she never saw Dave happier. Like he just got the best Christmas present ever." Dif waited for the quick response that usually came from Rosie, but there was none. He looked over at her. "Anything the matter, Rosie?"

"Oh, no," she said. "It's just that I was thinking about Dave and the new crib he put together for the baby. All the time he was working on it this morning, I could hear him whistling and talking. One time I walked out into the hallway to listen. He was talking to the baby. 'Daddy's making sure you are going to be safe and sound in this here crib. You're going to be sleeping here each night with all your little furry critters dreaming those nice dreams and Mommy and Daddy are going to be right next door."

"Well, I guess Edna's right. Dave's never been happier."

# 24

It was a little after five when Jimmy called. Virgil was sitting in the kitchen. Clara was starting to make supper. It had been a quiet day. He actually had a chance to get out to the barn and do a couple of things that he had been putting off. So now, taking a break, he poured each of them a glass of wine. He had just taken his first sip when the phone rang.

"Virgil." From the moment Jimmy said his name, a cold shiver ran through him. He didn't want to hear the next words. "It's bad, Virgil, real bad." There was a catch in Jimmy's voice followed by a gasp almost like he was choking.

"Where are you, Jimmy? Where are you?" There was a garbled answer in the static on the phone. Virgil knew Jimmy was in his cruiser. He had to repeat the question.

"Where are you?"

"Mrs. Summers . . . Mrs. Summers's house."

"Is Cecil there? Jimmy, is Cecil there?"

"Yes . . . yes, he's here."

"Jimmy, listen to me. Don't do anything, I'm on my way. I'll be there in ten minutes."

"But, Virgil . . . it's, it's—" Again the garbled sound, but this time more like a sob.

"Jimmy, I hear you, I know it's bad. Take some deep breaths, just hang on. I'm on my way." Virgil leaped out of the chair so quickly, Clara dropped the empty saucepan she was holding.

"Got to go." It was all he said. She knew by the look on his face that there wouldn't be another word out of him. He ran into the other room. When he returned he was strapping on his gun belt. She was standing by the kitchen door holding his sheepskin coat and his Stetson. Wordlessly, he slipped into the open coat she held, then grabbed the hat.

"It's cold out there, Virgil." Their eyes met for an instant. He knew she was talking about more than just the weather. "Take care." She spoke the words as he flew out the door and ran to his vehicle. Clara watched from the kitchen window as the car tore up the driveway, scattering dirt and dead leaves in its wake. Virgil had the siren and flashing red lights on before he reached the county road. She watched until he was out of sight, then sat down heavily in the chair Virgil had leaped from. She did not have a good feeling.

It was less than ten minutes but seemed longer when Virgil pulled up in front of the Summers house. He was a little surprised to see two cruisers parked one in back of the other alongside the curb. He thought Simon was out of town, but he didn't stop to puzzle it out. He jumped from the car. There was no sign of Jimmy. When he reached the small porch with the one step up Jimmy opened the front door. He was bareheaded, his gun holstered, and he seemed unexpectedly composed. He held up his right hand, stopping Virgil in his tracks.

"Sheriff, take a step back and listen." Jimmy's voice sounded different, almost as if it were coming from a much older man. "I gotta tell it before you go in there so you know what to expect, and I think I can only tell it once." Virgil took the step back, instinctively grabbing the nearby handrail of the small porch. Jimmy was holding on to the frame of the door like it was a life preserver. He took a deep breath. "This is what Mrs. Summers told me. Cecil busted into the house about an hour ago with a loaded shotgun. He said she was keeping him from his kids and accused her of sleeping around. He told her he was going to kill her and her boyfriend. She said she tried to tell him that the man in the kitchen was a plumber she called to fix the dishwasher but she said he was crazy mad. The more she tried talking to him, the crazier he got. The plumber tried to talk to him, she said, but when he took a step toward him, Cecil unloaded one of the barrels. I guess the plumber was holding some kind of a metal basin, probably to catch dripping water from the dishwasher. Anyway, it more than likely saved his life. Caught a good part of the shot from the gun, not all of it. He got hit. Looks like he took most of it in his side. He's on the kitchen floor bleeding a lot. Mrs. Summers is with him. The EMTs are on their way."

"So this sounds . . ." Jimmy held up his hand before Virgil could continue.

"No . . . no." His voice had an angry edge. "Not all, there's more." Virgil heard the voice from the telephone for a second time. He took a deep breath, gripping the handrail tighter.

"Dave was driving by when he heard the shot. Guess he was heading down to Redbud. That's his car in front of mine. He got here just before I did." Jimmy's eyes glazed for an instant as he glanced at Dave's cruiser. "Dave stopped when he heard the shot then ran into the house. Mrs. Summers said Cecil just seemed to react. He shot him as he came through the door. Dave didn't have a metal basin. Never even got a chance to draw his weapon. Didn't know what hit him. Caught the full load. He's dead, Virgil. Lying in there against the wall, soaked in blood. He's dead, Virgil . . . Dave's dead. I held him in my arms. He said one or two things then closed his eyes. "

As Jimmy repeated the phrase, it was like the air going out of a balloon. He slumped against the door. Virgil instinctively grabbed him. He felt his full weight, knew he would have gone down if he hadn't caught him. He heard the sound of a siren, getting louder as it came down the street. He could feel Jimmy shaking. Then he heard him sob. He held him tighter. There were voices now behind him, coming up the sidewalk. He heard someone call him Sheriff. He knew what he had to do. Two attendants came onto the porch in back of him. One tried to walk around him, to enter the house.

"No," Virgil shouted. "No. Don't go in there." His voice sounded strange to his own ears. "I've got to make sure it's secure. Here, help this officer." Virgil recognized the attendant. He shifted Jimmy to the waiting EMT, who, with the help of the other attendant, walked Jimmy off the step onto the path that led from the house to the waiting ambulance. Virgil looked at the opened doorway, took a deep breath, then drew his gun. Dave was crumpled up against the wall, as Jimmy said. He couldn't see his face, it had sagged to one side, but the spreading pool of blood had reached the edge of the throw rug that lay in the small entryway. To the right was the living room, while just beyond from where he was standing he could see most of the kitchen. The kitchen and living room area were separated only by an L-shaped breakfast bar. In the corner beyond the breakfast bar, in back of the living room, was the dining area with a table and chairs. Virgil could see Cecil handcuffed on the floor, immobile. His hands were cuffed in back of him. He was sitting, leaning up against a wall. Cecil looked at Virgil, his eyes glazed, a weird half grin on his face. Jimmy had done his job. Virgil holstered his gun, then walked through to the kitchen area.

The plumber was sitting on the floor against one of the base cabinets under the sink. Elvira Summers sat next to him, holding a bathroom towel to his side. Virgil could see it was soaked in blood. She looked up when she saw Virgil. He crouched down next to her. There was blood on her clothing, a vacant look in her eyes. She mouthed something Virgil couldn't make out. She tried to say something again. Virgil put his finger to his lips. "It's over." He said. "It's over," he put his hand on her shoulder, then stood up. He left the room, walked past Dave trying not to look, on to the front porch. He waved to the EMTs.

"Come on. Danger's passed."

Two of them immediately came up to him. A young woman stayed with Jimmy. Virgil told the two men what they would find inside, then watched as they walked by. He stood for a moment trying to piece it all together. A man who he had just let out of jail against Rosie's wishes had just killed her husband. Down deep he knew he had no choice. He didn't

95

make the rules. That knowledge was cold comfort as he stood on the small porch, moving to the side as one of the attendants walked by him to the inside, carrying a body bag. If there were no rules, he knew without hesitation he could have walked right back into that kitchen and put a bullet deep inside Cecil Summers's brain. For the first time in a long time he knew again the savage that was inside him, wanting to be unleashed. His new deputy, Simon, had spoken of it. Virgil heard his words echo.

I did things I never thought I could do. I became someone I never knew. And worst of all, when I left Afghanistan I brought that person home with me. I've been running away from him ever since.

Standing on the walk outside the Summers house as the second of two vehicles and the one carrying Dave Brand's body drove off, Virgil knew one thing. He was incapable of running away from who he was. He had never done it. He was not about to start now.

# 25

She was still there when he walked into the office.

"Don't say it, Virgil." She was the first to speak. He pulled his chair over to her desk where she was sitting. He sat down then reached across, taking one of her hands in his. Edna, Dif's wife, put a cup of coffee next to him on the desk then sat next to Rosie on the other side. Rosie repeated the phrase. "Don't say it, Virgil. You let Cecil out because you had to, I get that. Maybe Dave had to go so Elvira would be there for her kids. I don't know, but I know it's not your fault. You've got to know that too." Rosie looked at Virgil. For the first time tears flowed freely down his cheeks. Rosita choked back a sob.

"Where is he, Virgil?"

"He's with Ark at the hospital."

"Was it quick?"

"Dave never knew what hit him, never saw it coming. Jimmy was there almost immediately, after Dave was hit. He held Dave until the very end."

"Did he say anything? Anything at all?"

"Jimmy said he looked up at him and said, Tell Rosie it's okay. Then Jimmy said he just closed his eyes and went to sleep." Rosie put her head down on their locked hands. Her whole body convulsed. Edna put her arm around Rosie's shoulders. A wail straight from her soul filled the room, ending in muffled sobs. Virgil and Edna comforted her. At last she picked her head up.

"Where's Cecil?" It was an inquiry. There was no anger in her voice.

"I didn't want him here. Called the state police. They came and got him."

"How's Jimmy?"

"He did everything I would have done. Tore the heart right out of him but he did his job. It will take some time but he's going to be alright. "

"I've got to call the kids," Rosie said.

"No, you don't, honey." Edna drew Rosie close. "Dif is taking care of that. What you need to do right now is take care of yourself and that baby. You know that baby is going to help you keep Dave alive. Remember before, how you were telling me Dave was talking to that little girl. Well, he was talking for you too. Now, you will have to talk for him. That's how he is going to stay alive for her and you."

Rosie smiled at Edna, then let go of her and Virgil and got to her feet. "You're right, Edna. I'm going to have to tell her a lot about her dad. Most of all, how he loved her . . . how he loved us all."

# 26

Clara was watching from that same window in the kitchen when Virgil pulled into the driveway. Night had long since crept over the land. She had gotten a call. She had been waiting an eternity. She saw the car come to a stop alongside the corral fence. She heard as the engine quieted, saw when the lights shut off, how against the dark shadow of the barn the car became almost invisible. There was no moon or ambient light coming from the night sky. She waited. It was a long time before a door opened. The dome light fell on a figure that looked somehow different from the man who had left the ranch hours earlier. She watched as he stood up. He moved slowly. For a long time he just stood there next to the car looking into the darkness. She could see his expelled breath rise on the night air. Finally he turned, taking a few steps toward the house. As he got closer, he stepped within the arc of the porch light, which she had lit for him. She saw him reach for the railing. That movement told her all she needed to know. She had never seen him reach for it before. He stopped at the boot jack then hung up his sheepskin coat on the wall peg once he stepped inside. It was all rote. He looked around like he almost didn't know where he was. She wrapped him in her arms then led him to a chair. He looked at the bowl of stew she put in front of him, staring at it like he didn't know what to do next. Infused steam rose from the bowl. She put a spoon in his hand. He began to eat. Then he started, when the hot liquid touched his lip. He put his hand to his mouth.

"You've got a small cut on your lip. I can see it. You probably did that to yourself. I've done that, bit my lip when I got tense or stressed by something."

He looked at her directly for the first time.

"Dave is dead. Dave Brand is dead."

"I know," Clara said. "He was a good man, a close friend to you. You will miss him, but we will talk about it tomorrow. Now you need to eat. Then I want you to go upstairs, take a warm shower and go to bed."

The words in her soft voice washed over him like a salve.

He turned his attention once more to the bowl.

"Put the spoon in on the left side of your mouth, away from the cut." He did as she said. When he had finished she put a cup of hot tea sweetened with some honey in his hand. "I know you are not much of a tea drinker but drink this." Again he did as she said.

He drank the tea down in three gulps. It was not unpleasant. He tasted something in it other than the tea. When he had finished, she took the cup from him, then helped him to his feet. Then she walked with him to the foot of the stairs.

"Now, go take that warm shower then right into bed." He put his foot on the first step then stopped and looked at her. He looked like he wanted to say something, but for some reason the words would not come.

"Do as I say, Virgil. We will talk in the morning. It will be better." Virgil walked up the stairs. A couple of minutes later she could hear the pipes groaning. They stopped a short time later. Five minutes after that, she crept up the stairs and opened the door to his room. He was in his bed, never stirring when the beam from the hall light crossed his face. His clothes were in a heap piled on the floor. She gathered them up, laying his belt with the gun still holstered on the chair next to his bed. Quietly she left, closing the door, went back downstairs.

A little while later, after she had put the clothes that were bloodied to soak in cold water, she poured some of the amber liquid from the opened bottle on the counter over ice in a glass then took it inside to the living room.

• • •

Morning sun was working hard to diminish the glaze that had settled on the ground during a colder than usual night when Virgil walked into the kitchen. Aunt Clara was stirring a saucepan of oatmeal laced with brown sugar and sliced apples.

"Just in time. Sit down. I'll get your juice. Did you sleep well?"

"Better than I thought I would, like a dead . . ." He didn't finish the analogy. Before he sat down Virgil walked to the window.

"There was a heavy frost last night, but the sun has started to do its job." He turned to look at her when she spoke. She noted the pencil-thin scars on his cheeks seemed a little deeper, but he didn't have the haunted look of the previous night. She came away from the stove with the pot of oatmeal then began to spoon some of it into a bowl by his place. He started to protest. "Nonsense," she said. "It's a cold morning. You need a good start." Just then Cesar came in from outside.

"It's cold out there. That oatmeal looks good."

"Looks good, tastes better. Sit down, I'll get a bowl for you."

"Thank you, Senora."

"De nada," she responded as she set a bowl in front of him. Virgil slid into the chair opposite. Then Clara sat. The three ate in silence for a moment.

"Been a long time since I had homemade oatmeal. Tastes good," Virgil said. Cesar grunted in agreement.

"You men are all alike. Clyde was the same way. Left alone you won't take the time to boil water. Stand in front of the icebox drinking milk right out of the bottle because you're too busy to get a glass."

"Me, I cook sometimes, frijoles and chili. Also huevos for breakfast."

"Well, that's a start," Clara said. "What about you, Virgil?"

"Oh, I've been known to throw a steak on the grill. As far as that other criticism, I do drink milk from the container sometimes. Why dirty a glass? By the way, it hasn't come in bottles in almost fifty years, Clara. And that white thing over there is a refrigerator. We haven't had an icebox in seventy years." Clara reached over, slapping Virgil's arm. They sat over coffee trying to ignore the immediate past along with the impending future.

"Virgil, I have a suggestion. Things have taken a bad turn. I know you are facing a lot in the next few days. But it might be wise to take a step back."

"Not sure I understand where you're going with this."

"Well, all I'm saying is that when things get turned upside down without warning, we need some time to catch our breath. We need some time to readjust, get over the shock. Nothing is going to happen for another couple of days. Dave's not going to get to Simpson's before Wednesday. Alex called before you got up to tell you Simon and Dif are at the office. Everything is quiet down to Redbud and the state police are increasing patrols in the Hayward area for the next few days. So why don't you take a little time to regroup."

"Clara, I'm fine. Don't worry."

"I'm not saying you're not, Virgil. All I'm saying is give yourself a day or two, some breathing room."

"Sounds like a good idea to me," Cesar said.

Virgil looked from one to the other. He had never been hardheaded. The logic made sense. He knew he was still churning inside.

"But what am I going to do? Sit in a chair for the next two days, contemplating an uncertain future?"

"Maybe do some work?" Virgil looked at Cesar.

"You, Pedro and José pretty much got everything covered until calving in the spring."

"Pretty much, sure, but we never seem to have time to get into the backcountry to check fence and shelter for the cattle if we get bad snow."

"There you go," Clara put in. "Ride fence for thirty or forty miles. Get some calluses on your butt. Maybe check to see if Grandpa's old cabin is still standing. Get out in the country. Clear your head. That'll do you a world of good, Virgil."

Virgil got up from the table, walked to the window again. All trace of frost was gone. A barn cat was sitting on the top rail of the corral licking its paws. A clear blue sky framing the full sun beckoned. At last he spoke to the waiting listeners.

"Well, I guess I'm going to spend a day or two riding fence." He didn't have to look over his shoulder to see the satisfied looks of the two co-conspirators.

• • •

The ranch house was well out of sight when he pulled Jack up the first time. The chilled air felt good because it had been tempered by a rising sun. There was no wind. A slight steam rose off Jack's neck. Virgil reached into the pocket of his denim jacket. It was only a little after ten according to his cell phone. He had charged his phone before he left, just in case. It was his only link to what he left behind, what he had to face when he returned. He got off Jack, then relieved himself by a twisted cottonwood that was probably twice his age. He reached into his saddle bag, pulling out one of the apples that Clara had placed there. Jack had dropped his head to nibble at some bunch grass.

While Virgil sat on a nearby rock, he watched Jack move from tuft to tuft. He had chosen a hackamore for his headset rather than a bit and bridle, making it easier for Jack to graze. He got up, pleased that he didn't feel stiff, and gave a soft whistle to Jack, who immediately raised his head then started walking to Virgil's outstretched hand and the apple core that sat in his palm. Virgil took the reins, which he had double-tied around Jack's neck so he wouldn't step on them as he walked. Holding them loosely in his hand he led Jack to a perch on a rimrock that overlooked a scene of undulating landscape all the way to the far hills. He could have been the last man on the face of the earth. The land, untouched, looked like he imagined it had when his great-grandfather first saw it, well over a hundred years before, when he first came into this country. He realized as he stepped up into the saddle that Clara was right. There was a healing power in the land.

# 27

Simon had been sitting at Virgil's desk when Dif came into the office.

"I didn't know where to sit," he offered, almost by way of an apology.

"I know," Dif said. "It's almost like you are wearing someone else's clothes. Edna's cousin died about six months ago. He was older than me but we were about the same size. Anyway, Edna comes home one day with one of his coats. I put it on. It fit perfectly. It was a real nice coat, didn't make any difference. Wore it once. Couldn't get it out of my head that it belonged to someone else. Just didn't feel right."

"Yeah, it was a choice, between Virgil's desk or Rosie's."

"I got an idea," Dif said. "It's only going to be for a couple of days. Give me a hand." Dif went over to the long yard-sale table, which sat against the far wall. He unplugged the microwave and the coffeepot, then carried them to the counter next to the refrigerator. He put the microwave on one side of the sink, the coffeepot on the other side. Simon joined in, carrying the tray full of coffee cups, setting it alongside the coffeepot. Then they pushed the two desks together, Rosie's and Virgil's, in an L formation, creating an open area for the table. Then they moved the table. After placing two chairs next to each other, there was plenty of room between them for one of the computers and a phone. Dif even found two desk pads in the storage closet next to the bathroom. "Now we ain't jumping into somebody else's grave," he said.

Simon had just sat down when the phone rang.

"Sheriff's office. How can I help? Well, he's not here right now. No, actually he is going to be out of the office for a couple of days. I can take a message. It's likely he'll call in." Simon motioned to Dif for a piece of paper and a pen, then wrote down the name of the caller and a number. "Okay, I'll pass this along."

"Anything important?" Dif asked.

"Not sure. She wouldn't tell me any more than her name. I thought she sounded a little unsure, anxious." Simon fingered the slip of paper. "Jessica Allison is her name. She said to tell him Jessie needs to speak to him."

"Don't know the name. Can't say I've ever heard Virgil mention her. Guess we ought to pass it along to Clara. She said he would check in with her."

"Where is he?" Simon asked.

"I think he's taking a little time to get his feet on the ground after yesterday. Guess you know about that. He's up in that high country. Clara and Cesar talked him into it."

"Yes, unfortunately I do. But for the sheriff it's not just the personal loss but all the fallout. He is not only going to have to bury his friend but figure out how to replace him."

"Yeah, I think when he hired you, he thought he could take a breather for a while. Then the bottom dropped out. I remember Sam, Virgil's father, saying one time, when everything seemed calm that's when he would start to worry."

● ● ●

It was late in the afternoon by the time Virgil reached his great-grandfather's cabin. He had ridden the fence line a couple of hours, even though he realized pretty early on it was a ruse. The wire was tight as a drum. Cesar and the boys stayed on top of everything. The wind had begun to pick up again. By the time he reached the cabin, he was starting to feel the cold. Even Jack with his thick winter coat seemed ready to settle in for the night. When they came in sight of the small barn and corral he broke into an easy lope.

Virgil saw that the basic structure of the cabin and the small barn looked sound. The barn door was hanging open on one hinge. Some of the rails on the small corral had pulled free. One was broken, in pieces on the ground. He got off Jack, double looped the reins again, let him free to graze. For the next half hour he resurrected the corral and the barn door. He checked the interior of the barn. There were two rough stalls on one side, one on the other. The open space where there was no stall was used for hay storage. Virgil was surprised to see four or five decent-looking bales showing good color there. He figured at some point Cesar must have sent José or Pedro up there on an ATV. All part of the plan, he figured. The hay was still tightly corded, so Virgil put his knee into the middle of one bale, slipping the twine that held the hay tight as he did, then he carried a couple of flakes outside, dropping them in the middle of the corral. Jack at some distance nickered as he picked up his head and immediately trotted toward the corral. When he came inside he dropped his head, picked up a mouthful, began to chew. He continued eating while Virgil brought the tack inside of the barn, hung the saddle on what was a makeshift saddle rack, then hooked the headgear and reins over the pommel. When he left the corral he turned his attention to the cabin.

He knew he had been delaying going in, because the minute he stepped inside the bittersweet memory of the last time he was there would be waiting for him. He remembered what he had told Clara when she referred to the cabin. She knew full well why he had never returned to the cabin. Clara had known it had become a special haunt for Virgil and Rusty when opposition had begun to build from her mother about their relationship. Virgil didn't know until years later why Audrey had been opposed to the idea of them as a couple. Nevertheless, the cabin had become their go-to place. In the naïveté of youth and in the full flush of emotion, there they had talked about their future life together.

He stood outside the cabin door, a cold wind blowing at his back. The flood of memory had anchored him to the spot. He was reluctant to let it go. It was not unlike the feeling he had when he first entered the newly built barns a few months earlier, wiping out the childhood he had shared in the old barns with his parents. Now once again, when he stepped inside this old cabin, another door of his life would close. The lesson was driven home again and again. Nothing is permanent. Dave full of hope, not unlike Virgil twenty some odd years before. Virgil left behind after Rusty, now Rosie after Dave, each with a shattered dream.

Virgil threw open the door. As if on cue, a huge wind gust blew through the shuttered windows of the old building as though the opened door created a vacuum. Dust infused with miscellaneous debris, pieces of chaff along with age-old memories, flew into Virgil's face. He couldn't escape the symbolism as he brushed the debris out of his eyes and off of his clothes. He stepped inside the cabin. The wind was still coming through the windows, whistling around the eaves, tugging at any looseness it could find in the old structure. Virgil set his saddlebags on the homemade table that stood crookedly against the wall, then he went over to the old bed in the corner, stripping off a blanket that pretty much fell apart in his hands. He tightened the cord frame after he took what served as a bedboard off, then set it back down on the cord webbing. He threw the tattered, faded blanket that had been on top near the fireplace, then threw his bedroll on the top of the board that covered the webbing. The last thing he did was empty his saddlebags of the foodstuffs Clara had packed for him.

He grabbed another apple, biting into it as he stepped back outside. Light was fading fast, so after tossing the apple core into Jack, he quickly started to gather deadfall for the fireplace. By the time he had a pile stacked, waiting by the fireplace, the cabin was darker within than it was outside. He quickly built a fire, happy to see the ancient chimney drawing as well as it ever did. One more time he went outside while the fire started to work. In the last of the light he led Jack into the old barn, bedding him down in the first stall. He gave him some of the grain ration he had brought, spilling some of it into an old bucket. Then he got another bucket, filling it with sweet water from the old hand pump that had been outside the barn for as long as he could remember. After Jack was settled he took some random pieces of plywood sheeting he had found in the barn and headed back to the cabin. He spent most of the next hour patching areas of the windows that had been broken with the wood. When he was done he stepped back to evaluate his work. There was more wood than glass in the windows. They definitely were not airtight, but the wind that blew through was more of a whisper than a howl.

"It'll do for the night." His words in the semi-darkened quiet hung in the air. He threw a few more logs on the fire, then threw in the ragged blanket he had put to one side before starting the fire. It caught immediately, flaring up and disappearing in the flame in seconds. He had found a tin filled with beeswax and a thick wick. Lighting the homemade candle, he set it on the table then ate a cold supper. He thought about getting water from the old pump then gave it up as a bad idea. The wind was still calling. There was no moon. The likelihood of getting back from the pump in the pitch dark with water and body intact was slim. Besides, he was warm and comfortable, so he reached back into his saddlebag, took out a pint bottle that Clara had slipped in there and unscrewed the cap.

After a while, as he sat gazing into the flames, listening to the fire hiss and crackle as it discovered hidden pockets of moisture in the wood, the thought came to him that since he left the ranch house, he hadn't thought about the trauma he had left behind or what he would be facing on his return. He realized again that Cesar and Clara's advice was insightful. A kind of calm had restored him. It didn't change reality but gave him a little more ability to face it. He reached into his pocket and took out his phone, then pressed the On button. The artificial light came on. He saw that it was a little after seven. He tapped the face, then Contacts, watching the list of numbers come up. He tapped Home then held the phone to his ear, waiting for the ring.

"Hello, Virgil. Is Grandpa's cabin still standing?"

"Sure is holes in the walls and all. A little patchwork and it will be good for another hundred years. Any messages or calls from the office?" Jessica Allison. At first the name meant nothing to him. Then Jessie. The memory of standing outside the office of the sand and gravel company looking into those blue eyes came back to him, reminding him in the darkness of the little cabin that he was Virgil Dalton, a man still alive and the sheriff of Hayward. Tomorrow he would return, say goodbye to Dave, then pick up the pieces he had left behind.

# 28

"Jimmy, is Mr. Summers going to jail for a long time?"

"Probably the rest of his life, Abby."

"Do you think he meant to kill Mr. Brand?"

"Don't think it makes much difference. He had a gun. Even if he didn't do it on purpose, he brought the weapon. So to my way of thinking, he has to accept the responsibility for what happened. You know we all got to be responsible for what we do. Guess that's what Sheriff Dalton would call a life lesson."

"You really like Sheriff Dalton, don't you?"

Jimmy looked at Abby his young sister, who was sitting at the kitchen table doing her homework.

"Yeah. I really do."

"Why?"

"Well, I guess it's because I figure he saved me from myself. He helped me to become a better person."

"I think you were always a good person, Jimmy."

"Well, Ab. For a while there, it could have gone either way. Virgil, I mean the sheriff, got a hold of me before I did anything too stupid. That's why, when you think I'm bugging you, that's what I'm trying to do for you. Keep you from doing something so stupid that it messes up your life. Seen a lot of people do that."

"You don't have to worry about me, Jimmy. I ain't near as stupid as you were." Abby put her hand to her mouth. "I mean because you were always there. I didn't do anything too stupid."

"Good save, Abby." Jimmy smiled.

"I'm glad you're smiling again, Jimmy."

"Yeah, well, it's been pretty hard to find something to smile about lately." Abby didn't say anything. Just then Mrs. Tillman came into the kitchen.

"It's all done, Jimmy. Cleaned and ironed. You are going to look real nice." She held up Jimmy's uniform.

"Thanks, Mom."

"Am I going to Simpson's, Mom?" Abby asked.

"No, honey. I don't think so."

"Why not? I went when Grandma died."

"I know. But this is different. This isn't the natural order of things.

You've got plenty of time to find out how mean the world can be. Let's not rush it."

Jimmy took his uniform and went into his bedroom. After a few minutes he returned to the kitchen, buttoning one of his cuffs.

"Mom's right, Jimmy, you look real nice."

Mrs. Tillman brushed something from her eyes.

"You okay, Mom? What's the matter?"

She waved her hand.

"Oh, it's nothing, Jimmy."

"Ma, are you crying? What is it?"

"Mommy, tell us," Abby pleaded.

"It's just, it could have been you, Jimmy. It could be you, lying there in Simpson's. I just never thought . . . Oh, Jimmy, I know our life wasn't easy when you were growing up. I mean, I wasn't always the best mom. I tried, Jimmy, I really did . . . did the best I could. But these last few years have been so much better. It's because of you. Me and Abby have been, are, so proud of you, what you've become. Just this morning a woman I hardly know came up to me in the store, telling me how everyone was talking about you. The wonderful job you did, how you stayed with Mr. Brand until he passed. How the sheriff said he couldn't have done any better. I was so proud. Then the lady said it could have been you. When she walked away, I just stood there. That's when it hit me. I started shaking so hard I had to hold on to the shopping cart to keep from falling."

Jimmy could see the anguish. He went to her, wrapping her in his arms.

"Mom, it's okay. You did a great job with me and that little knucklehead over there. We always had a roof over our heads, our bellies were full and we had a soft bed to sleep in, because you were usually working two jobs. Now I'm helping to make things a little better for you. It's called payback. The sheriff has trained me well. Oh, sure, I know there's danger, but I try to be as careful as I can be. Besides, I'm tough. I mean, people falling out of the sky can't even take me out. Don't worry. What happened to Dave shouldn't have happened but he didn't know what he was walking into." Jimmy walked her to the table, then sat her down. "Now, why don't you sit over a hot cup of tea while Abby tries to figure out what two plus two adds up to, because I've got to get over to Simpson's. After a little while, when you are feeling better, you come over. Then we can come home together later." He leaned over, gave his mom a quick kiss, then reached over to pinch Abby's cheek and left.

• • •

Jimmy stepped outside of the trailer that he, his mom and Abby called home. The cold of the early January day didn't touch him but there was a cold from deep inside that did. He had been putting up a good front but the brief moment with his mother had his insides in a knot. It wasn't that what she had told him was some sort of revelation. He knew what being a member of law enforcement was all about. At least he thought he did until now. The woman who had come off the overpass in the middle of the night months before while he was doing a nightly patrol, crashing through his windshield, ultimately putting him in the hospital, had shaken him. For the first time in his life, he had come face-to-face with his own mortality. It threw him back on his haunches. Ultimately, though, it became part of his own personal learning curve, helping him to take a giant step away from his boyhood.

Up until that time, he had felt a rung or two down the ladder in his dealings with the adults in his world. In reality, he realized for the first time that he was inviting that perception. To a certain extent, that notion had been validated with the arrival of Simon. Simon was no kid and no one treated him like one. He saw it right away. Virgil, Rosie, Dif, everyone spoke to him and of him as an equal. There was a certain nuance that he had picked up on that was different from the way they spoke to him. He was Jimmy, the kid from town who they had all taken under their wing. He had always looked at Vigil as the father he wanted but never had. He was realizing that on some level the relationship had been reciprocal with Virgil and through his fostering with the others. It had been very comforting for a long time, but he was no longer the kid being picked up off the ground by the sheriff in back of Talbot's hardware store with a bloodied nose. He was no longer the kid who clung to Virgil and to the others who had reached into his life with caring and love. It was Dave, bloodied and dying in his arms, who finally propelled Jim into the manhood that was his destiny. That cold he felt deep inside, as he stood by the car outside of the trailer, was not just because of the death of Dave but of the boy he was leaving behind.

# 29

Virgil pulled into the parking lot at the back of Simpson's Funeral Home. There were no other cars in the parking area. He had come before any of the other mourners, even before Rosie and her children got there. He knew he was early. He had counted on it. The back door was locked so he rang the bell. He rang a second time. Just as he was getting ready to ring again, the door slowly opened.

"Hello, Boots." The man he greeted was reed thin, tall and bald. Virgil had known him all his life. Virgil glanced down at the highly polished boots he wore, which had given him the only name most people knew him by.

"Hello, Virgil." Virgil stepped inside. "You know regular viewing won't start for another hour."

"I know," Virgil said. "But I need some private time with Dave."

The old man, who wore every bit of his eighty some odd years lined deeply in his face, looked at Virgil through clear, brown eyes.

"I understand." He turned and Virgil followed him down a long hall. They stopped at the arched doorway of a room that was all too familiar to Virgil. Then they passed up the aisle between the rows of chairs that would shortly be filled, until they reached the closed casket that sat surrounded by the floral displays that had literally emptied out Kleman's Florist Shop. The perfume was overpowering. Virgil coughed twice.

"Yes," the tall man said. He left Virgil's side, went over to the wall facing the street, then opened the broadside of four huge windows, which bowed the wall into an angled alcove around an upholstered window seat that looked out on Main Street. He returned with the cold breeze that lifted the curtains and freshened the room. "I should have done that earlier." He stood next to Virgil alongside the coffin. "A decision has been made by Miss Rosita to leave it closed for the public viewing." Virgil nodded. Then the tall man stepped forward, reached out, raised the lid, then stepped back next to Virgil. He looked at Virgil, his brown eyes betraying nothing. He nodded when he saw Virgil take in a deep breath and left the room.

For a long moment, Virgil stood rooted to his spot. At last he took two steps forward. He was flooded with emotion. He looked down on Dave Brand, a man who had been part of his life all of his life. He tried to speak but he was struggling for his words. He took another deep breath before his next attempt.

"I am so, so sorry, Dave. I . . . I had no choice. I had to let Cecil go. I never thought . . ." The words hung in the air. Virgil reached forward, put his hand on Dave's shoulder. "I will never forget what I owe you. I promise that I will be there for Rosie and the new baby for as long as I live." He squeezed his hand until he could feel Dave's body beneath the fabric that he wore. He stood for another minute in total silence. Then he turned and left the room.

# 30

The wind that blew on the high ridges above the ranch where Virgil had been before Dave's wake and funeral continued to blow for the next three days. But by the third day, there had been a subtle change. The sky had clouded over. Moisture had also crept in on a change of wind direction. Virgil noted it as he stood with half the town as Dave was lowered into the ground. He felt if numbers counted for anything at a time like this, Rosie could take some solace in the fact that Dave had left his mark. One of the Simpson brothers had told him the night before they hadn't had a turnout like Dave's in the previous ten years. He looked around at the gathered mourners, ranging from town officials to state police, along with people representing every aspect of Hayward society. Cowhands he'd seen wrangling cattle down at Luther's stockyard in Redbud standing alongside shopkeepers and staff from the hospital. Dave and Rosie had thrown a wide net. Lastly, his eyes came to rest on Rosie and her family standing by the open grave, clinging so close they appeared as one. It did not escape his notice that Rosie was comforting her children. It was not a surprise. As he was leaving the cemetery a little while later, Mayor Bob Jamison caught up with him.

"How are you doing, Virgil?"

"I've had better days, Bob."

"Guess we've got to have a sit-down pretty soon. There's quite a bit we have to talk about."

"Yes, Dave has left a huge hole, but there is a lot more than filling Dave's slot that we have to talk about."

"How is the new man, Simon, working out?"

"Simon seems to be fitting in nicely, but as I said, this talk is going to have to be a lot more wide-ranging than a replacement for Dave Brand. The county is growing and changing. We need to address that."

"Well, the town council . . ." Virgil held up his hand.

"Listen, Ears, there are people on that council who are looking at Hayward through forty-year-old glasses. What they see doesn't exist anymore. Dave's death ought to drive that notion home. If it doesn't, I intend to, and I hope you relay that at your next meeting."

"Are you going to be in the office tomorrow?"

"I'm going to be in the office in ten minutes. That's exactly what I'm trying to get across to you. This ain't a once in a while job anymore. For quite some time now I realize that we have been like the song says, running on empty, and that's just to stay in place. That's got to change or you are going to have to get someone else to do this job. I'm not about to risk people's lives because the town council wants to live in the past." Virgil had reached his vehicle. He opened the door then turned to face the mayor. "Anything you want to say, Bob?"

"Guess we just had our sit-down, Virgil. For what it's worth, I just want you to know I'm going to deliver your message at the meeting next Monday with one addition."

"And what would that be?" Virgil asked.

"That if things don't change, in addition to looking for a new sheriff, they are going to be looking for a new mayor. You take care, Virgil. You are one of my favorite people." Then he turned and walked away.

# 31

He heard a voice on the other end after the third ring.

"Mesquite Sand and Gravel." There followed a litany of options. Virgil waited until he heard the extension for Human Resources then he punched in the number.

"Jessica Allison, how may I help you?"

"Virgil Dalton, Miss Allison . . . Jessie. Sorry I couldn't get back to you sooner but I haven't been in the office for the last couple of days, but I did get the message that you called."

"I'm afraid you are mistaken. I didn't call you."

Virgil was puzzled by her response.

"You didn't? Guess I got the wrong information."

"Well, it happens. Goodbye."

Virgil was even more perplexed by the dismissive note in her voice. He placed the phone in the cradle then sat back in his chair. He thought there had been something of a connection between them.

"Guess I'm not the stud I thought I was," he said to the empty room. He spent a few moments trying to read between the lines. He came up empty, so he pulled a pile of paperwork over to begin the process of catch-up. An hour later, when Simon came into the office, he asked him about the call.

"No, Sheriff. It wasn't Dif who took the call. It was me. I took that call. That was her name, I'm sure. Hold on, she gave me the number. I have it right here. He picked up the phone on the table that he and Dif had been working from, taking a folded sheet of paper from underneath a desk blotter. He read the name and the number aloud.

"Well, that's her name, but that's not the number of the company, at least not the number I called." Virgil was even more puzzled.

Simon left to make his rounds a little while later. He was stepping in for Jimmy to give him a little time with his family. Virgil worked alone in the office until the pile on his desk had disappeared, then he went over to Margie's for dinner. A few snowflakes were swirling in the light of the parking lot when he left the office. He pulled up the collar of his jacket and put his hands in his pockets. By the time he made the short walk to the restaurant, the snow had become a little steadier. When he stepped inside the door, he took off his Stetson then brushed the snow off it against his leg.

"First real snow of the season, Virgil," Margie's voice greeted him.

"Probably won't be the last," he replied. He realized he was the only one in the place.

"Didn't see you at Rosie's after the burial."

"No. Had to get back to the office."

"Guess things are going to get a little hectic for you without Dave and Rosie." Her comment caught Virgil off guard. He hadn't really thought about Rosie not being in the office. "Clara not cooking for you tonight?"

"No. I called her before I came over, going to stay late tonight. Want to make sure someone's in the office. Simon took over for Jimmy. He's making rounds. He thinks Jimmy needs some downtime with his family. I agree with him. That kind of an experience can set you back on your heels. I gave Dif the night off."

"Yeah, well, like you, I'm missing some people but it don't much matter. Lot of people want to be with their family. Dave's death sucked the life out of this town today, but I figure like you, someone's got to be here. Guess that's the boss. Well, Virgil, got some chicken and dumplings back there, you interested?"

"Sounds good, Margie. Don't usually come here to admire the artwork." Virgil nodded toward the calendar on the wall.

"Gee, Virgil, I thought you came because of my riveting personality and my insightful comments about the state of the world."

"Always that," he said. "Adds to the culinary experience."

By the time she returned, he realized how hungry he was, calculating that he hadn't eaten anything since breakfast. By the time she brought his coffee, he had wiped the last bit of gravy off his plate with the fragment of a dumpling.

"Don't eat the plate, Virgil. I'll get you a piece of pie."

"I'm good, Margie. No reflection on your pie but I gotta get back. Can't be gone too long." When he stepped outside, he was surprised to see a coating of snow covering the world. There was little activity to be seen. Only two cars went by on Main Street on the walk back to the office. He figured a lot of people were back home hugging their families after Dave's burial. The snow was making the world quieter. Once the cars passed the only sound was the crunch of snow under his feet.

The one light he had left on in the office only made it seem more dark and lonely. When he opened the door a gust of swirling snow followed him inside. He glanced at the wall clock. It was a little after eight. The thought came to him that at the same time one week before, everybody was celebrating Christmas at the first-ever party at the ranch. He remembered how much Dave was enjoying himself and sharing the news about the baby with anyone who didn't know. A week ago. It didn't seem possible.

After he hung up his jacket, he turned on the TV but saw nothing that interested him, so he scrolled through to the music channels until he found some jazz. Then he went to the holding cells, which were unoccupied, found a push broom and started to sweep. Half an hour later, he had swept out the cells and the office. Then he got a bucket and washed all the floors. He actually broke a sweat. The physical activity made him feel good. Finally, when he was finished with the cleanup, he got a cold can of soda out of the fridge and sat down behind his desk. He sat there listening to some jazz while he drank.

A loud knock at the door some time later startled him out of a doze. He glanced at the clock then dragged himself out of his chair. There was a second knock before he reached the door. A cold blast of snow greeted him when he opened it. She stood before him, the snow blowing at her back.

"I know it's late but I saw the light. I was going to wait until tomorrow, but when I saw your light I thought I'd try."

"That's okay," Virgil said. "Come inside, out of the weather." She stepped inside.

Virgil realized as he closed the door that there was at least three or four inches covering the parking lot. "Can I get you something, a hot drink?" She had brushed the snow from her coat, then took off her woolen hat, which she held in her hands until Virgil took it from her.

"Here, let me have your coat also." She took it off, handing it to him. Virgil hung it next to his on the rack of hooks on the wall alongside the door. "Now, how about that hot drink. Find yourself a chair. I'll be with you in a minute." He went to the cabinet over the counter, took out a couple of packets of cocoa. A couple of minutes later he set a mug in front of her. "Figured on a snowy night hot cocoa was the way to go."

"Thank you. This is great." She took a sip from the mug, which she held in both hands. He took a sip from his own cup as he slid into his chair.

"Guess you are wondering why I'm here, especially after the brush-off I gave you on the phone earlier."

"Yeah, well, you sure got my curiosity aroused."

"Well, let me start by telling you, maybe I'm more than a little paranoid. Maybe this is just a waste of time."

"What are we talking about? Tell me what's got you worried, then I'll judge whether or not you should sit down with a professional, to start talking about your early life and all the people who abused you."

"If it comes to that, I've got a list that would choke a goat." She smiled then took another sip from her cup. "Okay, here goes. After you left the other day I got to thinking and I remembered something Mrs. Stark said the last time she came to the office."

"Mrs. Stark, I don't think I know . . ."

"Mr. Stark, Michael, was Mr. Jessup's partner. Remember I told you that I knew him but I didn't know Mr. Jessup that well. I think he was the primary partner in the company. I met him, Mr. Jessup, on a few occasions, but Mr. Stark, well, he handled the accounting primarily for Sand and Gravel so I saw him pretty frequently. Remember, I think I told you he had an office in the building.

"Anyway, Mr. Jessup handled the housing development, that's why I didn't see him as often. That last day when Mrs. Stark came to the office to collect his personal belongings, I told her how sorry I was about the accident. I remember she looked at me in a strange way. Then she said, 'Miss Allison, you don't have an accident that kills you when you are driving along a road that you've driven so many times you could do it with your eyes closed.' She said Michael was an excellent driver. She said from the moment the state police called to tell her what happened, she told them that it was no accident, but she said when he died after being in a coma for a month, she could tell they had moved on, weren't interested.

"I didn't know what to make of it at the time. I guess I was kind of like the state police. I mean, I know that road well. Even a good driver can make a mistake. That road isn't going to give too many drivers a second chance. Then when you came by it got me to thinking. Even then, I was going to let it go, until Mr. Zambrano came by the day after you came to see me. He was obviously upset, not himself, even almost seemed a little angry that I had spoken to you. I was really puzzled by his behavior. It was like he was almost grilling me about your visit."

"But why didn't you tell me this on the phone when I called today?"

"Here's where the paranoia starts to kick in. A couple of times since that day, when I've been on my office phone or dialing an outside number, I've heard a click or what sounds like a click on my phone. I finally mentioned it to the receptionist because I never heard it before. She told me she didn't know why my phone would be affected but that there was a technician who Mr. Zambrano had told her to let into my office one day after I had gone. He said the man was going to upgrade my computer. I think whoever that was put a tap on my line."

Virgil got up from his chair, picked up her empty cup, then brought the two empty mugs over to the sink.

"Do you know anything about Mr. Zambrano?"

"You mean not work-related?"

"Yes, anything about his past life?"

"Not really. He has always been real nice to work for and is totally involved in the business. Everyone likes him and he has really taken the company to new growth levels. He is really hands-on. We've never really socialized other than at some work-related functions, like the office Christmas party. I do know he's from or lived for some time in Chicago. He made a comment one time when we ordered pizza for his birthday party that the pizza couldn't compare to the pizza you got in Chicago."

"So that phone number you gave to my deputy?"

"That's my cell. I wouldn't have closed you down so quickly today if you had called on my cell."

"Oh, that's a relief. I thought it was me, I don't handle rejection well."

"Somehow, I doubt that's something you've experienced very much." She brushed her hair back from her face with both hands. Virgil saw the mark on her left cheek, the one he had noticed at their first meeting, deepen when she smiled. Her eyes were as blue as he remembered. Virgil also remembered when they first met her hair was pulled back, now it hung free. He liked it better.

"By the way, I heard about your deputy. I'm sorry. Sounds like he was a good man."

"He was. We are going to miss him. He was a good friend. Knew him pretty much all my life, left a big hole around here."

"I didn't realize, again, I'm sorry. Well, I guess I better get home before the snow gets much deeper."

"Are you going to be alright? I mean, do you have far to go?" She had gotten up, walked over to the sink and rinsed out her cup and Virgil's.

"You didn't have to do that." Virgil joined her as they walked to the door. "I'm going to be here late, looking for stuff to do . . . quiet night."

"It's nothing. As far as the weather, I'll be fine. I'll just take my time. I am only about ten minutes away."

He opened the door as she slipped on her hat and coat. The wind had died down. The snow was falling in larger flakes, confetti dancing in the night air. "It is really pretty, isn't it?" She stood next to him in the doorway. He could feel her closeness.

"Yes, makes the world look a lot different."

"So, you never said. Do you think I'm paranoid? Should I make an appointment to see somebody to discuss the trauma of my childhood?"

"I am going to do some checking but I have a hunch you are seeing the world as it is. Now I've just got to see if your suspicions are in any way connected to the problem I'm trying to solve. In the meantime, if anything else happens or you need to get in touch, just call."

She took a step outside then turned.

"You can reach me on my cell if you need to or even if you just feel like talking." Then she turned away before Virgil could reply.

"I'll keep that in mind," Virgil yelled after her. She turned when she reached her car and waved.

Virgil realized as he was driving home that for the first time in the last few days he was starting to move forward. By the driveway turnoff, the snow had stopped. He almost hated driving through the untouched snow. When he reached the midpoint, he stopped his vehicle and turned off the engine. He got out. Clouds scudding across the night sky were breaking apart. Stars were emerging between the clouds, the moon trying to show its face. The fence rails were covered. The spotlight from the house stretched across the driveway to fall on the silhouetted barns. Virgil sucked in the crisp air. There was the lightest wind stirring the top layer of snow, some of it dancing in the headlights. A kind of calm invaded his soul. He was getting his balance back. It was time, literally and figuratively, to move forward. He got back into his car, turned on the engine, then drove down the driveway into the Currier and Ives winter scene.

# 32

Clara sensed the change when she saw Virgil in the morning. He was sweeping the accumulation off the steps when she came into the kitchen. She could tell by his body language he was back. Full sun flooded the landscape but there was no melting. It even looked cold. She looked at the thermometer mounted outside the kitchen window. Virgil's breath rising in small puffs had already told her what she would see. She watched him run across the driveway to the barn. By the time he came back twenty minutes later, she was flipping pancakes on the griddle. He was inside the door brushing the snow off his jacket.

"Cesar will be over later. I took care of the morning for him."

"Is he okay?"

"A little too much tequila," Virgil said as he pulled up his chair. "Snow paints a nice picture."

"It certainly does," Clara responded. "I wonder how the roads are this morning. I'd like to stop by the hospital to see Everett Jessup once more before I head back home."

"I would like to see his son." Virgil took a bite out of his first pancake. "I'm also concerned about Mr. Jessup going back to his place. Whoever put him in the hospital might call again."

"Did he know who it was that attacked him?"

"No. I saw him two days after he was brought to the hospital. He had very little memory of the incident but he said he had never seen either of the two men before. Ark said the fact that he had very little recall was to be expected after the beating he took."

"So you think they were looking for his son?"

"Nothing else makes any sense, especially when it happened right after the news was released that it wasn't Everett Junior's body in that burned-out trailer. The way I figure it, they were after Everett. They knew it was his trailer. They assumed that was him in it. So they staged that whole meth scene. It was only later they found out that the man inside wasn't Everett. That's when they went looking for him at his father's house. I've gone over it again and again, nothing else computes."

"Why are they after him?" Clara asked.

"That's the reason I need to find Everett before they do. He's the only one who can answer that question. But as far as you going in to see Mr. Jessup, I'm sure that by the afternoon the roads will be clear. Anyway,

Clara, you know we'll miss you. It's been a long time since Cesar and me had a mother."

# 33

The first thing Virgil did when he got into the office was to reach out to Kyle Harrison, his contact at the ATF.

Their relationship had been a little bumpy at times but in the last year or so he and Virgil had developed a mutual respect. That call ended with Virgil leaving a message for a callback. Virgil's next call was to the state police. Both a courtesy call and a request, this call bore fruit immediately. Virgil first thanked Major Travis for the increased patrols over the last couple of days then asked if it would be possible to help out with more coverage down in Redbud. He explained that until he got another deputy down there on a permanent basis, Alex was alone in the substation.

He had always had a good working relationship with the state police but knew it was a delicate balance. Not too many years back, there had been a push among some members of the community to disband the sheriff's office and just rely on the state police to save money. Then Hayward had a growth spurt, with the huge expansion of the hospital into a regional care facility, along with the surge down in Redbud, which resulted in the need for the substation. So the idea of the state police being the only law enforcement group in Hayward died a quick death. Too many people wanted to see the law regularly driving the streets of Hayward or knowing that after going into their homes each night that there was someone a phone call away who could be to their house in minutes if needed. Virgil was relieved to know he was getting the extra coverage but he knew this fix was only temporary.

Shortly after his phone call ended, he got a call back from Kyle Harrison. Virgil knew that Kyle had a lot more resources at his disposal than he did.

"Hey, Virgil. What's going on?"

"I was wondering if you could check on the background of someone for me. His name is Zambrano. I think he came here about four or five years ago. He either owns the Mesquite Sand and Gravel Company down in Cielo outright or is a partner. Anyway, he came to our neck of the woods from Chicago, James Zambrano."

"Zambrano, I'm not familiar with the name. I assume it's spelled like it sounds. I'll do my best, Virgil. Give me a day or two. Everything okay with you? I really liked Dave. I know this is a bad time and I know how close you guys were."

"It's been tough but I try to remember what my father told me. You're never going to ride the horse that threw you if you don't get back in the saddle. That's what I'm trying to do now, get back in the saddle."

"We all have to learn that lesson. Don't hesitate to reach out if you need help."

"Thanks, Kyle. I appreciate that. My next move is to find out if there's anyone who would be interested in a job replacing the previous deputy who died doing his." There was a moment of silence on the other end of the line.

"You know, Virgil, I might be able to help you in that regard. Sometimes we get candidates who look really good but for whatever reason they change their mind. I'll get back to you on that, along with that other thing."

Virgil waited a little bit to finish the last of the paperwork that was left from the night before then put in a call to Dif and Jimmy asking them to come in before Simon's shift was over. His next call was to the hospital to check on Mr. Jessup.

"Mr. Jessup is gone, Sheriff."

"What do you mean gone?" Virgil asked.

"Gone as in released. He was discharged this morning."

"He's on his own? I mean, he just walked out?"

"Oh, no. A woman came and picked him up." Virgil asked to speak to the doctor but Sam wasn't available.

A little while after he hung up the phone, Dif and Jimmy walked into the office together.

"What's up, boss?" Dif asked.

"I figured we ought to talk about some things today so we are all on the same page," Virgil said.

"Before you say anything, Edna and I had a talk. We both agreed that for the time being or as long as is necessary, I'll be available full-time."

"Me too, Virgil," Jimmy added. "I can pick up more time too." Virgil looked at the two of them.

"You know . . ." He was searching for the right words, when the door opened.

"Well, if it ain't the brain trust." Rosie stood looking at them from the doorway while taking off her coat. Dif was the first to find his voice.

"Rosie, what are you doing here?"

"Man, that dementia must finally be kicking in. Don't you remember, I been working here for over fifteen years. By the way, you are sitting in my chair." Dif quickly jumped up. "Did any of you figure out how to make coffee while I was gone?" She glanced over at the empty pot.

"Rosie, seriously, what are you doing here? I mean, I didn't expect—"

Virgil didn't get a chance to finish.

"Virgil, stop. I know where you are going with this. You think I don't know how you all feel about me, how you felt about Dave. But life goes on, Virgil, you know about that. We all do. Dave is dead and buried but I am not about to jump in the grave with him. He wouldn't want that. I know there are going to be some really tough days, some days when I don't even want to get out of bed, but he'd want me to move on for myself and for this baby that he loved. I'm not going to do that if I sit home crying. That isn't going to bring him back. That isn't living. So I'm going to be coming in here like always, making coffee that people can actually drink, seeing that the paperwork is taken care of, and hopefully keeping you guys on track so this little girl I'm carrying is going to grow up in a nice, safe town."

"Boy, why can't I find a woman like you?" They all looked to the door again. Simon was standing there

"Maybe you ain't looking hard enough or in the right places," Jimmy piped up.

"Out of the mouth of babes," Dif added. "Now, about that coffee."

"Okay . . . okay." Rosie walked over to the coffeemaker. "By the way, who is the interior decorator?" She looked at the rearrangement of the table and desks.

"Dif and I didn't feel comfortable sitting behind your desks, so we made a little change," Simon offered.

"Virgil, I think maybe we ought to get a third desk in here. Doesn't look too professional using that old table with all the coffee stains and dings in it for such a top-notch staff."

"I agree. We'll get a brand-new desk pronto. Meantime, let's sit down and get up to speed on a couple of things."

For the next forty-five minutes they worked on scheduling. Simon was going down to Redbud four days a week, Jimmy two, and one day Alex would be by himself. Then Simon would be one day in Hayward, Jimmy three days, while Virgil would pick up the slack. Rosie and Dif said they would work out their hours.

"By the way, Dif, if Edna thinks she is getting off the hook by sending you down here full-time, tell her I appreciate the offer but I couldn't possibly deprive her of so much quality time with you."

"That's always been my problem," Dif said. "Spreading myself so thin that people, especially women, can never get enough of me."

They all smiled at Dif's comeback. For just an instant, an observer passing by would never have known that they were struggling to escape the cold clutch of death, which had unexpectedly reached out to each of them.

Before he left, Virgil brought them up to speed about Mr. Jessup, along with his suspicions about the fire.

"So you don't think the trailer was a meth lab?" Jimmy asked.

"I was doubtful from the moment I met Mr. Jessup. The way he talked about his son. The way his son every year went over the top decorating for Christmas then inviting everyone to a big party. If you're cooking meth in your trailer, you keep a low profile. You're not outlining the trailer in Christmas lights. Besides, Mr. Jessup has a real close relationship with his son. He would have known about that. No. Somebody wanted it to seem like his son died accidentally in a meth fire. The problem was I think they were hired to do the job. Had the address but had never seen his son, so they killed the wrong person. I don't know why the young man was there but I think he was just an unfortunate victim."

"Is that why you asked the ME to hold the body as long as he could?" Dif asked.

"I figured I had to because once they realized they made a mistake, they would try to correct it. After seeing what they did to Mr. Jessup, I'm sure that's the case."

"So where are you going from here, Virgil?" Rosie asked.

"The only place I can. I've got to find Everett Junior before they do and keep Everett Senior safe."

# 34

It was late afternoon by the time Virgil got back home. He was surprised to see Clara outside in the cold brushing the snow off her car. He knew she had taken the pickup when she drove into town in the morning. Now that daylight was slipping away, he couldn't figure why she was clearing off the snow. By the time he got out of his vehicle, she had brushed off the last of it. He yelled to her as she was climbing the stairs into the house. She gave a wave then continued inside.

He saw Cesar in the barn. It had remained cold throughout the day. Temperatures never made it out of the thirties. There was little snowmelt, except in completely exposed areas where the wind had helped. Jack acknowledged Virgil's presence from the corral. Virgil walked to him, reached through the rails and stroked his neck. Jack responded with a soft nicker. While he was stroking Jack, Cesar came out of the barn and joined him.

"How did it go today?"

"It was good. I've got some very good people in my life, but we are going to be spread pretty thin for a while."

"Maybe, when you start looking for someone, try a new direction."

"What are you talking about?"

"Other day I was over to the Thompson place, High Lonesome. Miss Marian working hard over there to get that place back to where it was with Manuel and that boy you brought down off the mountain. He's a good kid, hard worker, teaching her some Mex. Got to thinking, lot more folks like me in these parts than when Sam brought me here. Not so many hiding in the shadows. They own stores, restaurants, becoming a regular part of the community. So maybe when you look for someone new, maybe you want to think about that."

Virgil took his foot off the lowest rail.

"You know, every so often you are a step ahead of me. This might be one of those occasions."

"Well, I'm just trying to keep you up with the times. I read the paper, watch the news. Diversity, I think that's it diversity."

Virgil looked at Cesar.

"You know, old man, I'm just sorry you're not thirty years younger. Hell, I'd hire you."

"I think they call that ageism," Cesar shot back. Virgil laughed so loud Jack jumped back from the rail.

"What was that all about?" Clara asked him when he came into the kitchen a few minutes later. Virgil told Clara about the exchange.

"You know, Virgil, he's not far off the mark. The world, this country, things are different, always changing. Can't ignore that."

"That's just what I told Bob, the mayor, the other day. I know it but some people are going to fight any change."

"Hell, you can't let that stop you. Those idiots are always going to be there." Virgil hadn't heard a swear word out of Clara in a long time.

"Guess I struck a nerve," he said.

"Oh, it's just that I get so disgusted when I'm faced with stupidity. And these days when I turn on the TV, I see that there's more than enough of it to go around. The latest I hear is that some nut wants to build a wall clear across the country to keep all the immigrants out. Is this a serious consideration? If it wasn't for the immigrants, this country never would have gotten a start. You know, I've watched a couple of these genealogy shows on television, people trying to trace their roots. Seems to be a big fascination of a lot of people lately. Some of them going all the way back to the pilgrims, but no matter how far back they go, I've yet to see somebody who didn't originally come from some other part of the world."

"I don't disagree. Anyway, my problem is a little more local."

"Well, I've got faith in you, Virgil. There's nobody on that town council that you can't drag, even if it's kicking and screaming, into the twenty-first century."

"I'll be happy if I can drag them into the twentieth century. By the way, why were you out brushing the snow off your car just now?"

"I'm heading home after supper."

"Clara, that's a long drive down toward El Paso. It's going to be dark pretty soon. Why are you doing it at night?"

"Well, you know what they say about under the cover of darkness."

"What are you talking about?"

"Well, you know I went into Hayward to see Everett one more time before I left."

"I know and he wasn't there. They told me he was released when I called."

"Well, he was there."

"But they told me he was released, some woman they said took him out of the hospital."

"Well, that part is right. I was the woman. On the way into the hospital I got to thinking about what you said, about Everett being in danger if he went back home. So when I got there, we had a little talk. Doc Sam came in, said Everett was good to go. So he's upstairs right now, taking a nap. After supper we're leaving. He agreed to spend some time down El Paso way as my guest. I figure going at night is safest if anyone is keeping tabs on him."

"Clara, I can't ask you to do this."

"You didn't ask. All you did was tell me about your concern for Everett's safety. He and I discussed the rest. It is one less worry you have. Everett will be company for me. We got a lot of catching up to do and I sure do like the idea that I can help you out a little. Virgil, you know you are as much to me as my own sons. So don't buck me on this. It is something I'm going to do. My mind's made up." Virgil saw the look of determination, heard it in her voice. He didn't argue.

By the time they had finished eating, all light was gone from the evening sky. Cesar and Virgil had loaded Clara's car.

"Don't worry, son. I'll take good care of your Aunt Clara. I'll make sure she keeps it under eighty on the way down to El Paso. By the way, thank you for making sure my animals are being looked after. That means a lot. Never been without a horse. He's a good one. Got good blood, trained him myself. Neck reins so quick he'll turn on a dime. Everett Junior says I'm too old to ride. What he probably means is not that I'm too old to ride, hell, I've been riding since before I started to walk. I think he means I'm too old to fall. He's probably right about that, but just knowing Ranger is there and ready whenever I can ride is important to me. Guess maybe like Everett, you're too young to understand. Anyway, thanks again. This is for you, by the way. Clara convinced me to give it to you." He handed Virgil a slip of paper. Then he got into the passenger seat next to Clara.

Virgil and Cesar watched as they drove the length of the driveway, then until the lights of the car could no longer be seen on the county road. When Virgil and Cesar got inside, Cesar asked Virgil what was on the slip of paper.

"Couldn't read it out there, too dark." He took it out of his pocket, unfolded it, then laid it on the kitchen table. "The Desert Rose, fifteen miles past the turnoff for Inscription Rock."

"Inscription Rock," Cesar repeated. "Isn't that the place they call El Morro?"

"I believe so," Virgil said.

"What do you think it means?"

Virgil hesitated before answering.

"I think it means if I want to find Everett Jessup Junior, I've got to go to a place called the Desert Rose two miles beyond El Morro."

# 35

Before he made the trip to El Morro, Virgil decided to drive once more down to Cielo. He had made an appointment at Mesquite Sand and Gravel. He wanted to meet James Zambrano in the flesh. He thought it was time. Clara and Everett Jessup were safely down in El Paso. The new schedule in the office seemed to be working out. Everyone was trying not to be overly solicitous to Rosie. They were failing miserably but she was managing to put up with it.

Kyle Harrison had called the day after Virgil had asked for his help.

"Okay, Virgil. Here's what I've got. James Zambrano is clean as far as I can find out personally but he is connected."

"Connected how, what do you mean?" Virgil responded.

"Well, it's interesting. Crime syndicates have evolved, changed with the times, a lot more sophisticated. This isn't twenties Chicago, lining up your competition in a garage and mowing them down. The family Zambrano traces his roots to has a long history, but this guy is third maybe even fourth generation. No record, clean as a whistle. Graduated from an Ivy League school with a major in geology, then went on for more study at the Montana Bureau of Mines and Geology. He has all the background for running the Mesquite Sand and Gravel Company."

"So what are you saying? This operation is totally legitimate?"

"What I'm saying is be careful. On the face of it everything says so. He may or may not be involved in something, but they, his connections, don't like too much scrutiny. If he is connected to something illegal, he might call in some outside help to stay removed from the action. These guys he may call in are dangerous. They play hardball. If there is anything going on it isn't running numbers in the barbershop on the corner, small-time crime, Virgil. He is not on our radar, otherwise we would be dealing with it, but if you get on to something definite, call us. Don't go it alone."

Virgil was replaying the conversation in his head on the way down to Cielo. He knew he was operating on instinct at this point, but until he spoke to Everett Junior there wasn't much else to go on.

When he had called for the appointment, he'd gone through the receptionist. He didn't want to involve Jessica Allison. Virgil needed to meet with Zambrano. It would have been hard to explain to someone like Kyle, who came at crime and criminals from a clinical perspective, but

Virgil was more instinctual. He wondered what his gut would tell him about Zambrano. What Virgil hadn't told Kyle Harrison was that if there was a solid connection between Zambrano, a burnt-out trailer with a charred corpse inside, along with a growing list of other factors, he very much was afraid that the "outside help" was already on the scene.

• • •

Kyle was right. Zambrano didn't look like a dues-paying member of any organized crime syndicate. As Virgil sat in the smoothly polished leather chair he was offered, a glance around the room suggested nothing other than the activities with which the company was typically engaged. There were photographs on the wall depicting different stages of sand and gravel processing, along with the framed diplomas and certificates recognizing the accomplishments of the man sitting on the other side of the desk.

"Well, Sheriff Dalton, how can I help you?" The man asking the question was younger than Virgil, but not by much.

"Actually, I don't know if you can. This is a bit of a fishing expedition for me. For the last couple of weeks I've been looking into the disappearance of one Everett Jessup. Turns out his home was set on fire. There was a body found inside but it turned out that it wasn't Mr. Jessup. It took a while to find this out because the fire was intense. The body was little more than a skeleton. It wasn't pretty."

"I can imagine."

"Anyway, here's what led me here. Mr. Jessup, it turns out, worked for you, or that is to say you hired him and his partner, Michael Stark. They worked for you as accountants for some time, I understand." Virgil paused for a reaction.

"Oh, yes. Jessup, I remember now. Michael Stark was the senior partner. We contracted with them and they did work for us."

"My understanding is they actually were your accountants from the time you bought the company up until this past year."

"Yes, well, we decided it was time for a change."

"Oh, can you tell me what led to that decision?" Virgil had the sense that James Zambrano was not comfortable with the inquiry.

"Well, as I remember, there was some question as to whether or not they could handle or keep up with the company's growth. The company has tripled in size since we purchased it almost six years ago. They were a small firm, after all, and I might add did a very competent job for us in the beginning. But I don't see what that would have to do with Mr. Jessup's disappearance."

"Well, as I said, I'm just trying to connect some of the dots at this point. There are some things that bother me."

"Well, I don't see how I can help you further. They did work for us but now we've moved in a different direction. It happens all the time in business."

"Probably you are right about that. I guess I'll just have to keep on digging. It's just that coincidences bother me. I am like a dog with a bone when I run into them."

"I don't exactly follow, coincidences?"

"Yes. First you discontinue your business relationship with the accounting firm. Then Mr. Stark, Mr. Jessup's partner, dies shortly thereafter."

"Yes, I know about that, but my understanding was that was the result of an auto accident. The road he crashed on, I've heard, is considered quite dangerous."

"Yes, all of that is true, but I'm considering having the state police look into that again, a second time. There are some questions as to whether it was an accident. I understand Mr. Stark had driven that road for years. Then of course there is the fire in the trailer, another accident? On the other hand, maybe it was made to look like an accident."

"But I thought there was talk of some illegal activity connected with that fire. Sounds like two very disparate occurrences to me. I thought I even heard something about a drug lab exploding."

"Now that's surprising, how did you hear about that? We never released any of that kind of information." Zambrano paused for a moment. Put his hand to his tie and cleared his throat.

"Oh, I think one of the drivers was talking about it. A couple of the workers in the company are volunteers at the fire department. We encourage civic participation. They must have been at the sight of the fire. In any operation like this, there is always a rumor mill up and running. That's probably where I heard it."

"In any event, once it became known that Mr. Jessup was not in the trailer when it burned, a couple of men paid a visit to his father looking for him. They didn't get the cooperation they were looking for, so they beat him real bad, then left him for dead. That really caught my attention, really pissed me off, because he is a very nice elderly man." Virgil looked for a reaction to his word choice but saw none. "Obviously, there is some kind of connection. I came here today hoping you might be of some help because the only link I could come up with was the sand and gravel company. I admit it's not much but it's the only link I could find."

"Well, I wish I could help you, Sheriff, but like you said yourself, it's not much of a connection that these two men once worked here. Probably, Mr. Stark's was just an unfortunate accident. As for Mr. Jessup, maybe he was involved in some other kind of activity. Owed money to the wrong people, something like that, not too uncommon, gambling, drugs, etcetera. That's about all I can offer. Personally, I think you are wasting your time. My advice would be to let it go before you get in over your head. It could be dangerous."

"Gee, thanks for that insight, Mr. Zambrano. I hadn't really thought of that. It's just that when my curiosity gets aroused . . . Maybe you are right. I'm in over my head. Maybe I ought to have the FBI look into it. I have one or two connections there."

"I know you might not be comfortable with this, Sheriff, but coincidences do happen." He stood up from behind his desk, extending his hand. Virgil stood also, then took his hand.

"Thank you for your time. You've been very helpful."

The winter sun was already sliding toward the horizon as Virgil walked to his car. He was mulling over the conversation dynamic. He hoped he hadn't overplayed the Mayberry role of small-town sheriff.

Mr. James Zambrano obviously was not easily rattled. On the other hand, Virgil didn't miss the subtlety of his warning. His gut told him that there might be a little more to that than concern for his welfare. Maybe that was also why he felt like there were a pair of eyes boring a hole in his back as he walked to the parking lot.

• • •

Virgil knew it was too late to go looking for Everett Junior by the time he got back to Hayward. Dif was in the office alone.

"How did that work out?" he asked as Virgil settled into his chair.

"Well, I got a vibe, not a particularly good one, but it could be that I'm counting too much on gut reaction."

"Oh, I don't know. I kind of think there's a lot to be said for first impressions or gut reactions. Most of the time in my life, gut reactions to someone or something have served me well. If I don't have a good feeling, I take a step or two back. Simon and I were talking about that earlier."

"Simon?" Virgil got up, then sat in Simon's chair alongside Dif, in back of the yard-sale table. The future desk for Simon and Dif was still a figment of the imagination. "You and Simon sharing these days?"

"Yeah, well, it took a while but he's been opening up. You know, speaking about first impressions, there wasn't much to go on initially with him. I mean, I liked how he handled the loss of his hand, but there wasn't too much below-the-surface kind of talk. Since we were alone in the office for those two days, we kind of got to know each other a little

132

better. Turns out, he is a nice guy who has seen and done a lot of not nice things. You know he told me that when he first returned after his second tour, for the first six months back he felt he could have been classified as certifiable. I could relate. I felt like that when I first got back."

"Gee, Dif, I forgot you were in Vietnam."

"Yeah, well, Vietnam, Afghanistan, different place, same experience."

"You never talked much about it."

"No. I don't think many people who go through those kinds of experiences get much out of reliving them. I know I don't. I do remember one time talking to my dad about his time in the South Pacific. I asked him if he thought he was going to survive. He said he didn't think about it. It was just about getting through each day. He said when they first came ashore on Leyte, you were surprised that you even made it off the beach in one piece. For the next couple of weeks, when the air raid siren would go off, everyone would run for the bunkers. Then as time went on resignation set in, planes would come in strafing the area, guys would stand outside firing at the planes with their sidearms, ten feet away from the bunkers. He said most by that time had the attitude it wasn't a question of if, it was a question of when. Simon said that was the way he felt. I did too. When you've seen a lot of your friends end up in body bags, you start looking for the one with your name on it."

"Guess I missed out on that kind of life experience."

"Don't think you missed out on anything," Dif said. "Wished I had missed out. Bet Simon feels the same way. Nobody ever returns from a wartime experience in better shape than when they went in, no matter whether they caught one or not. Oh, you hear all the stuff about the camaraderie, the great closeness. I made some great friends in Nam but I think it was because we shared the reality that each day might be our last. Like the man said, never was a good war or a bad peace. Takes a long time to put it behind you, what you did and saw. In some ways, you never do. Maybe going to some of those reunions helps. I don't know, never went to one. It wasn't a past I was anxious to remember. Until the day my father died, he always avoided loud noises. He wouldn't even go look at the fireworks on the Fourth of July. Time passing helps. That's what I told Simon, it'll get better. Rosie is going to find that out also. In the meantime, we got to take it one day at a time."

"Yeah, well, you did enough today, Dif. Get on home to Edna. I'm good here."

Dif got up from his chair and stretched.

"Been sitting too long. See you tomorrow, Virgil."

Virgil stood in the doorway long after Dif had gone. The cold air blowing in his face kind of revived him. It felt good. The snow in the parking lot had been packed down by the vehicles that had come in and out. He could see some bare patches where gravel showed through, along with a couple of places where the snow had compacted into ice, glistening in the glare of the overhead lights that flooded the area. He thought about throwing some salt on those patches but remembered he had heard a forecast of temperatures in the fifties for the next day. There was enough on his plate without doing an unnecessary job. He took one last deep breath then went inside. The next few hours passed uneventfully.

Simon checked in twice before Virgil decided to head home. It was ten thirty when he closed the office door. As he pulled out onto Main Street, he saw no sign of life. All the stores and businesses were in darkness. He thought about turning right, driving down to the Lazy Dog, getting a beer and whatever they could scare up in the way of food, but decided he was too tired, so he made the left instead. He passed by the hospital on the way out of town. It was the only place where there was any activity. An ambulance with red lights flashing pulled out, then went flying by him. He knew somewhere, someone was waiting. The flashing red lights would be a welcome sight. Dif's comments were still rattling around in his head. One day at a time, he decided. It was the best way.

# 36

The weatherman didn't lie. It was well above freezing when Virgil stepped out of the house the following morning. There was full sun. The last of the snow was dripping off the eaves. He knew by midafternoon it would be a memory. There was no sign of Cesar. Then he remembered the note he had left on the kitchen table. Cesar said Clara had called, also that he was heading over to the Thompson ranch, High Lonesome, to make sure that they would be able to get enough hay to get them through the rest of the winter if they needed it.

Virgil could see from where he was standing that all the horses were out. He could see them as mere specks, a dark bare profile against the white more than a mile away at the base of the low-lying ridge. They were hardly moving but he knew that each of them was pawing through the snow to get to the grass beneath. No matter how good the hay, it never took the place of grass, even snow-covered, dried-out grass that they had to work hard to get. Probably an evolutionary trait that had to do with depending on yourself for ultimate survival, not counting on a man for your sustenance. A lesson learned over thousands of years, a good one not to forget. He wondered how the cattle had fared in the first snow to amount to anything so far.

He was tempted by the need for some physical exertion so he grabbed the handle of an ax that was sunk into a log. For the next half hour he split some wood, ignoring the log splitter covered by the tarp that was sitting nearby. He was sweating freely almost an hour later when he sunk the ax blade deep into the same log from which he had taken it. There was a slight tightness in his right shoulder. He rubbed it as he stood back admiring his output. He scooped up an armful of the newly split logs and carried them into the house. Before he returned to the kitchen, he had placed most of them over some tinder in the fireplace in readiness for the fire he hoped to sit before that evening. Then he picked up the phone to call Clara.

The phone call changed his plans for the day. She told Virgil that Everett had been talking to his son. Everett Junior said Virgil should talk to Mrs. Stark. He said Michael Stark was the key to finding out about why someone wanted him dead.

• • •

135

Rosie was in the office by herself when Simon came in behind a man in handcuffs.

"Who is our guest?" Rosie asked.

"Near as I can make out, his name is Rosario, but he's not much of a talker. Caught him after he carved his initials into another guy. Said the other guy stole from him but wouldn't tell me what he stole. EMTs took his pal to the hospital." Simon took a glassine bag filled with a white powder from his pocket and dropped it on Rosie's desk. "I think this is what his friend stole from him. Guess we'll have to sort that out later."

Rosie got up from her seat then walked to the door leading to the holding cells. Simon followed, nudging the man in front of him. After they had him settled in one of the cells, they returned to the office. Simon sat down at the table and started filling out an incident report. Before long Rosie had come over, bringing him a cup of coffee.

"You didn't have to get that."

"Not a problem, just part of the service we provide to keep all our employees happy." She sat in Dif's chair next to him.

"Thank you." He took a sip from the steaming cup.

"Be careful, it's hot."

"I like it hot. I like things that are supposed to be hot, hot. Things that are supposed to be cold, cold."

"Dave always said that. One time I made gazpacho. He got halfway through it then put it in the microwave. Soup is supposed to be hot, he said." Simon took another drink from his cup.

"You know, I didn't know Dave that long, but I've yet to hear a bad word about him. Kind of feel sorry that I missed out. Think we would have hit it off."

"Yeah, Dave was pretty easy to like. I think you two would have gotten along just fine. I know Virgil was going to send you down to Redbud as we got closer to the baby coming. Dave knew about that. He said helping you to settle in down there would give you guys a chance to get to know each other. Too bad . . ." Rosie looked away for a second or two. When she turned back, Simon did not miss the glisten in her eyes. It was his turn to look away. He put the cup to his lips again, drinking until it was empty. A sudden quiet had infiltrated the room. He set the cup down on the table in front of him. Rosie stood, reaching over to pick up the empty cup.

"Listen, I just wanted to say that I know you are going through a bad time right now. I know what that's like. I mean, I don't know exactly in your case, but, well, let's just say I've gone through some rough patches. You think you're never going to come out the other side but somehow you do. The world doesn't look the same, probably never will, but I just wanted to say if you need anything done, like around the house or anything, I'm pretty handy. When you are on your own as much as I have been, well, let's say you learn to fix things, cars, appliances, so if you need any kind of help just pick up the phone. I'm just saying. I'm sure you got all kinds of friends, family, but I just wanted to make the offer." Rosie stood by the table holding the empty cup looking at Simon. Tears were flowing freely down her cheeks.

"Simon, thank you for that. I'm overwhelmed. That just made my day. You know, before you came in with our latest client, I was sitting here feeling real sorry for myself. You just made that all disappear. Oh, I know there are going to be bad days going forward, but to know there's someone you can count on, well, that makes the future look a lot less fearful."

When Virgil came in the office a little while later he sensed that something had changed. Simon and Rosie were talking about something totally unrelated to Hayward, its populous or anything local.

"She can't be sixty-one," Simon said.

"I'm telling you she is. I saw it in *People* magazine."

"Wow, she looks awesome. Billy Joel, eat your heart out."

Virgil let the conversation play out. Life was starting to look normal again. He picked up the incident report, which was on top of the papers on his desk. While he was reading it the phone rang. He got to it before Rosie.

"Okay, I'll be over in a few minutes." He got up from the desk. "I see we've got a houseguest." Virgil held the incident report in his hand. Simon gave him a quick rundown.

"Good work, Simon. I'll be back within the hour, hang out with Rosita, okay?"

"No problem."

"Virgil, I thought you were going on a road trip."

"Plans changed, Rosie. Tell you about it when I come back. Right now, I'm heading over to the high school. Seems one of the entrepreneurial students was caught trying to sell some wacky weed in the cafeteria."

"Looks as if somebody wanted to add to the menu choices," Rosie said.

"Charlie Pearson's kid," Virgil said.

"Virgil, get over there right away, before Cassie gets there. That boy will be safer in one of those cells in back with the knife wielder than if Cassie gets to him. Otherwise she'll be in there on an attempted murder charge."

Virgil grabbed his hat.

"Forgot about her." He headed for the door.

"Boy, sometimes this town reminds me of the South Bronx," Simon said as the door closed in back of Virgil.

• • •

Virgil was back in less than an hour with his reluctant hoodlum. The young boy went more than willingly into the cell when he heard his parents were on their way. While waiting for their arrival, Virgil called Mesquite Sand and Gravel to get a telephone number and an address for Mrs. Michael Stark. The receptionist surprisingly passed Virgil's call right through to James Zambrano. Virgil explained to him that he wanted to speak to Mrs. Stark but didn't have an address or a phone number.

"Why did you want to speak with her? I mean, I'm just curious."

"Just part of my investigation. People do things for a reason. I'm trying to get at the reason why someone would kill a man in a fire without making sure he was the right man first. It almost sounds like a hit, a contract killing. Maybe Mrs. Stark might know something that could help me to get at the bottom of this. Probably just spinning my wheels but figure it's at least worth a trip." Zambrano switched him back to the receptionist after another caution to Virgil about getting in over his head, telling her to give Virgil the information he was after. Virgil hung up the phone, then told Rosie and Simon about the conversation.

"That was not what I expected."

"Don't you think you ought to be more careful in giving out information like that?" Simon asked.

"Well, right now I don't have a lot more than some suspicions so I figure I'll throw a little bread on the water, see if I can get a fish to rise."

"Just make sure, Virgil, you don't become the bait. That's a door that swings both ways," Rosie added.

Before he left the office Virgil put in a call to Mrs. Stark but there was no response. He ended up leaving a message. He had picked up his hat to leave but never made it to the front door. It flew open with such force that Virgil figured there had to be a dent in the wall where the doorknob made contact.

"Where is he, Virgil? Where is he?" Even when she wasn't angry Cassie Pearson was hard to ignore. She was definitely not the lightweight in the family, literally or figuratively. The Pearsons were one of those incongruous couples that seemed an unlikely result of Match.com. Cassie was at least six foot and then some. In the parlance of some locals, she would dress out at close to three hundred pounds. Charlie, on the other hand, would easily disappear in her shadow.

"Hold on a minute, Cassie." Virgil threw his hat back down on his desk and let out an audible sigh. "Come over here. Have a seat."

"I don't want to sit, Virgil. I want to get my hands on that kid."

"I understand," Virgil said. "But you want to do the right thing here. I've already talked to your boy. He seems like a pretty good kid who did something dumb and got caught. Why don't we try to approach this as something other than a capital crime? We're talking about a young boy who was trying to make some extra money so he could buy a secondhand motorcycle from one of his classmates. He told me that you didn't want him to get extra hours at his after-school job since he had to babysit the younger kids for a couple of hours, because you have to be to work before Charlie gets home."

"That's right, Cassie." Charlie spoke for the first time.

"Why don't you just sit down for a minute, honey? Talk to Virgil." Rosie came over and pulled a chair next to Cassie.

"Just a little bump in the road, Cassie. We all have been there one time or another."

Cassie looked at Rosie.

"Oh, Rosie, I didn't expect to see you here so soon after . . ."

"I know. Sit down now. Listen to Virgil. You and Charlie don't want to make a mistake here. Virgil has a lot of experience. You should listen to him." Cassie sat in the chair that was offered.

"Okay, Sheriff," Charlie said. "How we going to keep this aspiring pot dealer from becoming a major criminal?"

# 37

"Well, that went better than I thought it would." Cassie and Charlie Pearson had just left the office.

"Yeah," Virgil said. "Thanks to you portraying me as the great and all-knowing Oz."

"Well, let's face it, because you know the law as a lawyer and you bring over fifteen years as sheriff to the table, you have a broad perspective to draw on. That's a plus, Virgil."

"Sounds like this town is getting two for the price of one."

"That's one way of looking at it but don't expect to double your salary. By the way, I called to get a requisition for the desk for Dif and Simon. The response was less than enthusiastic."

"Wait until I hit them up for the new personnel, along with the expansion of the substation down at Redbud, then the creation of a new substation to serve the southern part of the county. Sparks are going to fly."

"Guess Dave was the stimulus for that." Rosie looked squarely at Virgil.

"Well, let's just say he left a void, but what we're talking about is long overdue. You know this county is bigger than the state of New Jersey according to Dif. That's a lot of square miles to patrol, with a staff of four or five people." The door opened and Dif came in. "Change that to five and a half," Virgil said.

"Maybe on a good day," Rosie responded.

"Why do I get the feeling that somebody here doesn't understand how valuable I am to the efficient operation of this law enforcement outfit?"

"Okay, Virgil, five and two-thirds," Rosie said.

"What the hell are we talking about, anyhow?" Dif asked. Virgil was about to explain, when the phone rang.

"I'll be the voice of enlightenment," Rosie said as Virgil put the phone to his ear. She filled Dif in on their conversation while Virgil continued to talk.

• • •

Mildred Stark was standing on her three-season glass-enclosed porch, holding her second Riesling in her hand, looking at the reflected light of the full moon flooding the desert. It was cold but not cold enough to keep her from her favorite view. There was still some snow clinging to the joints of a couple of giant saguaros. She had always thought it somewhat startling to see the giants or even the much smaller barrel cactus covered in snow, almost a contradiction, snow in the desert. She guessed that was because her formative years were spent in a part of the country where snow covered everything for three or four months of every year. Whereas the notion of desert existed in her imagination as a place of palm trees, cactus, sand and sun. In that scenario, the sun shone all the time, while the heat rose in shimmering waves from the desert floor. It took her marriage to Michael Stark along with her moving to the southwest to dispel that image. After all these years, snow-covered mesquite and cactus still enthralled her.

As much as the image before her seemed out of place, so also did the two phone calls on the answering machine after all this time. The first was from the office of Mr. James Zambrano, the second from Sheriff Virgil Dalton. She could only wonder at the meaning of the two within minutes of each other on the same day. She presumed this had something to do with Michael, even though it was more than ten months after his accident. She looked at the clock she could see hanging on the wall in the kitchen. It was a little past six. She was tired. It had been a full day at the elementary school where she taught, followed by a faculty meeting that went on for twice as long as it should have, although that wasn't much of a surprise. Teachers as a group, she decided, more than any other were guilty of falling in love with the sound of their own voices. Halfway through the meeting, she had already settled on the Riesling over the Chardonnay, which she now held in her hand. She almost didn't play the messages she saw flashing on the landline when she came home but then thought it might be one of the girls. A little relieved when that turned out not to be the case, she had hesitated before picking up the phone. She figured the office of the sand and gravel company would be closed, so she opted to try the Sheriff.

• • •

"That was interesting. Mrs. Stark invited me to stop by. I didn't realize the Starks lived down in the Roscoe Flats area." Virgil made the comment as he hung up the phone.

"Oh, now I remember," Rosie replied. "I think she is the Mrs. Stark who teaches in the elementary school. She was Carrie's teacher. I think it was fourth or fifth grade. Carrie loved her but she was tough. I remember when her husband was killed in that car accident last year. I kind of knew that they lived outside of Hayward, in the desert somewhere. Are you going over there?"

"I told her I could stop by tomorrow. She said that would work for her. If it's okay with you guys, I'd like to head out now. Virginia's going to come by tonight. She is going back to school tomorrow."

"Not a problem. I have a few more things to finish then I'm going over to Carrie's. The baby has a rash, probably from teething, so I told her I'd stop by and look at it. She wants me to stay for dinner."

"Go ahead, Virgil. Jimmy will probably be in soon after Rosie's gone. I'm good," Dif added to Rosie's comment. A few minutes later Virgil was walking to his car when Jimmy pulled in alongside.

"You are early. Dif figured you wouldn't be in for another hour or so."

"I wanted to catch you before you left. Here, give this to Virginia, a little going-away present." He handed what was obviously a wrapped CD to Virgil. "It's Adele, *25*," he said. "She really likes her."

"Adele?" Virgil repeated, obviously having no idea who she was.

"Yeah. She's pretty big right now."

"I'll take your word for it." Virgil got into his vehicle, then rolled down the window. "If you want to stop by, Virginia will be at the ranch later."

"No. I know. She told me but I think she wanted to spend some alone time with you. Getting cold, I'm going inside now." He gave a half wave to Vigil and headed toward the office door.

Virgil spent a good part of the ride home wondering how many other current world-class celebrities there were out there of whom he was blissfully unaware. The realization aged him. He considered that he hadn't been to a concert since he became sheriff. Worse than that, he couldn't remember who it was performing or who he was with at the time. Bob Weir popped into his recollection but he couldn't recall whether Jerry had died already. Going over some of the timeline of his past made him more painfully aware of just how fleeting everything was. By the time he turned off the hard surface road into the driveway, he had resolved to make a connection with the present-day culture. For openers, he was going to ask Virginia to introduce him to Adele.

Virginia came through the kitchen door a little after seven. Virgil was setting some plates on the table. She waved a bottle of red wine at him.

"Thought this would go well with the steak. Grandpa gave it to me. It's a cabernet."

"Is that where you were up on the mesa?"

"Actually, I drove down to Redbud to say goodbye to my other father and brother along with the people I worked with down there. On the way back, on a whim, I drove up to the mesa. I don't think I'll be back here before the summer so I thought I would say goodbye."

"I'm sure everyone was happy to see you, especially that old Indian."

"He was asking for you."

Virgil paused as he was opening the wine.

"Yeah, I know. I haven't seen him since the party. It's been really hard to find the time. Dave, Rosita . . ." He didn't finish the thought.

"He understands all of that but he worries about you. He says you are one of those people who gives of himself until there is very little left for yourself. He says you need to become more selfish."

"He must be channeling Rosie. That's what I get from her all the time. Come on, sit down. The steak has almost stopped bleeding."

They ate mostly in silence, their hunger overcoming their need for conversation. Finally, Virgil pushed his plate away then half filled both of their wine glasses.

"That was really good. By the way, I'm sorry I didn't get to spend more time with you too," he said.

"Oh, I'm okay. I know you've had a lot on your mind lately. I think maybe Grandpa needs you more, because you are the last link to his daughter."

"I get that. I also know time is slipping away. That point has been driven home to me a lot lately. By the way, before I forget, I've got something for you from Jimmy." He got up from the table. When he returned he handed her the disc.

"Adele. I've been wanting this. Jimmy's a sweetheart."

"I'd like to hear it before you leave. I want to know at least one twenty-first-century voice so that I don't feel completely out of it."

"Back to not leaving any time for yourself."

"Let's not go back down that road."

For the next couple of hours the talk was random, about the town, the way it was changing, local politics, even how the pecan business was doing down in Redbud. At last, with the night closing in about them, they knew it was time to say their goodbyes. Virgil left the room for a minute. When he returned he handed a small box to Virginia. Adele's voice filled the room. "Nice, very nice," Virgil said.

"What is this?" Virginia asked.

"Open it and see."

She took the cover off, displaying a ring inside. A sapphire was the centerpiece surrounded by some small diamonds.

"I, I don't understand, this is beautiful but . . ."

"It was the engagement ring for your mother, which she never got to see, which I never got a chance to give her. It's not traditional but it's her birthstone. Think she would have liked it. I wanted to do something, more original. She was like that. I want you to have it now. She would have wanted you to have it. That box hasn't been opened in twenty years. Just never could bring myself to look at it. But now, well . . ." Virgil unexpectedly got caught up in the emotion of the moment. Virginia came to him, wrapping her arms around him. "If you squeeze any tighter I'm liable to lose that steak we had for dinner." She kissed him on the cheek, then stood back at arm's length.

"Do you remember that day when you dropped me off at Crow's Nest, the first time you brought me to meet my newly acquired grandfather?" Virgil nodded. "I told you then I didn't know how I felt about you, about us. Finding out you have a father for the first time when you are twenty, well . . ."

"I know. It worked that way for me too."

"Well, I know now. I can't think of my life without you in it. It's, it's like I feel whole. For the first time in my life, I have all the pieces. I mean, it's not like Uncle Micah and my grandmother, Audrey, didn't do everything they could for me. But the one thing they couldn't give me, you could and did. Where I came from, a starting point, a sense of being. My mother is real to me for the first time in my life. I see her in you. I hear how she was every time you speak of her. You know, for the last few years, I've gone back to school without looking back, happy, eager for what was waiting for me, anxious to move on in my life. That's changed now. I really don't want to leave. I am so going to miss you. Even though we get together only sporadically, you are always within reach. I'm going to miss that. I'm going to miss you. I love you, Dad."

The number of times Virgil felt engulfed by emotion in his life he could count on one hand. A tidal wave had caught him. All the feelings that he had worked to keep in check during the last couple of weeks rose to the surface in Virginia's words with such force that he felt like he was spinning, out of sync with time and place. He reached out to a nearby chair to steady himself, the room morphing, a blurred reality. Again, he had lost his words. Virginia read the look in his eyes. She came to him again. He clung to her like he had clung to no one, even Rusty. He realized the full import of her words, because he too had a sense of being whole for the first time in a very long time. Maybe this was what Grandfather meant about being selfish, he thought.

They walked together in silence to the door. Virgil held her coat, then they walked out the door and down the steps to her car.

"Dad, you should have put on a jacket. It's cold out here."

"I'm fine. It feels good to me, makes me feel alive. I'm warm inside." She smiled at the remark.

"I'll call," she said.

"And I will answer," he responded.

"Will you come to my graduation? I'd love to show you my school and Saratoga. We could make kind of a mini vacation out of it."

"I'd like that. No power on earth will keep me from being there, unless of course Rosie says I can't go. I pretty much let Clara, Cesar and Rosie run my life now. They all are convinced I can't make it on my own." A smile crossed both their faces.

"I've noticed. But that's only because you are so important to them. Fortunately, they all seem to like me, so I'll be expecting you."

Virgil gave her a quick hug then she got in the car. He stayed long after she had reached the hardtop road. It was cold, clear and cold. The night sky couldn't hold another star. He heard a coyote call. Could picture him running along the ridge, tail down, nose to the ground, trying to sniff out something that might fill the emptiness in his belly.

"Good hunting, partner." Virgil's words cut the silence. He took one more look at the empty driveway silvered in the moonlight, then turned and went in the house.

# 38

High Ridge Road was appropriately named. The houses randomly scattered along its length were tucked into the high ridge that ran along the north side. Each was sited so it had a commanding view of a desert riddled with contradiction. Flat landscape contrasted with deep canyons that held rare water pockets and showed unexpected green. While in the far-off distance, the unmistakable blur of distant foothills rose to meet purple mountains. Virgil immediately thought of his grandfather sitting outside of his trailer on the high mesa at twilight, watching the sun slipping out of view against a variegated sky.

Irrigated swaths of green surrounded some of these homes but they were dominated by the broad reach of the earthen-colored desert beyond that stretched to the horizon. Virgil was always surprised by how quickly the barren landscape responded to the addition of water. It also did not go unnoticed by him how there were more swaths of green evident since he had last driven this road. In a climate where the cold hand of winter did not last that long, the temptation to add water for more production was strong. He knew, like many others, that this came at a price. The Colorado, which had in the past vigorously splashed into the Gulf of Mexico, had been reduced some years to a trickle. In this environment he appreciated how unique his own land was but knew that could change if the flow of water on his ranch were ever diverted. Green belts could turn desert brown very quickly.

He found the Stark house without difficulty. He parked in the wide space that had been carved out alongside the road to accommodate four or five cars, then climbed the thirty or forty stairs up to where Mildred Stark was waiting.

"I don't think we've ever met but I've always heard good things about you." Mildred Stark extended her hand.

"Thank you for that. As far as the other, I guess most people don't mind not meeting me, especially in an official capacity."

"Well, come into the kitchen. I've got a pot of coffee and some muffins to go along with it." Virgil followed her inside.

"That's some view." Virgil made the comment when he reached the top of the stairs inside the front door. The formal living area ended at the expansive enclosed deck that ran across the front of the house. The wall of glass looked out on the seemingly unending desert.

"You've got to climb halfway up a mountain to see it but we've always thought it was worth the effort. When Michael and I first came here and decided to build up on this ridge, a lot of people thought we were crazy, but as you can see quite a few other crazies decided to join us over the years."

The next few minutes were spent informally at the kitchen table. Virgil at one point mentioned that Mildred Stark had taught Rosita and Dave's children.

"Yes, I remember the Brand children. I heard about what happened to their father. I know what a loss like that is, my girls are still trying to cope as I am with Michael's being gone, but death doesn't linger. Life is too demanding."

"That's probably a good thing," Virgil said.

"Yes, it is." A quiet moment passed. "What is it you wanted to see me about, Sheriff?"

Virgil gave a brief overview of his investigation, ending with the notion of him not being too comfortable with the coincidence of Michael Stark's accident, the disappearance of Everett Jessup, and the fire and body found in Everett's trailer.

"You know, it's funny you should say that, because your call to me is a kind of coincidence. Since Michael's death I haven't had any contact with law enforcement or Mesquite Sand and Gravel, then back to back phone calls."

"I understand you have suspicions about your husband's accident." Virgil could tell that even after all these months the wound was still fresh. She sat forward in her chair looking directly at Virgil.

"I have nothing other than a gut feeling. Maybe you as a member of law enforcement, like all the troopers I spoke to, are strictly fact-oriented, but I knew my husband. He didn't take chances, he wasn't a careless man. And he knew that road. He had driven it in all kinds of weather. I mean, I was with him many times when we had two little girls in the backseat fighting over a toy, when the wind was howling and the rain was torrential. He never missed a beat. He drove that road for over twenty-five years, night and day, good weather and bad. So now I am to believe on an ordinary day that was bright and clear when there was nothing going on in our lives that would register as even slightly unusual . . . On that kind of a day, he went off one of the few straightaways on that road, all the way down to the bottom of a canyon? I'm sorry, but my gut tells me that never happened. Michael's dead because somebody made that happen. I don't know who or for what reason, but somebody killed my husband." Virgil heard the raw emotion in her voice, saw her struggling for control.

147

"I'm sorry." The words sounded feeble to his own ears. "I wish I could have been involved in the investigation but it never came to me because the state police investigated. That probably isn't much comfort for you, but the reason I am here today is because of my gut feeling." Virgil spent the next ten minutes laying out in full detail the reasons behind his visit. It was not something he ordinarily would have done with any civilian, but he felt like he owed Mildred Stark something. It was all he had.

"So, you believe me?"

"Yes. Yes, I do, Mrs. Stark. But I need to find the reasons to substantiate that belief. So let's get back to what you told me earlier. What did sand and gravel want?"

"Well, I don't know. I didn't call them back. It was too late yesterday. I figured they were closed. That is why I called you instead. I thought I would call them back today."

Virgil took a bite out of the muffin sitting on the plate in front of him.

"Mrs. Stark, would you do me a favor and make that call now? I'd kind of like to know what that call is about."

Virgil was on his second muffin and second cup of coffee when she hung up the phone.

"That was the HR person, Jessica, Miss Allison. She is a very nice girl. I've met her a couple of times. Michael always spoke very highly of her. She told me that she had something for me from when Michael worked there."

"Did she say what it was?"

"No. That's the odd thing, she said she would call back in a couple of minutes."

"Do you have any of your husband's records from his work there?"

"No. I asked for them but they said that was company property. But Michael always backed up everything related to his business. Maybe that's what she was referring to." The phone rang. Mildred picked it up right away. "Oh, yes, Miss Allison. I'll be there this afternoon. Oh, are you sure? If you don't mind. Thank you very much." She replaced the phone in the cradle. "Well, I was right. Miss Allison says she has a couple of flash drives that were Michael's."

"Why didn't she tell you that earlier?"

"She said something about speaking on her cell phone rather than the company line. Sounds kind of strange, doesn't it?" Virgil didn't say anything. "She also said she would drop them off within the hour. I offered to go get them but she insisted."

"I'm going to need them, Mrs. Stark. So if you don't mind, I'll wait."

"You want to show them to Mr. Jessup, my husband's partner."

"Yes. They wouldn't mean anything to me."

"I understand. I just want to make sure I have everything related to Michael's business, in case the IRS has any questions. Document everything. Michael always drove that point home to me. Guess that's the mind of an accountant at work."

# 39

"Leaving, Miss Allison?"

"Yes, going out for lunch, for a change of scenery." She turned away from the receptionist and walked out the front door. The sun was bright. She squinted in the slanting light. It was at the highest point of its arc at this time of the year but still low enough in the sky that she reached up when she got in her car and grabbed her sunglasses out of the compartment above the windshield. She figured to be gone an hour at the most. There weren't that many cars in the parking lot. She knew if she used the cutoff to High Ridge Road she would save some time. As she pulled out of the lot, she noticed another car pulling out in back of her.

She had been driving for fifteen minutes when she came to that turnoff. She noticed the car turn when she did. For a moment she wondered if it was her paranoia on overdrive, then whether it was even the same car that came out of the parking lot in back of her. The thought only lingered for a moment until she came to the next turn.

High Ridge Road was not a road to get less than your full attention. It was one of those roads in high desert where straightaways were a luxury. It had more twists and turns than an amusement park ride, but if you could handle the navigation, those roads could shave time and miles off a trip. Jessie actually liked the road because of the switchbacks, which provided constantly changing views if you could go slow enough to enjoy them. The vistas were spectacular. She had hiked in this area many times. The road reminded her of the road she drove up to Jerome the last time she had been in the Sedona area and to a slightly lesser extent of the San Juan Skyway, which wound from Silverton down to Ouray, where she lived for a year after college while having illusions of becoming a professional skier.

Jessie remembered that it was off one of these ridges that Michael Stark had met a fatal end. She glanced in her rearview mirror. The car behind her was coming up fast, but she had made up her mind that she wasn't going to go any faster just because he was in a hurry. She crisscrossed a saddleback two or three times with the car right behind her. Her hands began to tighten on the wheel. Despite her vow, she saw her speedometer starting to edge up. It made no difference. The car was right on her tail, so close most of the time that braking wasn't even an option on these hairpin turns. At one point he was so near, she couldn't see his headlights. She hit a brief straightaway, thought about braking, but realized the straightaway was so brief that if he couldn't stop the crash would probably take the two of them right over the edge into a deep crevasse.

"What is his problem?" she said out loud. She leaned on the horn. Then, when she saw no response again and again, no result, she was becoming frantic. She vaguely remembered a hiking trail with a pull-off for one or two cars from the last time she had been on the road. She had thought she might suggest it to some friends on their next outing. She didn't remember passing it. Then on one of the hairpin turns, she saw a marker. She was going too fast to read it but she couldn't think of anything else it could indicate. When she came around two one-eighty-degree turns, she glimpsed another straightaway up ahead.

She felt the car behind actually nudge her bumper, and she glimpsed two men in the car. Coming off the final turn, she pressed the accelerator, opening a short gap after seeing the break in the shoulder up ahead. Her hands gripped the wheel. Her knuckles turned white. Thirty feet ahead she saw the cutoff. She pulled sharply to the right. The tires left the hard surface. She felt the gravel under the tires as she started to brake. The car yawed to the right, then to the left, tires spinning, dirt and gravel peppering the underside of the car, a cloud of it rising up in back of her. The car, brakes locked, slid for twenty feet before finally skidding to a complete stop only a couple of feet from the wall of stone marking the end of the pull off. The cloud of dust continued to rise in the car's wake.

Jessie had glanced in the mirror as she pulled off, just in time to see the other car fly by. She heard the screech of its tires on the hard pavement as it disappeared into the sharp turn up ahead, then it was gone. She sat clutching the wheel, gasping for long-overdue breath.

Minutes passed before she finally moved. She rolled down the window. She had thought she heard a distant noise. The cold air rushed in, blowing its freshness over her. She opened the door, almost falling out onto the dirt. She was shaking. She leaned against the car until the moment passed. Then she walked on legs that she could barely feel until she reached the road. There was no sign of the other car. Because of the twists and turns along with the changes in elevation, she could see up ahead for almost three-quarters of a mile. There was nothing. No sign. She crossed the road to the shoulder on the other side to get an even more expansive view.

It was then that she saw the smoke rising from the bottom of the canyon in a spiral. She walked further along the road to get a better view. It made no difference. The drop-off was so sheer that even when she had come in a direct line with the spiral of smoke there was nothing else to see. No sign of wreckage, nothing. The canyon bottom was so far away, while the piñons and scrub brush at the bottom were so dense that they obscured anything beneath them from view. She stood for a moment trying to process what had occurred, then turned and walked back to her car. At last she got back in, started the engine, put the car into reverse, then carefully backed out onto the road.

Ten minutes later, when the road straightened out, she saw a couple of houses tucked into the slope of the ridge. She slowed, then a little further on she saw a man standing by the side of the road. When she recognized Virgil she slowed even more, then turned into the parking area that had been carved out of the slope where it met the road. She pulled to a stop next to Virgil's cruiser.

"I told Mrs. Stark that I'd walk down here to wait for you. Didn't know if you knew the road that well." He made the comment as she was climbing out of the car. "Are you okay?" He knew immediately the answer to his question. "What happened? Take your time."

He reached out, taking her arm, then led her to the steps that led up to the Stark house. He lowered her down onto the second step. He felt her almost crumple as she began to sob. He sat next to her, held her close until her cries began finally to subside.

For the next few minutes she recounted what had happened. Mrs. Stark had come out onto the deck. Hearing the muffled sobs, she came down with a glass of water. While Jessie drank, Virgil explained what had happened.

"I guess I know now for sure why Michael went off that road. Thank god she didn't end up the same way."

Jessie sat up, handed the empty glass to Mrs. Stark. Then she turned to Virgil.

"Thank you. I'm a lot better now, especially seeing you, but the paranoia that we talked about in your office has kicked up a couple of notches." Jessie spent the next couple of minutes talking about her harrowing ride. Virgil listened without interrupting. She was obviously agitated and needed to talk, that was obvious. By the time she finished, he could see a subtle change in her. Her agitation had finally been replaced by a level of calm.

"Do you want to come inside?" Mrs. Stark had returned up the stairs to the house. They were still sitting on the stair. Virgil stood up and reached out to her. She brushed some nonexistent dirt from her skirt as she rose.

"Well, I have something for her. That's why I'm here."

"That is also why I am here. She is going to give me those flash drives. I want to have someone look at them."

"In that case, here." She handed a small packet to Virgil.

"It is probably best if I get back to the office. I don't want to be gone too long. Besides, I'm curious. I want to see if anybody is surprised when I return."

"Are you all right now?"

"Yeah, I'm fine. Just got to control my overactive imagination. Otherwise, like I said that night in your office, maybe I should make an appointment to see somebody about my past life traumas."

Virgil shook his head.

"No. I still stand by my initial diagnosis. I think your view of reality is pretty much what it should be."

"So, are you saying I should be worried?"

Virgil hesitated before answering.

"Worried, no. Careful, yes, like you were with those guys who were riding your tail on the way up here. They didn't know they were messing with a wannabe Indy driver. If I find out something that causes me to be more concerned for you going forward, I will call you right away. In any event, I plan to stay in touch."

"Thank you, Sheriff. That makes me feel a lot better." She opened the car door then slid inside. She turned the key. "I'll look forward to hearing from you, Virgil." She gave a little wave then backed out onto the road. Not one car had passed by the entire time they were talking. Virgil returned the wave.

He stood looking after her until her car was out of sight. Then he went to the cruiser, phoned in what had happened. He said he would meet the rescue vehicles at the site, not that there would probably be anyone to rescue. That was a one-way trip for whoever was in the car. He knew that. Her story of the incident on the road worried him but he didn't want to unnecessarily raise her stress level. He didn't know enough for that. Besides, he figured whoever was after her was no longer an immediate threat. In any case, there was an unexpected feeling that he now recognized. She had become more than just those blue eyes to him.

153

# 40

"Something bothering you, Sheriff?" When Simon came into the office he saw Virgil sitting at the desk staring at the flash drives that he had been given to show Everett Jessup. He was alone in the office because Rosie had walked over to Margie's for a late lunch. She told him she would bring back something for him. Virgil was at first unresponsive to Simon's question.

"Bothering me, no, merely wondering, hoping that these are going to offer a little insight. Evidently someone wants them bad enough to kill for. I know the direction they are pointing to but I don't know. There's something I'm missing, or I should say I feel like there is something I'm missing. By the way, what are you doing here? I thought today was an off day for you."

"It is. I left my hand in the drawer so I decided to stop by and pick it up." He held up his hook.

"Do you realize how bizarre that sentence sounds on so many levels?" The comment came from Rosita, who was standing in the doorway. "I left my hand in the drawer so I stopped by because I wanted to pick my hand up." She started to laugh. Then Simon and Virgil started laughing.

"Rosie's right, Simon. You should always watch where you put your hands, especially if you're on a date." The laughter continued for another five minutes, only interrupted by a couple of other punch lines contributed by all three.

"Well, we don't make much money here but we do manage to have some fun," Virgil said. "Now, give me my lunch. All of a sudden I'm hungry."

"Guess laughter is good for the appetite," Simon said.

"And for other things," Rosie added. "I haven't laughed like that in a while."

"So, Sheriff, what do you think is on those flash drives?"

"I don't know. I hope an accountant can tell me. That's why I have to make a trip up to a place called the Desert Rose and show them to Everett Jessup. He seems real anxious to see them. Evidently, these are backup records for the accounting work he and Michael Stark did for Mesquite Sand and Gravel during the last couple of years. I'm pretty sure I wouldn't know what I was looking at, so I'm hoping he'll be able to tell me. He said he really needed them when I called him from Mrs. Stark's. I understand they might be significant for him in terms of finding out what they contain, but it sounded somehow like more than that to me."

"The Desert Rose, what's that, some kind of resort?" Simon asked.

"I'm not sure," Virgil answered. "All I know is it's up near El Morro. Everett evidently goes there on occasion. His father says he has a friend there. I think his name is Randy. He was up there when his place was set on fire. He said that the boy who was there was hired to help him put up all the decorations for Christmas. According to Everett, he was hitchhiking back to the Rez after a thirty-day rehab stint. Everett picked him up one day and offered him a little work after he heard his story because he felt sorry for him. From what I've heard about him, it kind of sounds like something he would do."

"Hang on a minute, Virgil." Rosie had sat down at her desk. She started hitting the keyboard. After a couple of minutes she sat back in her chair. "Well, you remember when you told me that old Mr. Jessup told you that Everett wasn't inclined toward women. Well, I think Everett walks on the other side of the street."

"You mean that the Desert Rose is a . . ."

"A gay-friendly resort," Rosie said.

"Mr. Jessup gave me that slip of paper with Everett's number and directions. Guess I'd better make another call before I go up there."

"Yeah, Virgil. Folks might get a bit nervous if they see a sheriff's car pull up to their front door, or just get the wrong idea. On the other hand, a good-looking man like you in a uniform, well, who knows . . . maybe you'll get lucky."

Virgil grimaced slightly.

"Nice to know you haven't lost your sense of humor." He made the comment as he fished for his wallet. "Found it." He pulled the slip of paper with Everett's number on it from his billfold. He reached over and placed the call. While Rosie and Simon talked, Virgil ended up leaving a message on Everett's cell phone.

"Guess maybe it's not going to work out for today." Just as he took a bite out of the sandwich Rosie had brought back for him, the phone rang.

"Spoke too soon." He made the comment as he put the phone back in the cradle. "That was Everett. He said he knew Michael always backed up his work but he didn't know where the flash drives were. He said he had everything pertaining to the housing development, but Michael's record will complete everything. He almost sounded excited that I was bringing it up to him."

"You're not driving to the Desert Rose now? Virgil, it's almost two o'clock. By the time you get there it will be almost dark."

"Actually, he wants to meet me at El Morro. He must be on your wavelength and doesn't want a sheriff's vehicle showing up on his doorstep."

"He said that?"

"No, just figure you are probably right, as usual. He actually said he was planning on visiting El Morro. He said today is as good a day as any to do a little hiking in the desert."

"Well, thank you anyway for that left-handed compliment. But seriously, Virgil, that's a long drive. El Morro Monument, isn't that pretty much in the middle of nowhere?"

"A lot of places in this part of the world are pretty much in the middle of nowhere. El Morro may be a little more so, but all those people that stopped there to write their names must not have thought so. The Zunis actually lived on top for a couple of hundred years. Besides, Everett said it will knock twenty miles off my trip. That's something. Said he'll meet me near Inscription Rock at the base of the Monument, around six."

"Sheriff, if you want some company, I'll sign on."

"That's a good idea, Virgil. Instead of making that trip by yourself, take Simon with you. He might enjoy seeing El Morro."

"Are you sure, Simon?"

"I've got nothing special going on, don't mind seeing some of the country. Someplace I've never been, sounds cool."

"Okay. Let me finish my lunch."

Ten minutes later Virgil was standing in the open doorway. Simon had already stepped outside. He was standing by the car, not making any attempt to get in.

"What's the matter, Virgil?" Rosie saw the hesitant look on his face.

"Don't know." He looked out into the bright sunlight.

"Somebody walk over your grave, Virgil?" Rosie had come to stand beside him. "Hold on a second." She left him then went back into the office. When she returned, she handed him a rifle from the gun rack. "You know this was Dave's personal favorite. I know you've got your sidearm, but well, you never know. Dave took good care of it. Maybe it will take good care of you."

Virgil took the rifle, put it under his arm, then leaned over and gave Rosie a hug and a light kiss.

"Virgil, be careful. What happened today out on High Ridge Road pretty much tells you you're getting into deeper water here."

"Stop, you're scaring Simon. We'll be fine. I'll write Dave's name and yours on El Morro." Then he headed for the car.

# 41

"What happened today?" Simon asked as soon as they got in the car.

"I'll tell you on the way," Virgil said. They rode for a couple of hours, only stopping once for gas and a pit stop. Virgil brought Simon up to date on all that had happened.

"So you think all of this, beginning with the killing of Mr. Stark, has something to do with the sand and gravel company and this guy Zambrano. The only thing I don't understand is, if Mr. Stark discovered something, wouldn't he have told his partner, Everett? If Everett knew something, after Mr. Stark's death why didn't he go to someone with his suspicions?"

"You know, Simon, those are some mighty good questions. I have been asking myself some of those same questions. I have a hunch that Everett seems to have known for quite a while that someone was after him, so he went to ground rather than seek some kind of protection. I don't get it. Especially after his home was torched, his father beat up. It doesn't make sense. I'm kind of looking forward to hearing his answers to some of those questions."

The slanting sun was bouncing off the rugged cliff face when El Morro came into view. The sun was spotlighting it. An uncarved monolith, it dominated the landscape.

"Wow. That is impressive." Simon's words broke the silence. "This country is about as different as you can get. One minute you're in desert flat as a pancake then something like that jumps into the sky. Green, brown, purple, red, it's all there. In a strange way it reminds me a little of Afghanistan without the IEDs."

There was no sign of life in the visitor center. It was after hours. Virgil saw one car in the lot, which he figured belonged to Everett. Late on a January day, El Morro looked like it must have looked to those people who had managed to cross the desert to drink and renew themselves from the pool at its base.

Virgil pointed out to Simon that for them it represented a kind of salvation, a sign that the worst of their journey was behind them. It was no wonder that they had left their mark on its walls, a sign that they had been here. They had survived.

*"Paso por aqui,"* he said. "This was their proof. Graffiti was not a twenty-first-century innovation."

Virgil had pulled to the side of the parking area when he saw the other car. He turned the engine off and stepped out of the car. Simon joined him.

"Man, this is a lonely place." Virgil nodded an acknowledgment.

A wind had kicked up. Some small tumbleweeds were caught in its grip, hopscotching across the barren landscape. There was no sign of Everett, or anybody else for that matter. Outside of the dim glow of a light from the visitor center and the groomed parking area, the landscape was as it had been for hundreds of years.

"Guess he got here early, decided to hike in the desert or walk the trail to the top. Probably got bored sitting in the car. I'll go scare him up."

"You want me to come?"

"No. You stay put just in case he didn't go up top, decided to walk out into the desert. There's a pair of binoculars in the glove compartment. Look for him. Maybe if you scramble up on that huge boulder, you'll have a better vantage point." He gestured in the direction of a huge rock that sat off to the side of the trail that led to the base of El Morro. "I'll leave the laptop in the car, bring him down to use the flash drives."

"Okay. If you need anything or if he shows up, give a yell."

"You would never hear me," Virgil said. "If I don't find Everett within a half hour or so I'll come back. You fire off a round if he shows up here. Otherwise, we'll just wait by the car until he shows up."

It was a little over a quarter mile to the base of the mountain from where Virgil had parked the car. He walked along a well-worn trail packed solid by the many visitors who had come to see El Morro, along with the inscriptions it bore. Virgil had only been here once before with his mother and father. Thinking back, as a young teen on summer vacation it wasn't high on his list of places to go, but his mother had insisted. He remembered she had wanted him to see it through her eyes, as a revered place. She was trying to impress upon him that there were native cultures that existed long before the later settlers came across the prairie to drink from the waters at the base of this giant rock. His father had pointed out to Virgil that the first non-native, a Spaniard, had left his mark around 1615 but that some of the pictographs had been carved into its surface hundreds of years before. Even in his reluctant adolescence, Virgil could not escape the ghosts of this place. They lingered even now.

As he drew closer he had that same uneasy feeling that he had back in the office that Rosie had picked up on. He had never been particularly spiritual or a believer in omens. The eagle feather of his vision quest came to mind. His grandfather had given it to him, and only much later, after he had put years of faith into it, had it been revealed to him to be the feather of a dead hawk roadkill. But a gut feeling, a misalignment of the atoms that made up his universe, that was different. It had come to him rarely, unexpectedly, but when it had, he had been wise not to ignore it. He had that feeling now.

He had reached the base of El Morro, saw the pool that over the centuries had slaked the thirst of many, but saw no sign of Everett. A little further on he came to the first evidence of someone on the trail that began the ascent to the top, when he saw a cigarette butt lying on the ground. Virgil looked around, took a deep breath, then stepped on to the trail. The incline was gradual, but after ten minutes he had to pause for another breath. The air was getting thinner with the ascent. He also felt for the first time that he had broken a sweat. More evidence if he needed it that he had spent too little time lately in physical activity. He figured he was more than halfway to the top, so he gave a yell. Only the echo of his own voice against the sheer rock came back to him. He waited a moment, gave another yell, but there was no response. He began the final trek. Ten minutes later he stepped on top of El Morro. He had forgotten how big the expanse up there was until he saw in the distance the skeletal remains of the complex that had housed extended families of Zunis for over a hundred years. He walked over to the edge. When he looked down he could see far below in the distance the two parked cars in the visitor parking lot. He could barely make out the figure of Simon leaning against the large boulder alongside the trail. If he hadn't made a slight movement, he would have been indistinguishable.

"Sorry about hitting you in the head with that log in back of the trailer, Sheriff." Virgil was caught off guard by the words.

"Not as sorry as I was, Everett, but considering what had happened there, maybe I should have been a little more on my guard." Virgil looked at Everett Jessup in person for the first time. He was a little older than he had expected but he could see his father in him, the same square jaw, the full mouth and nose that looked like it might have been busted once or twice, not an unusual physical feature for someone who grew up on a ranch and might have hit the ground hard a couple of times after coming off a less than cooperative horse. In his mind's eye he could also see him serving up a fastball or a slider, but nothing inside. "Anyways, no permanent damage done. Doc says I've got a harder than average head."

"Glad to hear it. How is Pop?"

"He's good. Out of the hospital, down outside of El Paso, spending some recoup time with my Aunt Clara. Didn't know it before but seems like they have a lot of shared history."

"Good. I want to thank you for what you've done. Pop told me. He even told me how you arranged care for his Jersey cow and calf along with Ranger."

"Ranger?" Virgil repeated.

"Ranger, Dad's horse. He loves that animal, but I sure wish he would give up the notion of riding."

"I had forgotten his name. Yeah, well, I guess it's more than just the riding. Think your Dad likes the idea of being independent. That colt, the idea that he can still ride, goes along with that. I get it."

"I get it too. But it ain't hard to break your neck when you're Dad's age."

"I think he knows that too, Everett."

"So, Sheriff, did you bring the flash drives that you got from Mike's wife?"

"I did. They are down in my car along with a laptop, so you can plug them in and tell me what they have on them."

"Oh, but you do have them, I mean here."

Virgil reached into the jacket pocket of his coat, then held up a small packet.

"They were in this, but as I said, I took them out and left them down in the car with the laptop. Didn't see much sense in carrying the laptop around or up on top of this mountain."

"That's all we need." The voice, a different voice, came out of the shadows that had begun to spread across the top of El Morro. Some heavy clouds had swept across the monument, allowing only shafts of the setting sun to filter through, so the person attached to the voice was well hidden.

"I don't think I understand," Virgil said.

"You don't have to," the voice answered. "All we need are those flash drives. We already know what is on them."

"Who are you? And what do you mean 'we' need them?"

The figure in the shadows stepped forward. For the first time Virgil saw the gun in his hand.

"Everett, what's going on here?"

"I'm sorry, Sheriff. I, I . . . this is Randy. He's . . . he's."

"We haven't got time for this, Everett. Now we can get the flash drives."

"I'm not giving them to you, Randy, whoever you are."

"Don't think you are in a position to do anything else, Sheriff. In case you hadn't noticed, this is a gun."

"But if you know what is on those flash drives, I don't understand. Why do you need them?"

"I guess you can know that, not that it is going to do you any good. They are worth a lot of money to the right people. They are the proof that money was being laundered through Mesquite Sand and Gravel."

"You knew this, Everett?" Virgil asked.

"No. I didn't know it. Michael discovered it. He handled their books, did the final accounting. I just worked on the subdivision, then funneled my numbers to Michael for the final year end. He discovered how Zambrano in the last year had begun to launder outside money through the corporation. Those flash drives contain the hard evidence. Randy says we need them. Without them we got nothing. He calls them our bargaining chip."

"Bargaining chip. What are you talking about? Who are you bargaining with, what are you planning to do?"

"Don't you get it, lawman? This is our ticket to the good life. Zambrano will pay a ton of money to get these flash drives." Again the words came from the shadow man.

"Blackmail, this is all about blackmail. Everett, you are going to be part of this?"

"Well, Randy says it's only fair. It's illegal money. It's not like we are taking it from people. No one is getting hurt."

"Everett, what are you talking about? People have already been hurt, your own father, that boy in the trailer."

"That wasn't supposed to happen. I didn't know about that until later. Randy says that only happened because we didn't have the flash drives."

"What about Michael being killed?"

"We didn't do that. I couldn't do anything. I had no proof. I thought maybe it was an accident. It was Randy who put two and two together. Figured if we could find some hard proof . . ."

"No. Okay, maybe you didn't get it all, but Everett, do you know who you are dealing with?"

"What do you mean do I know who we're dealing with? Zambrano, he's the one who began funneling outside money through the company."

"Everett, you are not dealing with Zambrano here and Mesquite Sand and Gravel. Don't you get it? The money going through the business isn't Zambrano's. Zambrano is a go-between for the people that funded him. He's connected. I've been told his money, the money he got to probably buy the business, came from a Chicago family. Do you understand what that means?"

"We haven't got time for all this. Everett, we got to get those damn flash drives." Randy's voice echoed off the rock walls.

"Don't you know, Everett? Randy knows, don't you, Randy? That is why you stay in the shadows, hiding in back of Everett."

"What does he mean, Randy?"

"Nothing. He doesn't know what he is talking about."

"Everett, does Zambrano know anything about Randy?"

"No. Why would he?"

"Exactly. And that's the way Randy wants it. You worked for Sand and Gravel. As far as Zambrano is concerned, you are the only one who knows or might have evidence of the money laundering. That's why they came after you. Beat up your father, burned to death the young man in the trailer and probably killed Michael Stark. Everett, this is mob money, coming from Chicago. Randy has you in on a scheme to blackmail the mob. Even if it works and you get this money you're after, do you think it's going to end there? Do you really think they are going to forget about you? That is not the way they operate. They are going to come after you, not Randy. They don't know about Randy. They are going to come after you and probably your father. They are going to get you. Like they say, you can run but you can't hide. But Randy, he'll be fine because no one knows anything about him."

Randy ran forward to within a couple of feet of Virgil and Everett. He raised the gun.

"What are you doing, Randy?"

"You still don't get it, Everett. That's what this is all about," Virgil said.

"Okay, Everett. Go down to the car. I'll finish up here."

"What do you mean, Randy?"

"He means, Everett, he'll join you after he takes care of me. That gun isn't a decoration."

Everett took a couple of steps toward Randy.

"No, Randy. This was never part of it. We've got the flash drives. You said that was all we needed. We never talked about, about anything like this."

"Everett, get real. He knows everything. What do you think he is going to do if we let him go? He's a lawman."

"No, Randy. We can't do this."

"We aren't going to do this. I am. You go down to the car. I'll take care of him."

• • •

Simon had climbed up on the huge rock he had been leaning against a couple of times to look out over the uncluttered landscape for any sign of Everett. He had just jumped down from his last unsuccessful effort. Finally, he went to the car, got the binoculars from the glove box where Virgil said they would be. He thought about climbing back up on the rock but first started looking out at the desert, adjusting the glasses to his eyes while he stood by the car. At last, he looked up at the face of the monolith that had given the place its history. He was reminded of pictures he had seen of Ayers Rock in Australia. The monolith stood apart from everything else in the landscape, inescapable to the eye. Tracing the side closest to him, he saw the weathered surface carved by the ages. Niches, defying the onslaught of the elements, filled with windblown dirt and sand, supported life. Dwarfed mesquite and cottonwood along with clutches of desert grasses pockmarked the rock face. Simon traced his way up to the top through the field glasses.

His eyes finally settled on two figures standing fairly close to the cliff edge. One of them, closest to the rim, he took to be Virgil because of his Stetson, the other he assumed to be Everett Jessup. Dim figures, cardboard cutouts in the slanting light of the setting sun moving in and out of the shadows. He walked further down the trail until he could see some animation of their bodies, but distinctness of their features were largely lost to him. He kept walking watching them until he noticed that their attention suddenly seemed to shift toward something he could not see. As he continued looking, another figure came into view. Again, he could not make out specific features, but as the light for just an instant fell on the third party, Simon saw the glint of something unmistakable in his hand. He had seen the sunlight reflect off enough gun barrels to know that was what he was looking at.

Without warning, he saw the arm attached to the gun rise. A sudden quick burst erupted, the hint of a flash followed by the echo as it rolled off the plateau to the desert below. Simon saw the figure who had moved suddenly to stand in front of Virgil grab his side then take a step or two backward. Then he saw Virgil reach out and grab him to keep him from falling. The figure with the gun advanced a couple of steps, waving both his arms. Simon could see the agitation in his movements.

He reached over and picked up Dave's rifle, which he had taken with him when he left the car. It was an instinctive move. He looked again through the glasses. The armed figure on top of El Morro was still waving his arms, gesturing toward Virgil, who still seemed to be supporting the other man. Then he saw Virgil lay the man down. When he stood up he saw him moving closer to the edge of the rim, more into the fading light. The armed man followed closer, out into the full light, so that from Simon's vantage point he looked like a silhouette against the western sun. Simon thought of the black one-dimensional figures dancing on the wire on the firing range. He knew that he only had a window of a few minutes before the sun slipped below the horizon.

He took Dave's gun, quickly checking the magazine, then raised it to his shoulder. There was no telescopic sight like he had looked through many times when he was doing his job in Afghanistan. He took a quick look through the glasses, then through the mechanical sight, which he had

163

flipped up on the rifle barrel. He drew in a short breath, drew a bead on the black figure that was now aiming his gun at Virgil. He saw the scenario in his head, felt the trigger through the metal prosthesis in his hand, then squeezed the trigger. He heard the sound, felt the recoil, but in another sense didn't hear it or feel it but knew from his sense memory that it had happened that way. He picked up the binoculars quickly, expelled the breath he had held and looked. He saw the same silhouette frozen, unmoving for an instant, then a hesitation. The gun slipped from his hand. He took a step backward then reached up, clutched his chest, stumbled into the darkness and disappeared.

# 42

Simon slumped down against another boulder. He felt like a deflated balloon. All the air had suddenly gone out of him. Images that he had worked hard to put out of his mind from his not-so-distant past overwhelmed him. The crumpled figure that he saw fall was only the most recent in a long line. He tried to rise but his legs wouldn't support him. He thought he had turned a corner in his life, put his recent history behind him. Put it in that jar, where all bad memories should go, then place it high up on a shelf out of reach, where it would stay, until it was forgotten. But the tears rolling down his cheeks were a sharp contradiction to that illusion. He sat immobilized, detached from the world as it rotated on its axis, until he heard the sound of all-too-familiar distant gunfire.

In an instant, he grabbed Dave's rifle, then jumped to his feet in a reflex action, waiting to engage the enemy that was coming. Darkness surrounded him. He knew they were coming. They were out there, as they always were. He looked to see who was creeping up on his position. The shots ended. The quiet once again reasserted itself in the desert landscape.

Confused, he looked into the invading darkness. He glanced around, saw the single light glowing in the visitor center, the two cars parked in the lot. Slowly he remembered where he was. He shook his head, straining to bring himself back into the present. He looked at the cars in the parking lot and the visitor center beyond once again, reacquainting himself with the world and his new life. He realized that the shots must have come from Virgil. He ran back to the cruiser, put the rifle in back, got in, started the engine, then turned on the high beams, blinking them a few times to let Virgil know he was there and coming to his aid. He drove out of the lot onto the desert floor, heading for the base of El Morro. When he got to within a couple of hundred feet of the monument he could make out some figures. They had stepped into the arc of his high beams. Simon brought the car to a sudden halt and bolted from it. The closer he got he realized there were three figures.

"Virgil, are you hit? How were you able to get down here?" He looked at the two with Virgil, one still on his feet, the other being held up by both, obviously in bad shape. Simon reached out grabbed the one man and lay him on the ground.

"No. I'm fine. It's the other two. I think the one you got is in the worse shape. He might not make it, but Everett wouldn't leave him up there on that mountain, even though he tried to kill us both."

Everett Jessup, holding his side, had slid to the ground during the exchange. Both he and Randy were bleeding profusely.

"Help us into the cruiser, then see if you can get patched through to local law enforcement. Try 911. I think the best, closest hospital would be in Albuquerque. We can't wait for help to come here. If you connect, tell them we'll be coming east on forty so they can intercept us."

· · ·

A little more than half an hour later Virgil and Simon stood on the side of the interstate, watching while Everett and Randy were placed in the back of two EMS vehicles. One of the responders walked over to Virgil.

"Well, Sheriff, near as I can tell the big guy is in pretty good shape, got him stabilized, but the other is going to be touch and go. Got IV drips in each of them and each one still has some lead poisoning to be removed. If the one guy makes it through the night that will be a good sign. Check tomorrow. You both better get cleaned up. Anybody sees you, more than likely they will be calling for an ambulance for you." Virgil and Simon looked down at their blood-soaked uniforms as the attendant turned and ran toward one of the vehicles.

"Guess cleanup will have to wait until we get back to Hayward," Virgil said. They stood for another minute watching the flashing red lights speed down the highway until they were swallowed by the dark. Then they both turned and walked to the cruiser.

It was a long, silent ride back to Hayward. The stench of the drying blood caking on their uniforms was sickeningly strong. The car heater only made it worse. Finally unable to stand it any longer, Virgil reached the point where he had no choice but to lower the windows. The frozen night air rushed in, sweeping the stench out. Even with the heater going full blast, after a couple of minutes they both started to shiver. He rolled the windows back up. He repeated the process at least ten times before they finally reached Hayward. Virgil pulled into the parking lot in back of the office a little before three. As he got out of the cruiser he rolled down all of the windows.

"Simon, there is a fresh change of clothes inside."

"No. I don't want to change until I've taken a shower. I've got to get rid of that smell. New clothes alone aren't going to do it."

Virgil nodded in agreement. He also realized that those were the first words Simon had spoken since they had gotten in the car. Virgil also was aware that he had barely made a comment on the whole trip. He looked at Simon standing in the glare of the light that lit the parking area. His clothes bloodied, a distant look in his eyes. Virgil read the impact of the day's events on him. Leaning on Dave's rifle like a cane, Virgil saw him in a different light. He realized Simon was standing on a precipice. He moved to stand directly in front of him, inches from his face. There was no glint of recognition from Simon.

"Thank you, Simon. Thank you for my life. I know you didn't want to have to do what you did, but remember you saved a couple of lives today. I told you on the shooting range that morning I could never have made a shot like you did today. It's important for you to know that is a skill that breaks both ways. Today it broke for Everett and me. I'm glad you made that shot. So is Everett. I wouldn't be talking to you now if you hadn't. But I know the cost of it to you." He reached out his hand, taking Simon's prosthetic hand in his and raising them interlocked to eye level. "Go home. Take that shower and get to bed. You did a good thing today."

Simon blinked, then bent his head a little and turned without saying anything and walked to his car. Virgil watched until he drove out of the lot then he went into the office.

# 43

It was a little after eleven the next morning when Jimmy came into the office. Rosie wasn't too far behind him. He held the door for her.

"One thing about the cold, you move a lot quicker. Thanks, Jimmy."

"I kinda like it for a change. Those hundred-plus days in July and August sap your energy, especially when you get twenty or thirty of them in a row. You know, last summer Abby was invited to a birthday pool party. She told me they had to have an ice truck come down in the morning to dump cakes of ice into the pool so the kids could swim in the afternoon."

"Guess there's an upside and downside to just about everything. Right now I just appreciate being warm. The heater in my car sure picked a good time to crap out. Jimmy, aren't you going to hang up your coat?"

"Oh, I ain't staying. I'm on my way down to Redbud. Just stopped by to find out how the sheriff made out with that trip to El Morro yesterday. Today is my day down to Redbud. Simon will be here today."

"I don't know how I forgot about that," Rosie said as she hung up her coat. "Dif, what happened?"

Dif stood up from in back of the desk and stretched, an expressionless look on his face.

"I dunno, haven't heard a word from Virgil."

Rosie looked up at the clock.

"It's past eleven. That's not a good sign. Even when Virgil's not coming in early he always calls by eight." Just as she reached across the desk for the phone, it rang. For the next few minutes she listened while Virgil told her what had happened. "Okay Virgil, don't rush in here. Dif and I are here. Nothing much is going on. Jimmy stopped by, he is on his way down to Redbud. I will make sure about Simon. See you later." She hung up the phone, then sat down. For the next couple of minutes she filled in the narrative for Dif and Jimmy.

"I wasn't expecting that," Dif said.

"Don't think Virgil was either. He said they didn't get back here until three in the morning."

"Is the sheriff okay?"

"He's all right, Jimmy, but he's worried about Simon. Do you think you could stop by the hospital on your way out of town? You know Simon's friend, Chet. He's the intern."

"The guy with one eye. I know him. He's played basketball with us a couple of times."

"Sheriff thinks it would be good if he stopped by Simon's place, had a talk with him. Seems they went through a lot together."

"You mean the war."

Rosita nodded.

"Sure, I can do that. I'll stop by the hospital on my way out of town."

• • •

Virgil was sitting over a second cup of coffee when Cesar came into the kitchen.

"You all right, my friend?" Virgil looked up from his cup. "The clothes on the porch are covered in blood."

"Oh, yeah. I've got to get them into the wash. Left them out there because of the smell. Too tired to deal with them last night."

"Heard you come in real late."

"Yeah."

"Any of that blood yours?"

"No, no. I'm okay, don't worry."

"You want to talk about it?"

Virgil looked into the weathered face of Cesar as he sat down, then poured himself a cup of coffee. He saw the concern in his eyes.

"I don't know if going over it again is going to make any difference. I've got to figure out where to go from here."

"Well, maybe talking about it will help you figure that out."

Virgil hesitated, then spent the next ten minutes telling Cesar about the events of the previous night, ending with his concern for Simon. Cesar listened without saying a word. Then Cesar sat back in his chair, took a sip from his cup, reached his bony brown hand over across the table, covering Virgil's hand with his.

"I think maybe there are too many things crowding your head right now. That's why you can't figure out which way to go. Let's begin by getting rid of one of them. I understand your concern for your new man, Simon. Don't know him well but I liked him when I met him at the party. The fact that you took him on tells me he must be a good man. But his problems can only be solved by him. You can't do that for him. He has to figure it out. We all do, as we go through life. I was never prouder of you than when your mom and pop died. You met life head-on. You were devastated but you kept going forward. Simon has to figure out how to do the same thing. Keep going forward. Moving on from the bad things, the pain he has endured. Otherwise, he will have no life. But he has to do it.

169

You can't do it for him. He is very lucky to have you and the others in his life supporting him. We all need that, because none of us goes through life alone. Look at me. When Sam, your dad, brought me here, I knew maybe ten words in English. Now I even think in English. " Cesar withdrew his hand, sat back, then took another drink from his cup. Neither of them spoke for a while.

"You know, when you were speaking, I could hear my grandfather in your words. I wonder if I will ever get to be as wise as you and he."

Cesar smiled at the comment.

"You will. You just have to live long enough."

It was Virgil's turn to smile, recalling the same words to him and Billy Three Hats from his grandfather.

"Well, I don't know. If I have many more nights like last night, don't know if I'll make it."

"That's why you need men like Simon watching your back."

Virgil stood up and put his empty cup in the sink.

"Yeah, I've got to get more of those guys. Told Ears to speak to the council. Maybe I should bring that blood stained uniform to the next meeting, tell them about last night."

"That'll get their attention. Okay, got one problem off the table. Now for the next one, Everett.

Let Aunt Clara handle that one. She's got the old man down there. Call her. Tell her about everything that went down. Let her explain to him what happened, what's going on. I have a hunch the old-timer knows a little more about his son and his life choices than he has let on. He has lived in the world a long time. Besides, based on what you said about his son taking a bullet for you, I don't think it will go as hard on him as it will on his friend. Clara will know best how to tell him. She's the other side of Grandpa and me. Maybe the smarter side."

"I won't argue that point." Virgil left the house a little while later with a much lighter step. Now, he was down to one problem. He knew there was no handing this one off to someone else to solve . . . Mesquite Sand and Gravel, and Mr. James Zambrano. When he stepped out onto the porch, he looked at the pile of bloody clothes. He kicked at it, saw that it was a frozen mess, decided that the comment he'd made inside wasn't a half-bad idea. He stepped back into the house, got a plastic bag, picked up the tangle, took out his jockeys, which had even absorbed some blood, then stuffed the rest of the clothes in the plastic bag.

"Show and tell." he said. "Worked in first grade, not much different than a town council meeting." He smiled at his analogy then walked down to his vehicle and threw the bag into the back.

Before he left to get back on the horse, he took a little time to see how his own stock was doing. Remembering Clara's advice about taking a step back when he was feeling crowded, he caught Jack up. In less than twenty minutes he was up on the ridge. There were still pockets of snow in deep gullies. The ever-running stream that crisscrossed the ranch was full to busting its banks. He could hear its voice before he actually saw it. On the other side of the ridge he let Jack out into a full gallop. For the next ten minutes the cold air whipped his face. Jack flattened out into the run, exhilarated by the free rein. It was good for them both. Jack because he needed to stretch the muscles that hadn't been used in too long, Virgil because he needed for a couple of minutes to get away from the realities of what his life was at this point in time. He might not have consciously realized it but the ride was a kind of therapy. When he finally checked Jack's headlong run, it was with reluctance. He wished he could ride like that forever. Turning in a different direction to head back, he came upon some of the cattle, who took little note of him. They all looked fat and in good winter coats. He could already tell that most were well along with the calves they would drop come spring. It made him feel good to see them. He knew that if his dad was here, he would feel the same way. The reminiscence brought him down a bit but it passed.

At times like this, which occurred rarely, for he was not one to drown in the past, he wished he was a little more spiritual. He wished he could be content with the idea that one day they, his mother, his father, Rusty, would all be together again. But he could never get to that. He'd seen too much to believe in nirvana. His personal philosophy had gradually evolved over time, to getting through life doing as little damage to others as he could and maybe doing some good along the way. When it was over, it was over. If there was anything to come after, it would be a surprise. He never verbalized his beliefs to others. It was a secret he kept to himself.

# 44

Morning time with Cesar, along with the ride on Jack, had renewed him. It was a much different man who walked into the office a little after two from the man who had stripped off blood-soaked clothes, shivering in twenty-degree temperatures on his front porch in the middle of the night. His exhaustion had been compounded by the dread of dealing with the next day. Tired as he had been, he had spent most of the night tossing and turning. It had taken Cesar to settle him and gain some perspective. Rosie sensed the change right off. His was not the voice she had heard earlier on the phone. She and Dif were more than a little surprised when he dropped a bag of doughnuts on her desk.

"Figured we might as well keep up the stereotype."

"Trying to watch my weight, Virgil. My OB says every pound you put on now is just going to be another one you have to lose on the other end."

"Maybe you ought to get another OB," Dif said. "If every pregnant woman had that outlook, the population would be at a standstill and that guy would be out of a job. So if you are just going to look at that bag, pass it over here."

"I'll subscribe to that. But before you eat the bag, Dif, pass it over to me. I'll have one or two." Virgil looked at Simon, who had just come in behind him. The look of desperation he had seen on Simon's face the night before was gone. One look into his face and he realized that Chet was obviously Simon's Cesar. We all need one, he thought, recalling Cesar's words.

"C'mon, Rosie, pass that bag over."

"I'm thinking," she responded.

"Thinking, what are you thinking about?" Dif asked.

"I'm thinking about the benefits of immediate gratification, as opposed to denial, which might cause anxiety and be upsetting to a growing child. I think immediate gratification sounds healthier in the long run." With that, she opened the bag and pulled out two doughnuts, cream-filled and covered in chocolate. They all looked at her.

"Boy, that was a quick turnaround. I don't know, Rosie, maybe that OB of yours is on the right track."

"Maybe, but if you saw him you'd know he hasn't passed up a lot of doughnuts in his life." She tossed the bag to Dif.

172

"All right, now that we have solved the first challenge of the day, maybe we could move on."

"You mean we're not just going to hang out and eat doughnuts? What a rip-off," Dif commented

"Sorry, but the town has this crazy idea that they should get something for all the money they pay you," Virgil responded.

"What have you got, Virgil?"

"Well, Simon, it's about where do we go after last night?"

"How do you mean?"

"Well, Everett Junior and Randy are in the hospital. Law enforcement down in Albuquerque are going to make sure they don't go anywhere, but as far as I can see that still leaves us with a problem to solve. Those flash drives kind of make whoever has them a target. Before we considered going after Mr. Zambrano, I figured we had to neutralize that danger. They are important enough that people are willing to kill for them and already have to keep them from getting into the wrong hands. Randy and Everett thought they were just dealing with a local businessman. They had no idea who was in back of him. The people that came in to take care of Michael Stark, who also burned out that trailer of Everett's, are not likely to go away or stop if they think there is a chance of getting those flash drives. I think we have to recognize that. Zambrano I'm pretty sure had nothing to do with the actual crimes, other than as a go-between. We have to get at him through the money laundering. The two sets of books that Michael Stark discovered will take care of that."

"So you don't think it will end with those two guys who ended up at the bottom of the canyon?" Simon said.

"No. My guess is that we picked up a little breathing room, but that would be too easy. I think if we don't nail this situation down fast, there will just be a couple of new replacements showing up on our doorstep."

"When you close that operation down I'm sure going to be feeling really bad for all those people down there in Cielo," Rosie said.

"Yeah," Virgil replied. "I've been wrestling with that in my mind all night. A lot of people are going to be thrown out of work, lose their homes. The whole area down there is just going to take a huge hit economically. The worst of it is that from what I can tell, the company has been a huge success and the area is booming."

"Isn't there anything you can do to stop that from happening, Virgil? It's not fair. Again the innocent victims get caught in the crossfire." The room went silent at the impact of the words that came from Rosita.

• • •

173

The rest of the day was spent dealing with the day-to-day affairs of the office. Dif had gone home. Simon had begun making his rounds, while Rosie left for a doctor's appointment. Virgil was no closer to a solution to his problem when the phone rang.

"I guess you have been pretty busy since you haven't called." Virgil was caught off guard, almost didn't recognize the voice, but he couldn't forget those blue eyes. He took a deep breath. He wasn't dead yet. "I tried to come up with reasons to call, any danger to my life or something just as mundane but realized they would just be lame excuses. The truth is, I thought just maybe we had a bit of a connection. I wanted to find out if it was something only I felt."

"No . . . no. I mean . . . yes, but, but I've been . . ." He felt as if he was babbling. "Wait, stop."

"I don't understand."

"I'm talking to myself. Ignore me. I mean, starting at the beginning, yes. I felt it too . . . the connection. But things got a little crazy in my life. That night when you stopped by the office. Since then, I've thought about calling. I meant to but . . ."

"So I get it. You've been busy. But am I wrong? I think we at least figured out something here. Right?"

"Definitely," Virgil replied.

"So . . . so where do we go from here?"

"Tonight. When Simon comes back from making his tour I can leave. It would probably be around nine o'clock. Too late, is that too late?" He didn't wait for an answer. "If not, how about the Lazy Dog? A drink, a late-night bite, something to eat?"

"Sounds good, I'd like that, almost sounds like a date. Oops, maybe I shouldn't have used that word. I'll plan on getting there around nine. Don't worry if you're a little late. I'll wait. I've been waiting."

"I'll be there. You won't have to wait long. I promise. By the way, I can handle that word. See you then."

As soon as Virgil hung up the phone, he called Simon. "How is everything?"

"Quiet, real quiet. I think the cold has driven most people indoors. Is something happening, anything wrong? I mean, you don't usually call."

"No . . . nothing special," Virgil lied. "Wondering if I could get out of here by nine?"

"I don't see any problem with that unless something unexpected comes up. Like I said, it's real quiet. By the way, Virgil, I'm good. Thought a lot about what you said last night. Talked to Chet today. He's my anchor. Was trying to put my past behind me, but like Chet says, that doesn't really work. You just can't erase it. You are better off confronting it, that way you can move on. He says talk about it. He says that's what has helped him. Meeting Karen, he says, was the best thing that ever happened to him. Guess until I find that person, Chet is it for me."

"Well, I can think of some people you work with that might help you with that." There was a silent moment on the line.

"Yeah. I know," Simon said.

• • •

Virgil was thinking about what Simon had said on his way to the Lazy Dog, about it being important to have someone to talk to. Virgil knew that well. He had always had that someone. Simon was also right about there not being a soul in sight when he made his rounds. Maybe it was the cold driving everyone indoors, Virgil thought. When he stepped through the door of the Lazy Dog, he found all those missing people. The place was packed. He saw Florence behind the bar. She gave him a wave. There was something about seeing her there that made him feel good. He did a quick scan. His eyes locked with Jessie's in the third booth on the right.

"I see Florence gave you a wave." She made the comment as he slid into the booth across from her.

"You know, when life is crazy, especially if you feel a little out of control, it's nice to see something or someone who doesn't change, an anchor point, to use a word I just heard. I mean there she is, closing in on eighty, behind the bar night after night."

"And still wielding that hockey stick." Jessie smiled. Virgil could have sworn that her eyes got bluer.

"Technically, she told me that it's a hurling stick she got from an Irishman. It's shorter, thicker and has a broader head. She said when she can no longer swing it, it will be time to retire."

"I don't think that's happening any time soon," Jessie replied.

The last of the night drifted away while she sat over a couple of glasses of zinfandel. Virgil was washing down a burger and fries with a couple of beers.

"You sure you don't want anything to eat?"

"I'm about to steal one of those fries before you inhale them all."

Virgil pushed the plate across the table.

"I'm done. They are all yours."

"I wasn't hungry until I saw you attack that burger."

"Yeah, all of a sudden I was starving. Don't know where that came from."

"I have that effect on all the men I meet. Don't know what it says about me."

"Do they have the same effect on you?"

"Not usually, until now." Virgil felt a sudden rush of heat at the comment.

"So, do you want to talk about that out-of-control thing?"

"What do you mean?"

"You said a few moments ago about things being crazy, your life out of control."

"Oh, I meant, it's just my life, job. Wrestling with some things, trying to find my way. Nothing new. I spend a lot of time doing that, especially lately it seems. Now I'm wrestling with a way to do my job without hurting a lot of innocent people in the process."

"Maybe I can help you with that."

Half an hour later, as Virgil stepped out of his car he could still taste her on his lips.

# 45

When Virgil pulled into the office parking lot the next morning, he was pleased to see everyone already there, even Simon, who had stayed late in the office the night before.

"Guess you're pretty tired," Rosie said as she placed a cup of coffee on Virgil's desk. Virgil didn't respond.

"Yeah, I can't handle those late nights like I used to either, but of course I don't have the motivation of a single man like you," Dif said. The comment hung in the air expectantly.

"I don't believe it," Virgil said. He looked at the four faces focused on his. "It's a little after ten in the morning. How can you all possibly know?"

"Virgil, you forget Florence and Edna have been joined at the hip since before either one had their first date. You thought you were going to have a little interlude in the Lazy Dog without us finding out about it," Rosie said. Virgil shook his head.

"It wasn't an interlude. It was work-related."

"Oh, a couple of hours staring into one another's eyes over drinks and a late-night snack. We understand, Virgil, all in a day's work."

"Next time you have to work late, Sheriff, if you're not up to it, just give me a call. I'd be happy to take some of that late-night work off your hands," Simon offered. Virgil put his hands up in a surrender motion.

"Okay . . . okay. Maybe it wasn't all work-related. But she did give me some insight into James Zambrano. A lot of insight."

"But, Virgil, isn't it over? I mean, you've got the flash drives. The hit men are at the bottom of the canyon. What's left? Call up Kyle. Drop it in his lap. Let the feds take over."

"I could do that, but then a whole bunch of people are going to be hurt. I'm going to speak to Mr. Zambrano first. Here, keep these safe." He tossed the flash drives onto Rosie's desk.

It was a little after two when he pulled into the parking lot of Mesquite Sand and Gravel. James Zambrano was waiting for him.

"You know it's all over," Virgil said right off as he slid into the chair on the opposite side of the desk. Zambrano nodded.

"I never wanted this. You probably don't believe me. I get that. All I wanted was to build something of value. When I came here, this place was floundering. I mean, there was no eye on growth potential or expansion, much less innovating some new extraction techniques that were environmentally-friendly. No eye to the future. It was strictly run as a day-to-day operation. I knew I could turn it around. And I did. The business, the housing development, all of it growing and expanding. I tried to tell them in Chicago: This is a legitimate success. Leave it alone. They fought me, wouldn't listen. I could do nothing to stop them. I tried. I really tried. I made trips back to Chicago again and again to forestall what they wanted to do. Finally, Michael Stark caught on, and that was the beginning of the end."

"That's why we are having this talk. You are going down for this. I can't stop that, neither can you. I think you know, soon it's going to be out of my hands, even if I believe you never wanted it. But I'm hoping there is a way we can save a business, a lot of people's jobs, along with the growth that has happened in this part of the county. From what I heard about you, I don't think you would want that to happen. But when I turn the flash drives over to the feds, like I said, it's out of my hands. So I'm giving you a chance to do something special here. It might be the kind of thing that under other circumstances you would have wanted all along."

· · ·

Virgil was sitting in his office two days later. Kyle Harrison was sitting across from him.

"If what you say is on these flash drives proves accurate, we are going to make a lot of people in Chicago extremely unhappy. A huge revenue source is going to dry up. Indictments are going to follow. A lot of people are going away for extended vacations as guests of the government. You did a great job, Virgil. There's just one strange thing in this whole scenario that I don't get. After you called and told me what you had, I did a little preliminary checking. From what I've learned, I understand that James Zambrano has just sold the company and all of its assets to his employees for a dollar a share. It's become an employee-owned and directed company. My understanding is that they have already formed a board of directors. Because he did this before any arrest or indictment, I don't think we can touch Mesquite Sand and Gravel or any of its holdings, so I guess it will be business as usual for everybody down there. I just can't figure Zambrano out. It's almost like he saw what was coming and didn't want to bankrupt the company, throwing all those people out of work and out of their homes. Guess it goes to show you that not-so-nice people can do good things."

"Really strange, isn't it?" Virgil replied. A short time later, he stood in the doorway watching as Kyle Harrison pulled out of the parking area. Rosie was next to him.

"That was a really good thing you did, Virgil. It's a shame no one will ever know about it."

"That's the way it has to be. It will be, has to be, our secret. You know, I'm going to take the rest of the day off. I have to be at the town council meeting tonight so I have to get back to the ranch. There's a bag with some bloody clothes that I want them to see when I speak to them about how this area is changing."

"That should get their attention."

"You stole the words right out of Cesar's mouth."

• • •

Virgil's ride home was different. His mind was as clear as the cloudless sky overhead. He felt like he had just come out of a long, dark tunnel. There was still a lot of winter ahead, but the idea of more cold and snow didn't depress him. He actually looked forward to both. He was hoping for some long, quiet nights sitting in front of a roaring fire. When he rolled into the driveway, he saw Cesar leaning against the corral fence looking almost like he was waiting for him. He stepped out of the cruiser, took one or two steps toward the house, figuring Cesar would join him. Turning, he saw that he hadn't moved from his spot.

"What's up?" he shouted across the space between them. Cesar waved him to come over, then turned and started walking toward the barn. Virgil hesitated for a second, then ran to join him. He caught up to him just as he stepped through the barn door. He took a couple of steps, then paused at the first stall. Virgil was puzzled. Cesar motioned him toward the stall. Virgil stepped closer, then looked over the top. There, lying on top of a bed of straw, was a rust-red Jersey calf with big brown eyes who bawled when she saw Virgil. Cesar handed Virgil a note.

"She's the last Jessup calf left to represent the hopes and dreams of her ancestors. I hope she brings those hopes and dreams to you. Thank you, Virgil, for saving my son." Virgil smiled, then cleared his throat as he put the note in his pocket. He glanced at Cesar, who was shaking his head.

"What's bugging you?"

"Virgil, I just want you to know, I've done every job on this ranch you've ever asked me to do, but I'm telling you here and now that when the time comes, I ain't milking that cow."

Virgil smiled again.

"Tell me that again sometime, when we don't have any milk for your coffee." The calf bawled. Virgil smiled again then turned and left the barn.

# About the Author

Frank Hayes is a high school teacher who has started a new career as a novelist. He lives and writes in New York's mid–Hudson River Valley. He is the author of three Sheriff Virgil Dalton Mysteries, *Death at the Black Bull*, *Death on the High Lonesome*, and *Shattered Dreams*.